KALIFORNIA

Also by Marc Laidlaw

Dad's Nuke
Neon Lotus

KALIFORNIA

▲▲▲

Marc Laidlaw

ST. MARTIN'S PRESS
New York

This is a work of fiction. Names, characters, places, and incidents either are the product of the author's imagination or are used fictitiously. Any resemblance to events or persons, living or dead, is entirely coincidental.

KALIFORNIA. Copyright © 1993 by Marc Laidlaw. All rights reserved. Printed in the United States of America. No part of this book may be used or reproduced in any manner whatsoever without written permission except in the case of brief quotations embodied in critical articles or reviews. For information, address St. Martin's Press, 175 Fifth Avenue, New York, N.Y. 10010.

Design by Paul Chevannes

Library of Congress Cataloging-in-Publication Data
Laidlaw, Marc.
    Kalifornia : a novel / Marc Laidlaw.
      p. cm.
    ISBN 0-312-08830-2
    I. Title.
    PS3562.A333K34   1993
    813'.54—dc20   92-35531
                                                                                               CIP

First Edition: February 1993

10 9 8 7 6 5 4 3 2 1

It is not unreasonable to expect almost any kind of irregularities in so distant and neglected a department as California.

—*1 California Reporter 582 (1906)*

CONTENTS

Previews 1

Part One

1. Live Birth 7
2. Seascraper Soirée 26
3. A Hag-Ridden Coach with
   No Wood on the Sides 54

Part Two

4. Revolt of the Wage Slaves 67
5. Seersuckers 88
6. Poppies Will Make Them Sleep 101
7. Trauma in Tinsel-Town 124
8. Kalifornia, Here I Come 142

Part Three

9. The Meatpuppet Master 169
10. Ba-Ha-Ha 189
11. Who Will Baby-sit the Baby-sitter? 207
12. Zing! Went the Strings 223
13. Sequelitis 239

KALIFORNIA

Previews

Feedback.
 "Happy birthday, California."
 "Have a nice death. . . ."
 You'll thank me in kisses and credit.
 The forest of slick deformities loomed up like something vomited from the floor of the sea.
 "There's a hairball in your root chakra."
 "Tan, man. Totally tan."
 Kali-Kali-Kalifornia!
 "He wishes to have his wires removed."
 "People want to get inside her; they want to feel what she feels."
 —free of their dim ectoplasm.
 "Way tawdry . . ."
 "You can feel yourself being sliced limb from limb, while at the same time you're the one doing the slicing."
 "Suddenly I want sushi."
 —hot chocolate and fried onions.
 "Just because pleasure frightens you."

My daughter . . .
"Welcome to Libidopolis!"
Feedback.
—glittered in the dark entryway as candlelight went flowing up and down the slender rods and wires.
"This is Newsbody Ninety."
"But I felt you die!"
"Not a family show?"
"I forgot you weren't acting."
"Krrrawww."
"Madam, there's no need to slaughter innocent babes."
"But that's not her!"
"It's coppertone, baby."
"A dream, a dance. Maya."
"The child owes a birthdebt!"
"—food for giant buzzards!"
"And you call yourself a seal?"
"Kali-ma! Kali-ma!"
"Is it true you dogs have poor long-term memory?"
"You'll be blind and white as cave fish soon."
"I prefer to think of it as synthetic."
The Official Crone knew a penis when she saw one.
"Tumbling . . . with the tumbling tumbleweeds."
"I suppose you no longer utilize wardrobe consultants?"
"Sort of an Iron Toddler look."
"Jeez, now I know you were hatched in a tube."
"The only mother she'll know is our dark goddess."
—crashed against the office windows, sucking at limpets that clung to the glass.
"They study the things God doesn't bother with."
Flesh is so . . . *icky.*
"Men! Dogs and men!"
Shrimps and rice. Very nice.
"Daddy, make him stop! He's wrecking my sex toys!"
"She has complete control of the militia."
"Kali-Kali-Kali-ma!"

By then, the nuns were already firing.
"So few seals in the audience."
"Now look in my eyes."
"Elvis lives!"
Feedback . . .
                NEXT!

PART ONE
▲▲▲

1
Live Birth

Almost midnight.

Poppy lay in darkness. And out of it.

Sweat coated her face like a cosmetic mask. Her gasping sounded like the cries of a stranger. But that was only half of her.

The other half floated in a rippling, muscled silence.

Mother and child.

Giving birth to herself.

The blistered plaster and paper walls of the old hotel deadened her cries. Her fingers gouged holes in a crumbling foam mattress. Blood pooled in the plasticized sheets; warm liquid pulsed from her womb in rhythmic gushes, leaving her feeling drained but not yet empty. Exhausted, she couldn't imagine going on. But the hardest part still lay ahead.

The fetal wires had been live since the seventh month, broadcasting on a private umbilical wire that was shielded from any other receivers. She could enter her daughter through this wire, which served as a two-way channel until the cord was cut. Through infant eyes, heavy-lidded, she peeked at orange darkness, her fluid-filled ears picking up the pounding of her mother's and her own heartbeat. This part of Poppy was not entirely Poppy. The girl child, tentatively named Calafia, had a life of her own. Her soul was a bright fish that wouldn't be caught in the seine of wires. Sometimes Poppy wondered if her daughter ever crept up the umbilicus and into her mother's wires, to look out through Poppy's eyes, to listen with her ears.

There was nothing here worth seeing. Nothing she'd want a child to remember.

Ugly walls. A warm yellow lifebulb patched into an antique electric socket overhead. Bent venetian blinds hung like thin ribs among the folds of musty drapes. It seemed a shame that this would be her daughter's first view of the world—this decrepit room holding no trace of beauty, no sign of the modern time's wonders. Poppy's wireman, Clarry Starko, had dreamed up the juxtaposition of sleazy hotel with new life. She never had intended to let him talk her into it, but her contract favored him on such vague points of creative control.

Clarry was somewhere nearby, unseen as always; she could almost feel his fingers on her soul. He was busy in the studio van, monitoring all this, checking sensory quality, recording everything, yelling at the crew. A dozen people hung on her perceptions—millions more waited for the broadcast of this night—but none of them was any help. She was all alone here, in the grip of an ancient power.

She felt herself shifting, squeezed, squeezing.

The two sets of perception slid together, overlapping, growing confused. Her breathing seemed full of warm salt liquid. The room went dark and quiet, while her womb suddenly flooded with light and noise.

The clock chimed in her inner ear.

Midnight.

It was September 9, 2050.

Two thousand and fifty years since Christ, whoever he

was. Another god among the thousands worshiped in California.

From the streets came screams of celebration. Strangers welcomed the child without knowing it. California was two hundred years old tonight, and Calafia, ten seconds old, was being shoved out of darkness by a force as irresistible as that which would one day pull her back into it.

The pain eased slightly, promising release. This was it.

Like a watermelon seed, she squirted free. Light everywhere now; no part of her remained in darkness. Her ears roared with the sound of the sea. Two sets of ears heard the clamoring crowd. California on a warm September midnight. The midnight of her birth.

Even as Poppy collapsed, she felt strength surging into her. She closed her eyes for just a moment—

And a second pair of eyes trembled, flew open. Gaped at a blurred yellow brightness. She shivered in the dry air, so cold by comparison to the place from which she'd come.

She opened her mouth and began to wail.

Poppy sat up. Her daughter lay between her legs, gazing at the ceiling. For a moment she saw exactly what her daughter saw. Blurs of light and color, somehow beautiful and marvelous despite the reality of the room. Then a warm, scented shape; her own hands cradling her, bringing her up to peer into her own face.

As the eyes of mother and daughter met, a blinding pain raced through both of them. *Feedback*. Poppy nearly dropped Calafia. The pain poured through every sense, threatening to shatter both psyches, even the fledgling one.

Poppy set her daughter down. A gleaming, translucent coaxial cable, bright thin wires of several hues twined together, ran from Calafia's groin into Poppy's vulva. Poppy tugged a few more inches of cable from her womb, revealing a small black connecting ring. Twisting the ring in her fingers, she neatly severed the umbilicus, experiencing a dull twinge that fell somewhere between thought and sensation.

She felt . . . diminished.

Two eyes again, two ears. She was herself, alone, and no one else now. Nothing extra.

She tugged on the cable trailing out of her, felt corresponding twitches deep inside. Clenching her teeth, she jerked once more, as hard as she could, and the paraplacenta gave way with a sharp, tearing pain. A net of polymesh slithered out onto the bed, slick with blood, looking like the root system of an exotic seaweed. Except for the bruising memories of labor, fading already, she felt no further pain. And there was no danger of feedback now that her circuits were separate from the child's. In fact, no one would be able to monitor Calafia's wires until several adjustments were made, manually, to her wire system. The child now had a privacy not granted to Poppy.

Pain and exhaustion were replaced by joy.

My baby, she thought. My daughter.

The girl lay quietly stirring, tiny limbs pressing the air, mouth and eyes twisted up in soft knots. Poppy lifted her carefully, and the eyes tipped open again.

Orange eyes, bright as two flames. Molten, liquid, dancing eyes.

Figueroa eyes.

Poppy's eyes were the same shade of orange as those of her brothers, Sandy and Ferdinand, and her sister, Miranda. But it was her father, Alfredo, whom the baby most resembled. Like him, she was wrinkled and balding; even the sour, befuddled expression was Alfredo's.

Appropriate enough.

Calafia had been his idea, after all.

Only the latest and best technology for the newest addition to the Figueroa clan.

Calafia was the first child *born* to wires.

And already she was a star.

Poppy sighed, holding the infant close to her breast, thankful for these few moments of peace. The price of stardom was an intrusive plot. Clarry Starko was never one to linger on a tender moment. Long silences in his wirecasts were always broken by a scream or an explosion.

Sometimes she wondered if Clarry was the most suitable director for someone with her tropes. When he'd approached her with his idea for the series—at a time when she'd been desperate for work, doubting her whole career in the wires—she had been grateful for his enthusiasm. How could she have turned him down? And it had worked out well for her, so far. But something in the forced, frenetic pace of the program clashed with her natural inclinations. In the old show, the family show, she had always been the sensitive one. The task of raising her brothers and sisters had often fallen on her as their mother's ever more analytical schemes carried her farther afield. Her sibs had often looked to Poppy for what tenderness they needed, if they desired it at all. She often felt the need for quiet times, sentimentality, meaningful conversations. But Clarry was hooked on the breakneck pace, double-crossed plots, unexpected violence, reality distortions, and twisted endings. They made an unlikely pair—in short, exactly the sort of hybrid Hollywood was famous for. Tense. Unpredictable.

Sometimes she had to admit she hated it. But it was all she had. Her show.

And, now, her daughter.

"Come on," she whispered. "Let's get you clean and bundled up."

Towels and swaddling were stacked on the night table. She wiped Calafia carefully, giving particular attention to the genitals, such as they were. A length of cable ending in a shiny silver adaptor protruded from the skin of the baby's groin. Poppy unplugged the umbilicus still dangling from the child and dropped it by the bedside. She bundled the baby in a soft cotton cloth, then in a firm inner layer of Shock-Pruf (whose purpose she tried not to think about), then in more bunting. While she worked, she whispered.

"Calafia, that's a pretty name, isn't it? Your birthday is the same as California's. Tonight's the bicentennial of statehood. Isn't that a nice coincidence?"

It was hardly a coincidence; she spoke for the sake of the show. Livewires picked up everything but thought; she inserted loose bits of script when there was time, so that the eventual audience wouldn't experience these events in a void. All but the most cryptical livewire stars talked to themselves like madmen, busily keeping the audience up to date. It was the Golden Age of the Monologue.

Not that there wasn't plenty else to hear tonight. The streets of the city, the sounds of celebration, got wilder by the minute.

Any time now . . .

Somewhere near, glass shattered. She couldn't tell if it was inside the hotel or not.

Hugging the child, she went to the window, pulled the drapes, raised the blinds, and looked down at the street.

Eleven flights down, the world was far gone. She felt as if she were gazing into an abyss.

Behind her, in the hall, she heard whispering.

They had found her. The figures of Clarry's twisted plot, meant to add suspense to his bicentennial special. She could almost hear the promos: "Trouble for Poppy and her newborn babe, on the next episode of 'Poppy on the Run'!"

She tuned her ears to the slightest sounds. Was that a stuffy, rasping voice? Heavy panting? Footsteps?

A dog began to bay.

The sound was pure terror.

There was hope in the night, though. The building was old enough to retain a fire escape. Streetlights, neon figures, and the moving lamps of traffic winked up through slats in the old metal ramp, promising a moment's advantage. Better than none.

"We have to get out of here," she whispered. "Oh, poor baby. They found us. They always do."

She searched the windowsill for an electric switch but found only dust and dead spiders. The hotel was too old for automatic amenities. Paint clogged the ancient locks; no amount of prying would free them. She leaned against the pane, feeling the emptiness of night beyond. The glass had flowed like slow water down the years, rippling and distorting the view. If she broke it, the sound would betray her.

All her old tropes went into motion now, catching her up in snares of habit. She ceased to think of this as a livewire show, a performance. This was her daughter she carried, and the danger to both of them *felt* real.

So few places to hide. So many pursuers. Poppy was always on the run.

Poppy closed the drapes. The child kept quiet; clutched up close to her, she weighed next to nothing. Poppy set her on the bed and pulled swaddling over her face to shield the new eyes from broken glass. She looked around the room until her eyes settled on a rusted metal folding chair leaning against the wall.

From the hall, a low growl.

No time for further caution. She grabbed the chair, still folded, and rushed at the window, shoving the metal legs like battering rams through the glass. The drapes muffled the crash only slightly.

Footsteps padded down the hall, approaching.

She snatched up Calafia. "Out we go."

The dusty curtains protected her from the worst effects of jagged glass as she ducked through the window.

Outside, the sinuous stop-and-start flow of congested traffic, eleven stories down, dazzled her. Hand lanterns bobbed and swayed, vanishing through doorways; fireworks exploded between buildings, causing stark shadows to bloom on the brickwork and slide slowly upward as the rainbow flares descended. She looked to the night sky for relief and saw the full moon hanging like a hypnotist's pendulum frozen in motion. She flashed on all the hypnotic sessions she had endured to emphasize her tropes, immerse her in the action, intensify the believability of moments, and images, like these.

She stared at the moon, the tortious moon, the moon where everything had gone to hell.

Then came an explosion—

Fireworks!

Calafia's mouth and eyes dropped open. Staring up at a face of showering fiery gold pyrotechnics, the child began to scream. The baby's eyes and the face of fire were the same color.

More explosives shook the fire escape. Poppy offered a perfect target, acting like stupefied prey. After several moments, her mind sifted out a few separate components of the bicentennial chaos and realized that someone was breaking down the door of the room behind her.

She hurried to the first double-back and pounded down to the level below. All but one of the windows along the fire escape were lit. She hurried to the dark one and found it ajar; sounds of moaning issued from within. No help there. Her elbow brushed a liquor bottle standing on the sill; as it tipped over, it gurgled as softly as Calafia, who remained mysteriously calm.

Halfway down to the eighth floor, Poppy glanced up and saw a shadow untangling itself from the torn curtains of her window. It poured over the sill like spilled ink and quickened after her.

Poppy's steps caused tremors in the ironwork. The corroded structure, which had clung to the crumbling brick wall for a hundred years while the building codes governing it fell into disuse, began to quake as if an army were descending.

She stumbled to the seventh floor. This was the maximum height from which she could hope to leap and stand any real chance of survival.

Sixth. The odds were only slightly better. Broken legs and spine for her . . . and for the child, who knew?

From above came a screech and a thud. More shadows

roosted on the fire escape. Some dropped directly from level to level, ignoring the stairs, slipping over the rails and leaping.

Fifth floor. The street below looked like a doll street, a model awaiting her hand. Pedal cars, bikes, and wagons swerved around pedestrians who clogged the walks and teetered on cement columns that otherwise supported only flowerpots. Llamas and cows cried counterpoint to their owners' frustrated shouts. More pervasive were the cries of glee, of celebration. Every bar was full, the drug counters crowded with jostling bodies. Houses doubled as saloons. Celebrants packed onto the balconies of other buildings, jumbling from the habimalls. She wished for revelers on this fire escape, to offer camouflage.

From above, as she reached the fourth floor, she heard crumbling metal. A shape tumbled past her, followed by a rain of rust and particulate iron. It landed on the sidewalk in a heap of garbage, one of the night's many casualties.

Poppy hesitated. The third-floor landing was ragged and full of dangerous gaps like broken teeth.

As for the second floor ramp, it hadn't existed for years.

Whispering, screak of rubber, a breathy, bubbling voice called out: "Poppy!"

She must descend, futile as it seemed. Bricks and boards blinded all the windows of the third floor. The ruinous landing sagged beneath her weight, inching closer to the street. Old brackets tore from the walls, brick dust and iron flakes sifting down like poor man's confetti onto the revelers below. No one noticed. They brushed the grit from their shoulders and hurried on.

She stepped gingerly over the largest of the gaps, clutching the rail with one hand. The whole landing moaned. She was level with the streetlamps now, still dizzyingly high. As she shifted her weight to the far side of the hole, suspicious of the metal, two of her pursuers dropped into her path.

She threw herself backward, over the gap.

The fire escape screamed and broke in two.

Poppy landed on the edge of rotten metal, her legs dangling. The two pursuers watched from the far side, holding perfectly still. She stared into their dark, liquid eyes, saw their pink tongues lolling.

"You can't escape," one growled, extending a shaggy hand. "The child is ours."

It was the hoarse voice from the hallway.

"Tell the president to go to hell!" she cried.

They stared at one another, then sniffed the night. Both were transgenic—or teegee—dogs, leftover "Lassies" from the first days of animal-human hybridization. The SPCA had fought against creation of such unhappy teegee breeds, with limited success. Animal rightists argued that it was purest cruelty to subject innocent canines to the traits of humanity; cruel to instill the happy creatures with guilt, remorse, ambition, indecision. Other creatures arguably benefited from the humanimalism, but the change destroyed dogs, turning the mildest breeds into killers.

Loyal killers, true. Auggie-doggies made superb assassins, risking anything to please a full-human master. In this case, President McBeth.

Very carefully, the Lassies began to clamber upward. They would, she realized, run along the fourth-floor ramp and come down again beside her. They might knock the whole ramp loose. She would fall . . . she would probably die, or be too stunned or crippled to run.

She looked down at the street, the crowd. "Look at me," she murmured. "Why won't anyone see me?"

In the constant flood of traffic, in the unprecedented midnight clangor, the groan and collapse of the fire escape was little noted.

Rubber-soled feet tiptoed overhead.

She moved a fraction of an inch. The fire escape shuddered. Another fraction and the baby moaned, opening golden eyes. It was worth any risk to spare her from the president.

"You don't deserve this, baby. You weren't the one who cheated on your taxes."

Clarry Starko loved stories portraying President McBeth as a villainous tightwad.

"She owes a birthdebt!" called a dog from above. She looked up, about to argue with him, then realized that he was only trying to distract her. "Hand her over!"

The fire escape protested the addition of another dog's weight.

She leaned forward, over the dark-bright street, over the agitated stew of people and creatures and cars and contraptions. She clung one-handed to the cold iron rail, holding the child out before her in midair.

Not yet . . . not yet.

The landing swayed with too much weight. She would lighten it in a moment. The dog at her level moved cautiously, though not fearfully.

Not yet . . .

An old gas-powered station wagon appeared directly beneath her. The top was sawed away, leaving an open bed. The horn blared as the driver pulled up on the sidewalk to negotiate a stalled clump of singers and beasts. Bundles and baskets jostled in the bed of the wagon, fat soft sacks and heaps of black cloth. The wagoneer cursed and slammed on the brakes. The vehicle stalled for the moment, awaiting an opening.

Now.

Poppy let go and watched Calafia fall. Her daughter made an acceptably soft landing on a bale of cloth, then slipped down among baskets and bundles as the wagon started up again, moving off through a clearing in the shifting crowd.

The shock of what she'd done almost broke her from trope-trance. She had dropped her baby daughter. As if this were a real threat, and not a mere wire show.

The landing had looked safe enough. The Shock-Pruf in the swaddling would protect her. But still . . .

Behind her, curses.

Poppy looked back. Time to face the Lassies.

Her free hand stole into her garment and pulled out a gun. The dog on the landing growled when he saw it, lips peeling back from inhumanly sharp teeth. She knew he wouldn't ask for mercy. Not now. Nothing could keep her from firing.

Nothing but the weight that hit her from above.

The second dog caught her by surprise, crushing her in furry arms. She relinquished the rail and both of them fell. People screamed, catching the show at its climax. An instant later, they struck cement.

Poppy lay stunned, pinned beneath the dog, wondering where she would find the strength to push him off and flee. The Lassie moaned and tightened his grip on her throat. The world went black. She couldn't breathe, couldn't move. He was choking her, really doing it now, caught up in the tropes, believing the role, a canine actor overcome by his innate ferocity and hatred of humanity.

They should have used a man in a dog suit, she thought. He's really choking me!

The weaker half of the fire escape, rigged to fall, tore away from the wall. Clarry had meant it to create a convincing end for her attacker. But as she toppled into blackness, she knew that it would come too late.

"Kai," she tried to say. "Kai, it's me. It's Poppy!"

He didn't seem to recognize her, and she could hardly speak. He was strictly the president's dog now. And she was a fugitive. His legal prey.

Blackness. Light nowhere.

"Kai!"

Calafia . . .

"God!" exclaimed a gawker. "This is *so* realistic!"

* * *

"Cut! That's enough, Kai. Let go of her, you fucking mutt!"

Poppy felt as though she'd been washed up on a reef, drained and exhausted. Clarry Starko and a few hands dragged the Lassie away. Kai looked cowed, timid now, his vestigial tail tucked up between his legs beneath baggy trousers. They led him off. Clarry crouched and helped Poppy to her feet.

"Feel okay?"

"Dizzy." She clung to him for a moment, looking around at the crowd. People only now were beginning to realize that they had seen a livewire session.

Several men pulled the fire escape aside. It was hollow, almost weightless, and couldn't have crushed a puppy. The sidewalk was padded to cushion her fall, though at the moment she'd hit, caught up in the tropes of the chase, it had felt cruel and hard as real cement. So much unreality made the hotel look fake; its bricks seemed to turn soft and waver in the damp night wind. This whole back alley, with its lights and revelers, could have been just another set.

"You look way tawdry," Clarry said. "Way pale. Here, have a twist and tan out. 'Grats, by the way. You did a great job as a mommy."

He handed her a cool silver vial. She started to push it away, but he folded her fingers around it. His large, black, long-fingered hand dwarfed her small, pink one. "Go on, you deserve a break. I'll take care of the cleanup."

"I don't want a twist tonight, Clarry. I want my baby."

"That's tan. I'll go get her. You stay right here."

He walked off past the studio van. The street was busier than it had been during the recording, but down here in the midst of the crowd it all seemed two-dimensional, as if pieces of cardboard were cut into people shapes, all sliding past each other in shifting planes. She felt a bit flat herself tonight. Painted eyes followed her. Recognition. Everybody knew Poppy. Her spin-off was scaling the ratings, though it might never be as popular as the "Figueroa Show," in which her whole family had been wired and continually live. She should bask in the recognition, not cringe from it. But tonight fame didn't satisfy her. Was this any kind of life for a child? Poppy had been brought up for the wires, but not born in them. Her youth had been inviolate; she'd been neither sender nor receiver. The media surgery, the teasing growth of polynerves, had been (more or less) elective on her seventh birthday, which was older than most kids were when they got their wires. But then, most kids were RO—receive only—and she had been a sender all the way.

But Calafia never had a choice.

She sank back in an alley between a drug shop and a sushi-taco stand, twisting the halves of the silver vial. Clarry was right. A twist would help clear her thoughts. She glanced up at the hotel across the street, seeking out the broken window of the room where Calafia had been born. Maybe she would get a room and sleep up there with the baby tonight. She didn't want to stay with the cast and crew again. The baby deserved better.

Clarry found her again just as she was setting the twin halves of the twist against her temples. He slapped one arm down before the current could hit her wires.

"Hey," she said, mildly irked. Then she saw his face. "What is it, Clarry?"

Clarry was a smiler: he rarely quit grinning unless something awful had happened. Now his face looked as gray as old cloth. He was chewing on his vitamin-fortified tobaccorish rope at an alarming rate, unspooling hanks of it from his deep vest pocket.

"Poppy, I don't know how to say this. There . . . there was some mistake."

"Oh my God. The baby." She started past him, but he caught her by the elbow.

"Where you going?"

She spun about to face him. "What do you mean? Where is she? I want to see her."

He shook his head. "Poppy, when you tossed her . . . where did she go?"

She felt herself collapsing inwardly. Everything coming apart. Alone. The wires carried none of this; no one could share the fear she felt, the growing panic. What was happening?

"What do you mean?" she asked. "I dropped her in the wagon, right on the padding."

Clarry shook his head. "It wasn't our wagon, Poppy. I told you there'd be coordination problems in this crowd. *Our* wagon got stuck in traffic half a block away. No one knows where the other one came from—or where it went."

Clarry caught her to keep her from falling.

"Hold on now, babe. It's gonna be tan, totally tan. We'll find her."

"You lost her?" she whispered.

He sighed, drawing her into the street, toward the studio van. A pack of mangy Lassies—street dogs, *macho canés*—trotted past, sniffing obscenely in her direction.

"Do you remember what kind of wagon it was?" Clarry asked. "What was in it? Who was driving?"

"It was just like we rehearsed. You recorded everything! Play it back!"

"Settle down. I wondered if you had any other impressions." He shook his head. "I'm sorry. No one knew what happened till our wagon showed up empty."

"You better find her, Clarry."

He gnawed on his rope ferociously, hardly stopping to spit the chewed bits and brown juice. He gulped and swallowed before speaking.

"How hard can it be with those eyes of hers? If we can't find the wagon tonight, we'll advertise—we'll go global. She can't slip through the net, Poppy. We'll offer a reward, how about that?"

She nodded, but she was hardly listening. A ransom was more like it.

"I never wanted her involved in this."

"Come on, Poppy, tune it down, we've been over this. There's no danger to the kid. She's safe, I swear it."

"I didn't want her in the recordings. I've got the stuff to draw an audience by myself. But you had to have one more tawdry gimmick. You had to have my baby!"

"Look, we're getting her, it won't take an hour."

"If you lose her, Clarry . . . Goddamn you." She stopped in the middle of the street and covered her face. "I want my baby back!"

"Sh, sh, now, baby. You're making yourself pale. Hey, Poppy, look who's coming! Isn't that Cornelius? The seal from your old show?"

She turned around, searching the crowd for the familiar face.

Yes. Here he came, in his customary pinstripe suit and liquid tie. Black fur neatly oiled, long whiskers combed, pointed teeth polished and gleaming. The usual scent of sushi and Old Spice attended him.

"Good evening, Miss Figueroa."

"Cornelius," she whispered, putting her hands on his shoulders. "What are you doing here?"

"Your father sent me to inquire if you and Calafia would like to attend a birthday party. To celebrate her birth as well as the state's bicentennial."

"My daughter." She started to back away, but Clarry caught her from behind.

"Hey," Clarry said. "We haven't met. I'm Poppy's wireman."

Cornelius bowed slightly. "Clarence Starko, how do you do? I've enjoyed the series so far . . . in the flat versions."

"You're not wired? Oh, sealie, you're missing most of the show."

"I was never wired, not even for the Figueroas," Cornelius replied. "I don't suppose anyone missed my point of view, had fallen while several strong men hauled Kai off. The seal's suit was in shreds.

"I only want an autograph!" the dog snarled. "He's my favorite fur star!"

Clarry Starko reappeared from the crowd. "Shit. That Kai's crazy. He's a mad dog."

They stared as the transgenic Lassie was led away, still snarling. Blood speckled the faces and hands of the men who'd collared him. Poppy knelt beside Cornelius. His snout was badly gashed, his clothes in ruins, but he managed to smile and sit up.

"Dogs are always chasing me," he said.

Clarry whistled. "We may have to put that teegee down."

Cornelius stiffened, leaped to his feet. "He didn't ask for the life you gave him. And now you mean to snatch it away?"

"Hey, it wasn't my idea turning animals into people. No offense, I'm all for animal rights, but I don't think it was good for either party."

Cornelius gave Starko a cold stare, which warmed only slightly for Poppy. "I'll tell your father you can't make it. Please call him when you can."

"I will." She stood up on tiptoes to kiss him on the snout. "Get some healant on that."

He bowed his farewell and wove away through the crowd. Several people approached him hesitantly for an autograph, but he passed without acknowledging them.

"Don't worry about the baby," Clarry said around his baccorish. "We'll have her safe and sound."

"She's not gonna be in any more shows."

Clarry wanted to dispute this, but the night's events had proved her fears real enough. He only shrugged.

"You've got *me*," she said. "It's my show, and that should be enough. I won't have my baby subjected to this kind of life."

He shrugged, spreading his hands. "Tan, Poppy, totally

there being so few seals in the audience." He turned to Poppy again. "The delivery went without trouble, I take it?"

She started to shake her head. "Cornelius . . ."

"What is it, miss? You look frightened."

"She's fine," Clarry said. "Just a bit burned from her busy—"

"Leave us alone, Clarry."

"I'm telling you, Poppy, an hour, two hours at the most. Don't turn all pale over this."

"Clarry, just leave us alone."

She waited until he was gone, then took Cornelius by the elbow and led him down the street.

"The baby's missing, Cornelius. Missing."

"I don't understand."

"I can't go anywhere tonight. I'm sorry. I don't know what to do. I have to stay here and look for her. Maybe she's somewhere nearby. Maybe it was all an accident. I can't believe it. I don't know what to do."

"Missing?" Cornelius said.

She couldn't answer him. An accident. What else could it be? Why was she afraid it might be something more sinister? What if someone had kidnapped her baby?

"Is there anything I can do, miss? Have you called the police? Your father will want to help."

"I haven't done anything yet. I just found out."

A sudden eruption of barking and growling interrupted her. Cornelius jerked around, startled by the sound. A Lassie rushed toward them, unrestrained, fangs bared, saliva dripping all down his shirt. It was Kai, the dog who'd nearly strangled her.

"Kai, what's—"

He struck her aside, leaping at Cornelius, teeth snapping at the sealman's neck. Poppy screamed for help, so loud that every head in the crowd turned. People converged on them, trying to pull the humanimals apart. Cornelius lay where he tan. It was just such an irresistible idea, you know? The bicentennial. The birth. A chase scene . . ."

"A kidnapping."

"Whoa, now. What's that? Don't go saying stuff like that. This isn't a crime. This is a bit of bad luck."

"You mean there just happened to be an identical station wagon in the place of the studio wagon? And it just happened to be under the fire escape when I dropped my baby? That was bad, but it sure wasn't luck."

He looked embarrassed. "Well . . ."

"I don't think it was an accident, Clarry. But just in case it was, you'd better keep looking. Meanwhile, I'm calling the police."

"Not yet, Poppy. What if she comes back?"

She smiled, though her thoughts were bleak. "She's twenty minutes old, Clarry. You think she's gonna walk to us? No, I'm calling the police. You should be glad, though. It's free publicity."

2

Seascraper Soirée

Prone on his warm squishy Jell-O-bed futon, Sandy Figueroa filled his lungs with tasty, resinous, redweed primo, inhaled and kept inhaling, gulped a little bit more, lungs cramping now, like a pearl diver filling his chest before a particularly deep and difficult plunge. Then, lying back, releasing the hookah's filter tip, he closed his eyes and let his body channels switch at random.

Getting zee'd to ride the wires was his favorite indoor pastime, and he rarely did one without the other. The livewire frequencies modulated in accord with his thoughts, which, after the deep drag, had turned totally chaotic. Half a thousand channels flipped through him in half a second, none quite in synk with his mood. He waited for something to grab him.

Most of the broadcasts were garbage, a polluted ether of advertising and you-are-there game shows. Bad media lurked in his polynerves like an Alzheimer's prion, waiting to crystallize. He lost a little control and a bit more discrimination when he was zoned. That was part of the fun, but it made for a hairy ride. The redweed put an edge on his mood, making it easier for the freak shows to grab him. Now, for instance, he was snared by—*Bugs!*

Jessie Christo! They crawled from his pores, tickled his feet, cast off his nails like manhole covers and scurried for the shelter of his face and genitals. He didn't know whether to cover his nose or his crotch. In a panic, he tried to change channels, but his fright mired him in the signal, making it virtually impossible for him to tune anything else. There was no waking from this nightmare until it had run its course.

This was no horror show; they didn't grip so ruthlessly. This was a commercial.

Suddenly, a cooling aerosol spray covered him from head to foot. A purple-brown cloud of lilacs and chocolate dissolved the chittering little monsters an instant before they reached his face or pubes. Iridescent wings, scaly carapaces, manifold eyes, and quivering antennae—all vanished, leaving him limp and grateful for the spray, whatever it was.

"Doctor McNguyen's Soothing Antipsychotic," whispered a sexy voice in, curiously, only one ear. *"Now in aerosol cans."*

Sandy was too drained to tune another channel. He stayed on the line, letting the peaceful feeling and comforting scents fade. The wires carried him straight into a regular wire show.

"Look at Sandy," someone said, and immediately he felt his diaphragm convulsing with canned laughter. It was a disorienting sensation. His older sister Poppy stared at him, one hand over her mouth, suppressing her own unforced laughter. If he let go of his identity, he would slide over into her point of view. And it was tempting, since his body was wrapped python-tight and getting tighter. This was as bad as the bugs. He was starting to suffocate. Despite this, his father stood at Poppy's shoulder, observing him with an expression that edged on hilarity.

"Where'd you two come from?" Sandy tried to ask. But his mouth wasn't quite in his control.

Instead he heard himself say, *"How do I get out of this?"*

More laughter. His ribs ached when he resisted it, but they ached even more from the splintering grip surrounding them. As he struggled, the pressure altered slightly, becoming less violent but still threatening in its way: it was as if his clothes were beginning to pulsate, especially around his groin. Clasping and relaxing, like an exploring hand.

This was all starting to seem familiar.

A flicker. His identity wavered and he became someone else—someone taller, heavier, with a deeper voice. Someone who was saying, *"Sandy, what are we going to do with you?"*

He was his father.

Oh no. As the redweed rush passed, he realized what was going on.

Reruns.

For some dark reason, he had tumbled into the twenty-four-hour Figueroa channel.

From his father's POV he saw himself quite clearly, tangled in a contraption of Playtex, leather straps, and chrome manacles. He looked about fifteen years old, so this episode of the "Figueroa Show" dated from about five years back. He couldn't remember making it, but he'd spent most of those days zipatoned on weirder drugs than redwood marijuana. By age twelve he'd needed a dose of ET to get out on the right side of bed; then he'd sprinkle his cereal with MMSG for more paisley visions with every crunchy bite; by noon he'd be totally brain-soaked from sipping ESP-3 and TAB-synth; and he would only taper onto mild, relaxing weed or BeastMaster around midnight, to get to sleep. None of his internal stimulation carried through the wires, of course; in this way, drugs supplied him with the nearest thing to privacy that a wire star could purchase.

His baby sister Miranda toddled into the rerun room, bawling her head off when she saw Sandy caught in the straps. *"Daddy, Daddy, make him stop! He's wrecking my sex toys!"*

Sandy couldn't bear a return to his own wretched POV. He watched his younger self fumble with the straps for a moment longer, then drop his hands in exasperation. *"I give up,"* that Sandy said, his adolescent voice still brittle. *"I thought it was a Chinese puzzle-suit."*

A warm hand fell on his father's shoulder, and a warmer voice said, *"He certainly takes after you, Alfredo."*

Sandy, startled by the voice, slipped back into his tangled, gawky point of view. From this vantage, which fit him about as well as a child's neoprene wet suit, he saw his mother for the first time in years.

"Mom . . ."/"Mom . . ."

Both of them spoke, Sandy-then and Sandy-now. She came forward carrying the key to the manacles. His eyes brimmed with tears as she knelt to release him. Her own eyes were dark brown, for she was the only Figueroa to have shunned the orange iridic implants.

"Mom," he murmured. "Mommy . . ."

He couldn't take any more. The initial zee'd confusion passed, leaving him enough control to detune. He jerked himself free of the broadcast and lay breathing heavily. Every now and then, his inhalations caught on the ragged edges of a sob.

Mom. Seeing her alive again was the cruelest sort of torture, worse than being devoured by insects. No spray can of psychic balm could heal that pain.

He couldn't bear to ride the wires again tonight, though there were a million other shows that might have cheered him. He didn't want false cheer right now. If he'd really wanted that, he wouldn't be sitting alone in his apartment, smoking dope and riding the wires while the rest of California celebrated its two-hundredth birthday.

He checked the antique Kit-Kat clock above the futon, next to the old signed photograph of Danny Bonaduce. Rhinestone eyes and a switching fur tail—the clock's, not Danny's—told him it was well past midnight.

Happy birthday, California. From me and Danny.

The faded picture had been his father's—"*Hey, Alf! Roll with the punches! Danny B!*"—but even over the gulf of years, Sandy felt a spiritual kinship there. They were sitcom brothers, separated by nearly a century, but still, without "The Partridge Family," would there have been a "Figueroa Show"?

It was hard for you, too, wasn't it, Danny boy? Hard when the lights shut off and the wires went dead and everybody thought of you forever in that frozen zone of rerun adolescence. You were out raising hell and divorcing that Japanese babe and teaching karate, and people meeting you years later (even the cops taking your DNA prints, I suppose) would do a double take and say, "Hey, you're that brat from 'The Partridge Family'!" *Was*, you asshole. I was that brat.

Yeah, Danny. Like me. I'll never get older than seventeen. Except in real life, of course—but what does that count for?

He got up and raised the bamboo blinds a fraction of an inch to peer out the window. By day, he would have had a view of fields, tractors, and towering redwood-marijuana hybrids, a dense forest of mighty, smokable trees. Tonight he saw lights in the field, heard music and laughter. The mulch hands and trimmers sure knew how to party. They banged out odd, percussive rhythms on steel drums and played their band saws like dangerous kazoos.

It was stupid of him to sit here all night when his employees were out there having a good time. They would think him pale indeed if he didn't put in an appearance.

So, out the door and down the creaky stairs he went. From the porch, the smell of pine, pot, and fresh-trampled earth was invigorating. He watched the workers dancing outside their long, low quondos, whooping and hollering, leaping high. Rather than break the festive mood, he sank down on the porch of the two-story shack he called home, and simply watched. It was like gazing at another planet. No matter how dirty he got, no matter that he dressed in blues and grew his hair long and snarly and talked in a weird patois, he just never fit in with the regular folk. He was ever and always the wire-show star, intimately known to all—the most private moments of his youth soaked up by strangers whose lives would forever be a mystery to him. No one understood why he'd given up S/R status. What sender/receiver would choose to become a receive-only like everybody else? They couldn't comprehend why he wanted to be one of them, a plain RO, after tasting the luxury life of the world's most popular broadcast family.

But people knew only what the wires told them, and the wires were polynerves, not real ones. What the audience perceived as pleasure, Sandy had experienced as hollow and meaningless. His whole live life had been a string of situations dreamed up by a board of "creative consultants" and then enlarged upon and improvised by his family. He had dreamed of an existence where things simply *happened*, without contrivance; where he could ride the waves and do only what had to be done, or what he felt like doing, and never again need go looking for "situations." A lazy life, if necessary. A life of lying around, getting zipped, tuning in whatever stupid shows were on the wires—and never, ever sending again. The *wonderful* life of a simple RO.

He had wanted to retire as early as possible, but his parents wouldn't consent. He'd intended, as soon as he turned eighteen, to pull out and leave his family to fend for themselves.

He never had to wait that long.

When he was seventeen . . .

Oh, Mom.

He didn't want to think about it. Not now. It didn't bear considering at the best of times, let alone tonight, when the sound of laughter and music already had him feeling depressed.

He had wanted the show to end, sure. But not that way. Not on the moon.

Well, he had patched together a life for himself, like the

rest of them. Poppy had her spin-off and was welcome to it. Dad was in big business, though Sandy couldn't feature him as the executive type. That had been more Mom's style; she'd been the real pusher in the family, the ambitious one who cut the hard deals with the network execs. No wonder without her they'd lost the heart to carry on.

In a way, Sandy was happy now—as happy as he could hope to be owning a ranch that ran itself and living off the proceeds. And his royalties.

His main problem these days was boredom. Too much time on his hands: time to think, to surf, to twist, to zero in, to ride the wires, to deepen his tan. He owned the plantation, but didn't exactly run it. He wouldn't have known where to begin. He lived on the edge of the farm, communed with the workers, attended board meetings, and accepted his dividends. The rest of the time he rode either the wires or the icy waves of the rock-gnarled NoCal coast.

Such was life without creative consultants and situation mongers. Ten years, half his life, had been planned out for him: he still wasn't sure how to invent meaningful routines of his own. His younger sibs, Mir and Ferdi, were even more lost, having been born when the show was well underway, raised in the context of a wirecast routine; even before they went S/R with wires of their own, everything they had known was an artifice, a contrivance, though they didn't know it. Still didn't, in fact. For them, certain borders had never been properly drawn.

Footsteps padded toward him.

"Mister Figueroa?"

At first he didn't recognize the voice. He insisted that the farmhands call him Sandy and pretend to be his pal.

A figure in a tattered suit stepped onto the porch. A bandage decorated the visitor's long snout; his doglike whiskers were twisted and bent like used pipe cleaners.

"Corny?"

The sealman bowed as low as he could, an apology on his

thin black lips. Sandy let out a glad cry and threw his arms around him.

Cornelius remained characteristically stiff. He reciprocated the embrace, but awkwardly, as if it pained him. He had always been uncomfortable with human displays of affection.

"Greetings, young sir. Excuse my appearance. I had a run-in with an autograph hound."

"Who cares about your appearance? You look great to me. But what are you doing here?"

"Your father is throwing a birthday celebration tonight, and he misses you and Poppy terribly. I offered to do my best to convince you to come along."

"So where is she?"

"I, ah, couldn't convince her."

"Is this a big party? I mean, like, really big? Or is it just a family get-together?"

"It's rather large, sir."

Sandy sighed. "I hate those things. You think he'll be upset if I don't make it?"

"He'll be very disappointed if both of you fail to attend. And it will look very bad for me."

"Oh, all right," Sandy finally said. He was suddenly eager to go, although he knew he would hate it. "I suppose I should dress for the occasion." He swept a hand at his threadbare jeans, which stank of sweat and marijuana resins. "Or would this be appropriate?"

"You know your father's tastes, Santiago."

Cornelius followed Sandy into the house and upstairs to his room. The sealman was more than slightly neurotic after all the gene tinkering and mental programming that had gone into his creation. He stayed in the exact center of Sandy's room, as if reluctant to come in contact with the grimy walls or furniture or even the cluttered floor. Stuffed and mounted, he could hardly have looked less lifelike. Corny's obvious discomfort prompted Sandy to make a diligent search for clothes. He was rewarded with two moderately scent-free tabi-socks (one red, one green) and a pair of worn sponge thongals that made his ankles tilt inward. His only clean pants were swim trunks bearing shimmering tropical patterns. He found a reasonably fresh black chamois teashirt, over which he pulled a vest of very fine (if somewhat tarnished) chain mail. He crowned his efforts with a Greek fishing cap.

"What do you think?" he asked.

Cornelius trembled slightly. "I suppose you no longer utilize wardrobe consultants?"

Sandy grinned. "You kidding? Everything I wore had to be brand name when they were dressing me. Keep the advertisers happy! Every time I dropped my drawers to take a crap, I was supposed to look down at the label on my underwear." He deepened his voice to imitate a livewire voice-over. " 'Yes, Santiago Figueroa wears Ample Briefs, the shorts of the stars.' "

Cornelius made no comment. He pivoted on a polished heel and held the door open.

Sandy said, "Shall we take my truck?"

"Not unless it has wings. We're running late as it is."

The dark cannabis preserves of Humbocino passed quickly beneath Cornelius's airborne Jaguaero and the view gave way completely to the state-spanning metropolis of SanFrangeles. From Tijuana in the south to the bustling northern factories of Weed, the Frangeles "Franchise," or "Lunatic Frange," stretched with little interruption. Sandy often skipped up in the company SkyScout to ogle the pretty colors. Normally the sight was spectacular enough to keep him enrapt for a zoned eternity, but tonight its beauty was beyond belief.

As far south and east as he could see (which was fairly far, this being a fogless night), the city was fired up for celebration. Gouts of flame rocketed from the hearts of habimalls, exploding harmlessly (one hoped) amid the air traffic. The sky was full of giddy cars, all circling and spiraling to take in the sights, and consequently becoming part of the spectacle. The land looked like a carpet of burning jewels, heaped into hills and terraces, some spilling out upon the water. And it was seaward that Cornelius steered the car, away from the thrilling chaos of the Franchise, into the near total dark.

On the wet western horizon, Sandy saw a string of lights, perhaps a parade of nuclear yachts moored offshore to observe the continent's festivities.

Approaching the lights, the Jaguaero lost altitude until it skimmed the water. Sandy watched Cornelius to see if he gave the sea a wistful look, but apparently the sealman harbored no tender sentiments for the cradle of his ribosomes.

One sea-flung form loomed directly ahead of them. In a moment, Sandy saw the lights for what they were: windows in a massive offshore office building. The forward beam of the aircar showed wind-whipped wavelets lashing at the sea-level panes. Sandy gripped the edges of his seat, expecting to crash at any moment.

Cornelius brought up the Jaguaero in a smooth motion; they soared five stories in the time it took Sandy to gasp, then poised motionless over the roof while an aircar below them taxied into the indoor garage, freeing the landing pad for Cornelius. A minute later they were humming down fluorescent corridors. Cornelius parked in his reserved space near the elevators.

"This way, Master Santiago."

As they stepped into an elevator car, Sandy caught a whiff of powerful female pherofumes. His head filled unavoidably with the sights and sounds of sex, all called up by the smell. He shoved his hands into his swim trunks to hide a sudden woodie from Cornelius, who probably wouldn't have cared.

As the doors closed, he tried distracting himself with equations and mnemonics. Sandy knew he had a closet full of sexual anxieties from his years in the wires, when he couldn't so much as scratch his crotch without exciting legions of horny teenage wire-hoppers. Even now, as an RO, privacy was something he couldn't believe in.

The scent maddened him. He wanted to tear off his shirt and trunks. Even Cornelius was starting to look good in the stuffy compartment.

The doors opened. Laughter and music washed into the car and swept them out. Cornelius took hold of his arm, leading him firmly around the edge of the crowd, though Sandy would rather have dived in and followed that smell to its source. He knew intellectually that the pherofume was completely superficial, but the knowledge did him little good in the face of olfactory lust. He wanted to find that woman, whoever she was, pull her into a dark office and bury his face between her—

But Corny kept tugging him along, toward the smell of food and fainter perfumes. Many guests wore osmodelic pomanders around their necks; as he passed among them, the air filled with trails of light and his nose began to vibrate with desire. The multitude merged into a boundless blur of colored cloth and jewelry, a single, buzzing, hive-mind party insect.

They passed a row of tall windows at sea level. Waves broke against the panes, throwing phosphorescent foam and spray like wide, lacy fans above the heads of the guests. Kelp clusters rose and fell on the water, barnacled root systems trailing away beneath. Periwinkles left gleaming trails on the glass.

"Suddenly I want sushi," Sandy said.

"Haven't you eaten?"

Sandy shook his head, and Cornelius pointed out a long serving table.

"If you care to serve yourself, I'll find your father."

As the sealman disappeared into the crowd, Sandy grabbed a handful of honey-glazed prawns from an icy tray and hurried to lose himself. It was difficult being a Figueroa. Guests broke off chattering and smiled at him, some bowing slightly, some greeting him with hearty halloos that meant nothing to him, coming from total strangers.

"Sandy! Hey! How's life?"

"Very lifelike, thanks."

He was halfway across the vast room when a syrupy voice said, "Sandy, my boy!"

The voice was unmistakable. Turning, he put on his phoniest smile. "Reverend . . ."

The Reverend Governor of California, Thaxter H. J. Halfjest, waited with his arms spread wide to embrace Sandy. His crown of gold wire glittered with huge precious and semiprecious stones. His thick, red-gold hair stuck out through the crown, giving him an unkempt look. His clothes were gold, to match his shoes, and a golden mantle descended from his shoulders. Diamonds pricked his earlobes, more clustered at his nostrils, and bands of stones at his wrists and throat clicked together when he moved. "I'm *so* glad you could make it!"

He slipped his arm through Sandy's and patted his wrist. Sandy feigned a coughing fit, freeing himself before the Rev-Gov could smother him.

Halfjest was impossible to offend; nothing bothered him. His life was perfect. Not only was he governor, but he was perpetually live as well. His wire show had been second in popularity only to the Figueroas', and since Marjorie's death he'd been number one in the California ratings. No other politician was so open to global eavesdroppers. Living inside Halfjest, receivers conned themselves into believing they were gaining a political education, seeing the workings of government firsthand. But this was a well-orchestrated illusion. Actually, they rode in the tanned and scented skin of the most flamboyant entertainer since Liberace. It was showmanship, and not politics, that gave Halfjest his appeal. He treated his audience to a rich diet of caviar and champagne that few of them could have afforded (although, as taxpayers, they managed to somehow), leading them through the spectacle of his ever-changing Sacramento palace with its rich carpeting, scented lawns, and indoor waterways, inviting them to glamorous parties like this one, marked by meetings with the world's rich and famous. Halfjest had opened the corridors of power to his constituents—and taken them roller-skating down the slick marble halls.

He pretended to be continually open to the opinions of his audience, occasionally reversing the flow to look in on their lives and listen to their opinions. This was the perpetual promise of the wires: the simultaneous involvement of all citizens in the state, their opinions and desires constantly tallied and monitored and taken into account, then enacted personally by their most popular representatives, the elected embodiments of their will. However, Halfjest—like other politicians—opined that he was one lone man, without the superhuman ability to field and synthesize all their desires at once, and lacked the discrimination to separate momentary urges from deep conscientious longings. The task of processing, making sense of, and acting on so much input was beyond the ability of any computer of the day, let alone any one person.

And so the wires, with all their potential, were put to the endless task of distraction.

Had he cared to, Sandy could have flipped into his wires right now and picked up the governor's broadcast. Could have stood here talking to himself through Thaxter's POV.

But that was sick. It was bad enough to do it singly, let alone in duplicate. Besides, feedback was an ever present danger. Had their eyes met . . .

"Have you been keeping well, Sandy?"

"Tan, Thax. Totally tan. You?"

"I've been frantic preparing this birthday bash. Listen, we're having a contest. We need a new name for California. Something splendid to mark the bicentennial."

"A new name? Are you kidding, Thax? What's wrong with 'California'?"

Halfjest, disdainful, pressed an oiled hand to his breast. "You mean you don't know? I've been telling everyone what a horrid name it is. I mean, the associations, the imagery! Ghastly!"

"I guess I missed it."

The RevGov tried to reclaim Sandy's hand, but he got it into his pocket just in time.

"The California myths are all so terrible. Why, Calafia was a dreadful Amazon queen—not even a libby-lezzy! She only tolerated men as food for her giant buzzards! It's an awful story, and I hate our lovely realm to bear such associations. Imagine, they came looking for gold and ended up on the bottom of a birdcage! What were those Spaniards thinking when they came up with the name?"

Sandy shrugged. "They must have been pretty disappointed when they came looking for El Dorado and found Los Angeles instead."

Sandy searched desperately for another familiar face, any excuse to get away from the Reverend Governor. This was like one of his childhood birthday parties: hundreds of strangers smiling and calling him by name.

He was about to baldly excuse himself when someone came up behind Halfjest and slipped her arm around his crystal-clad waist.

"Ah, there you are, my darling," said Halfjest, turning to kiss the young woman. "I'm sure you remember Santiago Figueroa."

For a moment, as their eyes met, Sandy thought she was the one wearing the sex pherofume. But she didn't need to wear anything to arouse him; in fact, when she wore nothing it was best of all. He grew warmer, pulse quickening. The sight of her, and the memories that came along, made him blush.

She had her father's red-gold hair, but hers was long and thick, flowing down in waves to break on the backs of her thighs. Bare thighs. Her short skirt and blouse were striped gold and black. Like her father, she was decked from head to toe in crystals and diamonds, a delicate tiara woven through her hair, jeweled ankle bracelets tinkling, and little stones of ten colors gleaming on her toenails.

"Dyad," he murmured, his throat dry.

"Hi, Sandy. Where you been?"

"Up . . . up in Humbo," he said. "On my ranch."

Dyad took Sandy's hands in hers. She lifted them to her mouth and kissed each palm. It was like plugging his arms into a wall socket.

"Three years," she whispered. "Seems like forever."

"I was just telling Sandy about the contest, darling."

"Yeah, Dad." She moved closer to Sandy, putting one arm around his waist; her fingers ran down to grip his ass. "Come up with anything?"

"No, but something's coming up."

She brought one of his hands to her mouth again and began to suck on the back of his thumb, nipping at the skin of the first joint. Sandy's legs turned to water, but he was torn with indecision. The last (and first) time he'd gotten involved with Dyad—the night he'd lost his virginity—had started as the best experience of his life and ended up the most humiliating. Like her father, Dyad was live. When she had fucked Sandy, so had legions of horny teens (he tried not to think about his large audience of elderly adorers) who'd been waiting for the moment. OUR NIGHT WITH SANDY! For months afterward, their fanzines had been full of lush, overblown, almost worshipful descriptions of the act. SUPER SEX WITH THE SANDMAN! It was recorded and duplicated and traded among the teenie fans while Sandy went crazy with embarrassment. TASTE HIM YOURSELF—TONIGHT AND EVERY NIGHT! He had avoided Dyad ever since. And although he was no longer wired, she most certainly was. Some of his old fans, no longer quite so teeny, might still be waiting for a second chance to get it on with him vicariously. That thought was enough to shrivel his orchids quicker than a plunge into a penguin's swimming hole.

"What do you think, Sandy?" Thaxter asked. "I haven't heard anything very imaginative yet, but I'm sure we can outdo those old Spaniards. Goldia, Orangette, New Atlantis."

"Libidopolis," Dyad mumbled around his thumb.

He had not taken his eyes from hers for nearly a minute.

"See you later, Dad," Dyad said, breaking off her ministrations. "Sandy and I have some catching up to do."

"I need his opinion, Dyad. Maybe he'd like to be one of the contest judges."

"You can talk later." With that, she pushed Sandy into the crowd.

"I thought we'd never get away," Sandy said with a laugh when they were free. "But look, Dyad, I don't know if this is such a tan idea."

"Oh, it's coppertone, baby. I'm not S/R anymore. Haven't been live for months. I'm RO like you. We'll have some real privacy this time."

"Tortious," he said. And then: "Oh, no."

Cornelius had appeared at Dyad's shoulder.

"Your father is ready to see you, Sandy."

Sandy swore under his breath, cursing the time he'd wasted on Halfjest's filibuster. He and Dyad should have been downstairs, in a dark office beneath the waves, making up for lost time.

"Can't you put him off a while?"

Cornelius looked uncomfortable. "I'm already bringing him enough bad news. I would greatly appreciate your support."

Sandy sighed.

"That's tan," Dyad said. "I'll find you later."

He nodded. "I'll look for you." Turning to Cornelius he said, "You owe me one."

Dyad ducked away without so much as a kiss. Perhaps she

thought it would make their parting simpler, but it only added to his frustration.

This floor at sea level, and a few more in the bright waters just below, belonged to the CEO, board chairman, and seascraper owner—in short, to Alfredo Figueroa. Executive windows looked out upon green glimmering vistas of fish and dangling seaweed, while lesser employees spent their days staring out at a cold perpetual darkness, where not so much as a flashlight fish relieved their unrewarding vigil. At the bottom of the building, mail-room and cafeteria staff labored under extremes of pressure. A course of psychic decompression was a necessary part of employee orientation.

The hall to Alfredo's office was lined with ferns and potted palms, with here and there a humanimal—mainly seals, teegee bodyguards and butlers—standing motionless among the plants.

Cornelius opened the door. "After you, Santiago."

Sandy hesitated, sniffing. He had tracked the lusty pherofume to its source. It belonged to someone in his family. And he thought he knew who.

Inside, as on a vast flatscreen, the hated moon shone over the restless sea. Foam slapped the full-wall window and fell away, seeming to drip from the baleful, bone-colored ball. Anger and grief rose up in him as always at the sight of the satellite.

A semicircular desk was pulled up nearly to the glass so that the old man seated there seemed trapped between sea and sky and seascraper. Alfredo Figueroa's face seemed to glow with an inner light, like a carved pumpkin, every wrinkle etched deep by a knife of fine Swiss steel. But this pumpkin was rotten, pouchy and soft on the outside if not within. The gold eyes flickered like candle flames, still youthful, though the hair was so sparse that at first Alfredo looked completely bald. When his head moved, a few strands glinted against the pate like fine cactus needles.

"Shut the door, Santiago. Have a seat."

Sandy looked for a perch. His younger brother Ferdinand, engulfed in a huge orange Jell-O-chair, waggled a finger at him. Miranda, nine years old now, lay stretched out across a loveseat. He couldn't help staring at her. Somehow, surgically, she had acquired a hypervoluptuous body in the last year. Her breasts were enormous, her waist wasp-thin, her hips wide. Facial augmentation had given her a sultry, sexy expression: thick lips perpetually gleaming, eyes like coals in a barbecue. The smell that wafted from her, a distillation of pure sex, was totally terrifying in this context. The room reeked of incest. Not to mention pedophilia.

Mir gave Sandy a satiated smile and stretched luxuriously, then pulled her legs up to make room for him. Patting the cushion, she said, "Come sit here, bro-bro."

Sandy choked on the pherofumes and backed away sweating, his chain mail clinking. "I'm all right."

"What's the matter, Sandy?" said Ferdinand sarcastically. "Don't you love your sister?"

"Ferdinand," said their father warningly.

"Never mind then," Ferdi said. "I'll sit with you, Miranda. Sandy can have my chair."

"All right, I'll accept that. Even though you're not much of a man yet, Ferdi."

"How do you know *I* haven't been to the body shop?" He dropped down in the loveseat and they began to explore each other with their hands. Ferdi nibbled Mir's throat till she began to purr.

"God," Sandy muttered. "You two are worse than ever."

Miranda gave him an icy look. "And what are you? A born-again Puritan? Don't tell me what to do. Just because pleasure frightens you . . ."

"That's enough," Alfredo said. "I didn't bring you here to argue."

"Then why are we here, Father?" asked Miranda. "It's what we do best."

"I wanted to be with my family. I wanted to feel some of

the old magic." He rubbed his knobby fingers roughly, as though trying to work the knuckles out of them.

"You're pathetic," said Miranda. "If you want old magic, you should've summoned demons. Speaking of witch, where's that gypsy slut of yours?"

"Maybe you're my demons." Alfredo looked sharply at Cornelius. "Where's the baby?"

"I'm afraid there was some trouble, sir. Poppy wouldn't come with me. I don't know exactly what happened, but—"

"Were you in a fight, Cornelius?"

"Couldn't be helped, sir."

"Poppy wasn't violent, was she?"

"Good grief, sir, no! There was trouble on the set of her spin-off. It seems the baby—"

A sudden pounding on the door startled them. A sealman poked his head into the room and said breathlessly, "Sir, the news! Channel Ninety!"

"What are you on about?"

"Poppy's child, sir. Your granddaughter."

"What the . . . wait a minute." Alfredo pressed a button on his desk. The seascape faded from the window, to be replaced by a live projection of a wild Franchise street. Revelers raised their glasses to the wall as if toasting the Figueroas, hamming it up for the cameras. Sandy was grateful for the flatscreen image because he didn't feel like riding the wires at the moment. Most news programs were broadcast both flat and by wire, so that viewers could either watch a sometimes violent reality at a comfortable remove, or enter a wired journalist's body to participate in fast-breaking stories. He certainly didn't want to rush into a mob scene like the one on the wall. It looked a bit too real.

A newscaster stepped into view. The body was female, but, like all Channel 90 'casters, she wore the trademarked androgynous Channel 90 plastex mask. *The News You Need From the Face You Heed!* Only the voice and choice of attire betrayed any slight individuality, but they weren't enough to make any one 'caster less indistinguishable or trustworthy than any other.

The newscaster was saying: ". . . followers of the popular program, 'Poppy on the Run,' will get an unexpected surprise when they tune in for their regular feature tomorrow. The crew was recording a special bicentennial episode in the building behind me, when trouble struck the set tonight. We've known for some months that the newest Figueroa has been growing in the womb of Poppy Figueroa, but not even industry tattlers knew until now that the baby's birth was timed to coincide with California's bicentennial."

"I knew it was a bad idea," Alfredo growled.

"It wasn't your choice," Miranda said. "She *carried* the twerp. Her contract *ruled*."

The camera pulled back to show the exterior of an ancient hotel. Lights glowed in some of the windows. People crowded the upper ramps of a rickety fire escape. Below, children bounced on the padded sidewalk.

Newsbody 90 went on: "The session went as expected, according to the crew, with young Poppy pursued down this fire escape by actors playing the henchmen of President McBeth. But something went wrong when she dropped the newborn daredevil into a passing wagon."

"She did what?" Alfredo leaped to his feet. "What kind of stunt is that? I never heard—We never allowed anything so stupid on our show, so dangerous! The baby's injured, isn't she? God, this new vaudeville is monstrous. . . ."

"There's more, sir," said Cornelius.

"The baby Figueroa landed safely, as far as we know. Unfortunately, no one knows much. The unidentified wagon vanished, along with the child. Until she's found, the story of the Figueroa baby, like the plot of 'Poppy on the Run,' will be shrouded in mystery."

No one in Alfredo's office spoke.

"Is this a publicity stunt dreamed up by Poppy's producers?" the newscaster asked. "Another plot twist awaiting resolution in a future episode? No one is saying at this time, particularly not the program's creator, hot new wirist Clarence Starko. Starko is busy tonight, apparently coordinating search efforts and comforting the infant's mother, glamorous Poppy Figueroa."

And here an insert appeared, a wall-sized image of Poppy slumped with shut eyes against a dirty brick wall, her head lolling sideways as two halves of a silver vial fell out of her palms onto slimy asphalt.

"My God," Sandy whispered. "All this going on and she's twisted?"

"This is Newsbody Ninety, 'Facing the Facts' live from Snozay."

The image switched to another live report, a male Newsbody in a party hat covering the bicentennial opening of a databank or yet another habimall.

"Whoa," said Ferdinand. "Way tawdry. Hella dramatic."

Alfredo shut off the picture. Waves crashed against the wall. In all this time, the moon had hardly moved. Yep, I'm behind this, it seemed to say. This and every other sad, sour development.

Alfredo turned on his sealman. "You knew and didn't tell me?"

Cornelius trembled visibly. Sandy moved closer and put a hand on his shoulder. "Dad . . ."

"I assure you, sir, I knew next to nothing. I'm as amazed as you are to learn the details. It . . . it seems impossible."

"What's wrong with her?" Alfredo asked them all. "Why won't she come home even now? She needs our help more than ever."

Ferdinand stood up, lit a kelpie, and blew yellow iodinic smoke across the room. "Maybe she's afraid to face you, Pop. After all, she just wazzed your investment."

Alfredo slumped over his desk. "I never should have listened to her. Giving birth in the middle of a thriller. It just isn't done! She has the tropes of the grand tragedians. She's a dramatic actress, not . . . not a human target! *This,* children, is what the industry does to you when you go up against it alone. Oh, Chevy Chase was right. Hollywood eats its young. We were so good together; we kept each other safe and sane. That's all Poppy knows. She can't handle independence. She grew up in a troupe, with a whole company to cushion her. I tried to warn her how hard it is alone."

"Who listens to you?" said Miranda. "Look at yourself, skulking around, afraid any moment someone'll find you out and boot you out of the boss's chair. Are you really happy sitting here in a seascraper? Are any of us happy since we got out of the wires?"

"Is that what we were?" Sandy said. "Happy?"

She sneered at him. "You were only happy when you were ozoned or twisted, or popping your peenie in a Dyadic duo. Which was most of the time."

"That only happened once!" he shouted, making himself hoarse.

Alfredo's overdramatic sobs cut through their argument. He hung over the desk with his face in his hands.

"I thought Calafia would bring us back together. She was your mother's last project before . . . I thought it would be like having a little bit of Marjorie here with us again."

"Oh, wonderful idea," Miranda said. "A born S/R. Just the sort of thing to take our minds off the wires. What good is that baby anyway, except to star in her own show? How's that gonna help us? She's just competition. You think anyone listened to the Beatles once they heard Ringo work solo?"

"We . . . we have to educate her. She'll grow up in the company of fine actors. Just think of what she might do."

"She might hate us all, for starters. Excuse me, Alf, but I don't see you as any great paternal programmer."

But Alfredo was deep in a trance of delusion and hope. "She'll be such a beautiful child. We'll find her, wherever she is. If there's a kidnapper, we'll pay the ransom. It's just a matter of time till she's back with us. Marjorie's little angel . . ."

"My God," said Miranda with unveiled disgust. "You haven't even seen her and already you love her more than you love us. She's the perfect star you always wanted—or will be till she gets too close, too real. God forbid she should turn out to have a mind of her own—"

"Leave him alone, Mir," Sandy said, unexpectedly stirred by his father's grief; though perhaps more moved by the sight of Poppy in the alley, twisted and in a state of despair he knew was no advertising gimmick, no hypnotropic act. "Pop, we'll find her. We'll find that baby. Miranda doesn't know what she's saying; she's all spun out on her own smell."

"*You're* going to find her?" said Ferdinand, crushing his kelpie on the orange carpet. "Is this Santiago speaking? What was your old motto, Sandy? *'Turn Off, Tune Out, Drop In'*?"

"You little spaz. I'm not the reason we folded."

"Oh, sure, blame it on Mom now that she can't defend herself. Do you really believe that?"

Sandy's cheeks burned. He looked away, his lip twitching. But he wouldn't show his humiliation; he wouldn't show a thing.

"The fact is," Ferdinand went on in his squeaky voice, "we could have carried on without her. It was a tragedy, but hey, that's what pulls the ratings. Five of us was plenty enough—and you, too, Corny. Dad could have remarried once things cooled down. There's plenty of babes out there who could've been as pop as Marjorie. Maybe popper."

"Easy for you to say," Alfredo moaned.

"But we couldn't do it without you, Sandy. You *deliberately* blew it apart. Mom would have wanted us to carry on. She was *into* the wires. But you, you stupid druggie wimp, you took her death as the excuse you'd been looking for. You turned it into a cheap and easy chance to grab your freedom. You make me sick, Sandy, offering to find the baby. You pulled out years ago. Left Alf with the responsibility of raising us. So you can just stay out of it now."

"That's being slightly cruel, Ferdi," Miranda said. "Slightly."

"No," said Ferdinand. "If anything, it's too soft. What do you say, Sandy?"

"I'm afraid to open my mouth. I don't want to get your flying bullshit in it."

"All right, that's enough!" Alfredo cried. "Shut up, all of you!"

The children fell silent, uncomfortably aware that they had been slipping into the old situational tropes again: cruel banter, character assassination, spurious motive plumbing, crude comebacks. Ah, the good old days were here again, without the broadcasting to make it all pay for itself. It dawned on him that they were all RO now. For all Ferdi's talk, he left the airwaves to Poppy alone.

Alfredo pursed his lips and gazed at the surface of his desk. "We've all made mistakes. The biggest I made was getting into this business. You're right, Miranda, I've never been happy here, playing executive. Once I thought . . . well, it was hard for me to keep on without your mother. But I think maybe now's the time to try again. I've still got some power in Hollywood. I can use it to make the world safer for my granddaughter—as soon as I find her, I mean."

"So who's going to take care of the business, Dad?" asked Ferdinand. "You've got a seascraper to look after now. You can't just drop it."

Alfredo gave Sandy a questioning look.

"Oh, no," he said. "I've got my own business. The plantation takes all my time."

Lies.

"Can't you help out here for a little while, Sandy? So I can devote myself to looking for Calafia? I pray to God it won't take long. I could use you here, son, if you're willing. I'll teach you what I know, though it's not much."

"Let *me* find her," Sandy said.

Ferdinand scoffed. "You're hopeless."

Sandy turned away, as he had in the past, cursing them for the way they made him feel. They didn't appreciate his talents and never had. Wrapped up in themselves, groping at old roles, each of them grabbing for star billing, stealing the scene even when no one was watching. His father was the aging hero, striking out through dangerous territory to rescue a baby girl. Sandy supposed he might have been guilty of the same motivations. He told himself he genuinely wanted to help, but he didn't think that was possible here. Too many egos in the way.

"Talk about babies," he heard Ferdinand say as he walked out and closed the door behind him. The party sounds, the smell of osmodelics beckoned. He needed to get lost in the crowd; he needed a heavy-duty mind change.

He needed Dyad.

Dancers moved with erratic grace on a circular floor of patterned marble. The Reverend Governor occupied a dais in the center of the floor, sanctifying the crowd with a swinging gold censer, sipping champagne. Where Thaxter smiled down with particular emphasis, Sandy saw Dyad's hair and tiara. He headed toward her, stumbling over heels. He hadn't danced in several years, but even recent knowledge of the archaic steps was useless for finding a passage through the intricate, unpredictably whirling crush. They were doing the Chaotic Attraction.

Dyad hopped, backslid, then rushed, spinning, toward him, one hand joined with that of a tall, sepulchral young man with unfashionably pale skin, jet black hair, and thin lips cosmetically crimsoned. Sandy, backing off, collided with a bejeweled old woman and her adolescent partner. By the time he'd worked himself free with apologies, the dance had ended and he heard Dyad calling his name.

"Sandy!" she cried. "Over here!"

No avoiding them now. He put on a smile and faced her partner, submitting to an old rush of jealousy.

"Sandy, you remember Raimundo Navarro-Valdez?"

Raimundo's eyes flashed, and not with amusement. He kept the same expression, keen as ever, his lips like twin razors grown sharper with the years. His eyes bespoke a mind even narrower than his mouth.

"Yo," said Sandy, putting out his hand.

Raimundo refused the gesture, instead bending slightly at the waist, tapping the heels of his polished black boots sharply together, then returning his full attention to Dyad. One of his hands remained around her waist, in a touch that was light yet possessive.

Dyad said cheerfully, "Raimundo and I are getting married next month. *That's* why I'm not sending anymore." She shrugged. "Actually, I'm not even receiving. Raimundo's family doesn't believe in *any* wires."

Sandy felt a cold surge in his stomach. Undertow. "Married?"

Raimundo smiled for the first time in Sandy's memory. "An antiquated tradition, but one that still finds followers in the Old World."

"Which old world is that, dude? And what's wrong with the new one?"

Raimundo ignored him, still smiling at Dyad.

"We're not totally old-fashioned," said Dyad with a wink at Sandy. "I mean, it *is* an open marriage."

Raimundo's smile vanished. "Open? In what way?"

"I think you two'd better talk that one over," said Sandy, the words scalding his mouth. He backed off as though wading from a riptide. This was why he'd fled to Humbo, wasn't it? People got so weird on you; situations kept inventing themselves, even without a board of paid consultants. "Later, kids. 'Grats to you both."

"But Sandy," Dyad called, "we were supposed to get together tonight. Just like old times."

This was too much for him. He fled through the crowd as fast as he could and finally found a couch in a relatively quiet corner, near a dark window sheltered from the brunt of the waves. There he sat, staring at his reflection in the dark glass, becalmed in a mental Sargasso.

He felt a light tap on his shoulder. "Mister Santiago?"

In the black glass, Cornelius's reflection swam up suddenly.

"Hey, Corny."

"I came to see how you were feeling, sir."

"I'm fine, Corny, fine. I've been thinking."

"Thinking, sir?"

"I know I don't have much of a reputation for it, but sometimes it's hard to avoid. Maybe I will take over here for a while. I mean, I might as well learn an honest trade, right? I'd make a pretty good executive. Dark suit, conservative tie, Aramis. A new image. Let Dad go look for Calafia. It might be good for him."

He turned from the glass, expecting the news to please Cornelius. But the sealman looked dejected; his thoughts were elsewhere.

"What's wrong, Corny?"

"Nothing, really. It's just that, well, being with all of you this evening has made me nostalgic. I remember the days when we were together, living out the show. It must be the tropes."

Sandy sighed, then clapped Cornelius on the shoulder. "Guess memories aren't part of a seal's natural state, huh?"

"I wouldn't know, sir, but they can be painful at times. Unnaturally so."

"You're telling me?"

Cornelius stared at him, blinking back tears.

"Come with me, Corny, okay? While I talk to Dad? Remember, you owe me one."

"Certainly, sir."

"And don't call me sir. You're not our butler anymore,

remember? You're a self-employed man—or seal, or whatever. You're my friend."

"Your friend? Do you really mean that?"

"Why would I say it if I didn't?"

Cornelius looked puzzled for a moment, then shrugged. "I'm sorry, it's the tropes again. I forget that you're not acting."

"No way, dude, this is real. More or less."

3

A Hag-Ridden Coach with No Wood on the Sides

A black sawed-off station wagon rattled through thinning crowds and progressively emptier streets. It was not that dawn grew near and the revelers sought their beds, nor had the celebrants wearied of their activities, for this was an occasion that came but once and most Californians were anxious to prolong the novelty of the bicentennial while it felt like something more than another reason for sales spectaculars. No, there were better reasons for the growing silence and the infrequency of humans where the wagon went.

The streets grew steadily fouler; damper and darker the decay on all sides. Buildings had fallen here, but souls had lofted high.

The driver of the wagon was a thin old woman, so frail and bird-boned that she would have banged against the dashboard every second if she hadn't been strapped to her seat. Her ancient fingers, thin and tenacious as ivy creepers, clutched the steering wheel with desperate vigor; her arms, protruding from the depths of a billowing black robe, were scarcely thicker. She drove at full speed, although it seemed impossible in the cluttered streets. Sometimes she swerved to avoid black patches, unsure if they were puddles or bottomless tarns; more often she relied on ferocious speed to plow her over or through a variety of obstacles. Pieces of barbed wire, rusty rubble, broken tubes of phosphor-powdered glass, the occasional sluggard rat, such tokens could always be found in the wagon's radiator grill at the end of her wild midnight rides. Once a sister mechanic had found a human foot in the spoked hubcaps, severed just beneath the ankle. Its advanced putrefaction had been a relief to all, offering assurance that the Official Crone had not yet struck down an innocent being. Her license was in perpetual danger of being revoked. Yet, for all her frenzied speed and demonic, gutter-spanning leaps, she was at heart a gentle soul who always wept at the sight of a rat tail in the wiper blades. Nothing, however, certainly no tender sentiment, could slow her down.

Which was why she of all the Daughters had been chosen for this errand.

Over the unmufflered din of the old gas engine and through the perpetual ringing in her ears, she heard the infant wailing among the sacks of grain and kipple in the wagon's bed. It sounded like a siren, a noise foreign to these sacred precincts, since police never enforced profane laws within the boundaries of the Holy City.

She glanced over her shoulder to make sure the jolting ride hadn't thrown the child from its nest. The babe appeared safe, but it made her uncomfortable to leave such things to fate, especially after the trouble she'd endured to catch the little dear.

Before long, she was forced to slow the wagon. The street had narrowed until it was no better than a track for feral dogs. It was wide enough for the wagon in most places, but there had been some slippage during the day (or perhaps the Valis sect had slyly rearranged it), and rubble thicker than usual posed a hazard. She shut off the motor, dismounted, and peered into the back of the wagon, after first checking to make sure that no one was lurking about, waiting to fire pink light beams in her direction.

Ah, the healthy wailing of a baby girl. The Official Crone's old nipples ached and itched a little. Dry memories. She hadn't heard the sound in many years. The Daughters bore no children, having no contact with men—Goddess forbid!

The baby had worked her way down among the sacks, but after some exertion the crone retrieved her. She screamed vigorously, waving her tiny fists more fiercely than any tot in the old woman's memory. Cooing, she pressed the child to her breast, wishing her eyes were better, wishing (for once) that the night were not so dark. The buildings were so tall and congested that light rarely carried from brighter parts of the Frange. She couldn't make out more than the plainest fact of eyes, nose, and mouth. The High Priestess had promised that the girl would have orange eyes, but there was no evidence of that in this darkness. Still, this had to be the babe they sought.

The swaddling was loose; the child now kicked free of it. The crone set her down on a sack of cereal, bent painfully to retrieve the cloth, and, when she stood up, screamed.

Somewhere nearby, fireworks had exploded. Their light danced over the ruined towers, bits of it bouncing down to these drear depths. In the fitful flashes, unmistakably, the Official Crone beheld a child's dangling pee . . . pee . . . penis?

Penis?

It was a male. . . .

Her heart nearly stopped beating, but her thoughts moved so quickly that they tugged her blood along out of necessity.

The child's masculinity was a disaster. It meant she had somehow stolen the wrong child. A changeling. She would suffer the cosmic wrath of Mother Kali, not to mention the more painful and immediate anger of Kali's High Priestess.

But worse than this to the Official Crone was the knowledge that she had touched the . . . the male. Her fingers had very nearly brushed that, that, that, that *thing*, that terrible item of sickening masculine flesh! All this was forbidden. More than forbidden, it was disgusting, it revolted her. She had lain with men once, long before Kali called her. She'd had a husband and even male children, but that was long ages behind her now. To think that somehow a male member had risen out of nowhere and practically fallen into her lap—it filled her with horror. The Official Crone didn't know where to turn.

First, half out of her senses, she threw the soiled swaddlings over the child to spare herself the sight of his tiny pizzle in case of another fireworks flare. She didn't know whether to scrape the boy into the street and leave him there, or simply shove him back deeper into the wagon and pretend she'd never looked, leaving all hard decisions to the High Priestess. True, that would mean desecrating the temple, but at least she could hold to her story. She had fulfilled her mission to the best of her ability. How was she supposed to know that the wrong child would fall from the fire escape?

But if she ditched the child and came back empty-handed, she would have no excuse. The High Priestess would think her a doddering, blind old fool, and say her infirmity made her imagine a penis in place of the pristine apricot folds of the female gender. The Official Crone knew a penis when she saw one, but what if the High Priestess didn't believe her? It just wouldn't do to insist on detailed knowledge of such a blasphemous object!

That decided her. She would do no more and no less than the High Priestess had directed. If she ended up with the wrong child, so be it.

It wasn't her fault. None of it. It was an honest accident. How many infants were tossed from fire escapes at midnight on the state bicentennial?

She clambered back into the seat, trying to keep her mind off the thing that squalled behind her. Once the station wagon started moving again, the baby would slip down among the sacks; that would explain why its swaddling had come undone.

She wasn't going to risk impurity by touching it again.

With a fresh, impatient eye, she examined the pile of loose rocks and cement that blocked her way. She decided that ultimately nothing would carry her through better than a burst of honest speed. And if the child tumbled overboard, well . . .

Accidents will happen.

While the bicentennial was of great concern to many Californians (particularly those on the payroll), such temporal matters fell far below the notice of the Holy City's sacred squatters. Festivities couldn't offer the escape from care they sought. Governors had come and gone with hardly an impact on the precinct, except when their policies had plunged it even farther into poverty. A President of the United States had inspected the region more than forty years ago and declared it a disaster area, uninhabitable, worthy of federal assistance—had there been any spare change in the Union coffers. But money there was none, and the aid never came, and eventually even the toughest of the poor found good reason to leave. Life was hard enough elsewhere. Why suffer unnecessarily?

A few, however, ventured into the urban no-man's-land and found it to their liking—spiritual cousins of the hermits who wandered into deserts to live on locusts, into arctic wastes to subsist on lichen and flavored ice, or off to the weightless asteroid colonies, where a dedicated man could simper and suffer self-righteously while his bones slowly softened and imploded for want of gravity.

The forgotten city's new inhabitants were pioneers of decay who found in the tangled ruins of once-modern cities enough meaningful symbols to propel their souls beyond the reach of gravity. Atop slumps of slag from which NO VACANCY signs protruded, fire-eyed, speed-eating monks divined Zen prophecies whose meaningless runes they scribbled in spray-can poetry on gray, smog-eaten walls. These were the first temples and the first rites of the new visionaries.

Next, of course, came followers. Some were orthodox ruin-skulkers, professional jackals who prowled the shadows in search of the occasional senile citizen or mendicant monk so deep in satori that he couldn't be bothered to protect himself. Prides and packs of juveniles, beasts warring for territory, tore up streets that the priests had hoped to make their own. In such an atmosphere, religion could not help but flourish.

Eventually the gangs themselves were initiated into the mysteries of this new Eleusis, brought in as guardians of the fallen temples. Outside officers of the law found ever fewer reasons to enter the inner city. The defending angels kept the avenues dark and ruinous, inculcating the mood most helpful for a zealous pursuit of salvation. One could not tread these streets without acknowledging the flesh's vulnerability, the meager meaning of mere existence. Savage spiritual predators contributed to such insights. The gangs defended those who sat on girders high in broken buildings, staring at sun and moon till blindness stunned them and they fell. On occasion, the gangs were even said to roam beyond the sacred city's bounds searching for acolytes, offering a bloody baptism to those whom fate tossed into their filthy-pure hands.

None of these defenders disturbed the Official Crone's wagon, having watched it come and go night after night. She in turn accepted them, and tried not to dwell on the fact that some were men. Men did have their uses, she supposed. Life was all balance, all compromise. Only death, black mercy, was totality, a perfect bargain sealed.

At last, just ahead, she saw the black temple of her sect. Some Holy City residents made their homes in ancient condominiums, blasted supermarkets, laundromats, car parks, banks, and bowling alleys. But the Daughters of Kali had found themselves an actual church, of uncertain denomination but clearly intended for worship. Above the entrance was a wide marquee on which the Daughters had arranged the name of their goddess in black plastic letters. COMING SOON: KALI! A small booth stood below the great sign, from which the priests of old had declaimed to passersby and plucked acolytes from among the unwary. The doors were mere metal frames, empty when the Daughters inherited the temple, although they had since filled the frames with dark, translucent scenes in stained plastic. The crone had joined the temple several years before, when the High Priestess first opened its doors. Before that, she had served Kali in other ways, less knowingly.

She drew up in an alley alongside the church and rapped the secret code on the dark rear door. It opened creakingly, pulled back by a black-cowled Daughter who greeted the elder with a respectful curtsy.

"Get the High Priestess," the Official Crone said. "The errand is done."

"But it's nearly time for mass," the younger protested.

"Tell her now, before it starts. She needs to know."

The young Daughter scurried away, leaving the Official Crone to take her post. It was closer to dawn than she had thought. Inside the temple, Daughters scurried to finish their tasks before sunrise and the night's last ceremonies.

The tattered rows of temple seats were full of worshipers. Their shadows leaped on the painted walls where bits of dirty gilt glimmered, caught in the light of a hundred votive candles that burned in alcoves around the room as well as on the wide stage at the low end of the slanting floor. High in the wall opposite the stage was a tiny, square window, the fane of the inmost mysteries, where burned the most sacred flame of all.

Suddenly that high flame snuffed out. Three Daughters hurried over the stage, extinguishing votive candles, plunging the entire sanctum into darkness.

I'm too late, thought the Official Crone.

The morning mass began.

A light brighter than any flame sprang from the shrine's high window, cleaving the dark air, casting its radiance on the screen of dingy pearl above the stage. The Daughters cupped their hands together, beginning to moan. For a moment the light was too hot to bear; they squinted, not daring to turn away. Then, mercifully, a bit of shadow obtruded, softening the glare.

Black fingers fluttered across the white field. A sinuous black arm eclipsed the screen.

Now appeared the head, shoulders, and arms of a dancing woman. Her whole body followed. Snakelike she writhed against the screen, blacker than the night sky, banishing the hated sunlike glare. Once again the temple sank into blackness, but this was deeper, darker, richer than the puny shadows that had come before. This was the blackness of Kali, whose very name meant black.

The Official Crone's eyes rolled up in her skull. She sank to her knees. She was not the only one in rapture as narcotic smoke poured from the ventilation shafts and whistles wailed in the hollow heights.

"Kali!" they whispered. "Kali-ma!"

"Daughters!" cried the High Priestess, her voice falling all around them. "Daughters, the age of the sun is coming to an end. Tonight is Kali's time. The governments tumble, the nations will crumble. Tonight, even this decadent land of poppies and lotus-eaters has felt the force and cunning of Her wrath. While California sings and laughs, her golden hair is gripped in the black fist of the Goddess!"

"Kali-Kali-Kali-ma!"

Shadows crept like inky smoke into the convolutions of the Official Crone's brain, rooting out her secrets and her sins, feeding on her shame. They poked and prodded till she knew she must vomit out her guilt. Still she held her tongue, choking down the bile of her blasphemy.

"Truly, Daughters, the long night is falling. Kali's age is upon us. We live in the center of the storm, in Kali's eye. Our mother will preserve us when she brings the black balm of total annihilation."

"Kali spare me!" the Official Crone shrieked, unable to bear any longer the raking of black claws. "I have sinned! I have touched a man!"

Silence.

At her words, even the High Priestess fell silent. The darkness felt more ordinary now, though it remained ominous. A few candles sprang to life and the mother flame was rekindled in the high window of the most holy fane.

The Official Crone began to tear at her hair, begging silently for mercy. Oh, how the Goddess would punish her. Now she might never die. She would live forever beneath a searing noonday sun, in a California of chrome and plastic, enduring the smiles of young men with skin of bronze.

Suddenly the High Priestess, appearing out of nowhere, clutched her shoulder and dragged her to her feet.

"How have you sinned, old woman? Did you fail in your mission? Why didn't you come to me directly? How did you fail? When did you get back? What man distracted you? Can't we trust you on your own anymore, or are you determined to disgrace this temple with your vile hag-lust?"

"Please, please," the Official Crone gasped. "In the wagon, it was there I touched. Oh, forgive me, Kali. Forgive me, Priestess."

The High Priestess shoved her through the door, into the alley. "Stop your wailing. The pain you feel is nothing compared to what will come as your punishment."

The wagon sat silent in the alley. The child made no sound. Perhaps he had bounced out after all. Would that make the High Priestess any more merciful? Allow the Official Crone to doubt it.

"A man, you said. Where?"

The crone pointed with a trembling finger. The High Priestess and two Daughters advanced to the wagon, while others—fierce guardians—held the elderly woman erect. The

High Priestess began to sort through the sacks. Finally she found what she sought, and let out a bitter laugh.

"A man, you said?"

"A male, Priestess! I meant a male! I did as you asked, everything went perfectly, the other wagon was delayed, the child fell from the sky—but still, still, this is what came to us. I didn't mean to look, but how could I avoid . . . *it*?"

A commotion spread through the Daughters. Some cast their eyes fearfully to the sky, but thankfully there was no flush of dawn between the corroded towers.

"Not a man," said the High Priestess, chuckling. "Not even a male, dear old Crone, though I see how you made such a mistake with your bad eyes."

"A mistake?" the Official Crone said hopefully.

The babe began to bawl. The High Priestess tore away the swaddling and raised the child aloft. In the pale light falling from inside the temple, the Official Crone saw once again the thing that had terrified her in the streets.

But now, in steadier illumination, she saw where she had made her mistake.

The child possessed female genitalia, a hairless cleft, a tiny mound. All this and something more: not a penis, but very like one.

"Do you see, old woman?" The High Priestess shook the baby. "Do you see what you mistook for masculinity? It's nothing to be afraid of. In fact, it's a triumph. This is the child I sent you for; no other comes so specially equipped."

The Official Crone could scarcely take her eyes off the tiny wisp of . . . well, not flesh exactly. It looked more like plastic cable, shiny and clean, ending not in an irrational foreskin-covered glans, but in a reasonable metal tip. A simple prong.

The High Priestess's laughter echoed from the buildings. Far away, one could hear an unwitting answer in the revels of the Franchise.

The Official Crone let out a sigh and sank to the street.

"Yes, old woman, you have served Kali well." The High

Priestess signaled to the other Daughters. "Let her have the reward Kali promised. The Black Needle—Kali's blessing."

The Official Crone let out a cry of relief and delight. The Daughters crowded around, helping her to her feet, excitedly proclaiming, "Isn't it wonderful? Kali's blessing! Tonight you die!"

"Oh!" she cried. "Thank the Goddess!"

"Have a nice death," the High Priestess bid her. "You well deserve it."

While others took the Official Crone to her reward, the High Priestess remained behind. She held the child close to her cheek, inhaling the sharp scents of night that clung to the warm, damp flesh. She smelled sulfur, gunpowder, the brassy taint of human fear. Not the child's fear, no, but the fear of others who had touched her during the night.

Her own mother must have feared her.

The High Priestess gazed at the night sky, a black maelstrom of smoke.

"Kali is your mother now," she whispered.

The baby gave a startled cry.

"Yes, Daughter, we are all her children. But for you she has reserved something special, something quite unique."

The child quieted, staring at the High Priestess with deep golden eyes. The girl was more beautiful than she had imagined. Her eyes glowed like the sun. But this sun would bring an end to the other.

"In honor of this night, we have a special name for you. Yes, Daughter. Henceforth, you shall be known as Kalifornia."

PART TWO
▲▲▲

4

Revolt of the Wage Slaves

Alfredo Figueroa stood at his sea-level window, thumbs hitched in suspenders that never stopped chafing, looking out at a distant figure with long, sun-bleached hair who seemed to be standing on the waves. Sandy had found something to amuse himself in the corporation: he surfed the break that peeled off a corner of the seascraper. Alfredo, on the other hand, never took a moment's pleasure from the business. He'd thought working would distract him from grief, but it had proved an added burden. Thoughts of Marjorie never went away. They couldn't be papered over, not even by a bureaucracy.

He'd given the corporate world its chance to heal him, to return all the favors he'd done for commerce when, as America's favorite father, he'd lived the life of a walking, talking sponsor. Three years, and no improvement. What's worse—for the public—since the Figueroas there had been no family with a fraction of their appeal. It was as if the audience itself had lost a mother and seen its family fractured. Which was true enough. Most members of the audience had never had a real coherent family of their own, certainly nothing with the clear and stable lineaments of the Figueroas.

We were a force for stability, he thought with more than a little pride. We were always there for folks; with all our problems, they could count on us. Our wires were their moral fiber. And then . . . we let them down. We wimped out. Ran away. Skedaddled. No wonder I've been sick with myself ever since. At a time when they needed us the most, we abandoned them, ignoring the fact that our problems had become their problems. It really wasn't fair to tear our support away from them like that.

Who knows what other influences might have rushed in to fill the gap we left? At least we were wholesome and traditional—we had the network censors to see to that. We were living therapy. Might they ever take us back? Would they trust us now—or what remains of us? Are they waiting for a sequel or have they lost interest?

Do they need us as much as we need them?

No. The healing I needed isn't here, in isolation from the world. You have to be within the world, and let it into you. That's the only fair way to involve yourself in change.

"Mr. Figueroa," said a voice, "your Seer is here."

He turned away from the glass. "Send her in, please."

His stomach fluttered as if he were a boy again. It felt like wire fright, although he wasn't sending, and the building's anti-wireshow field prevented him from receiving all but specially coded business signals. The Seer always made him nervous and excited. Anticipation of her presence often turned his thoughts to metaphysics and philosophy.

She stepped silently into the room.

"Seer," he said, bowing a bit. He fought his nervousness with formality. He restrained himself from blurting all his doubts at once.

She glided up to the desk and extended a hand from beneath a baggy gauze of multilayered and many-colored fabrics, all of them more or less transparent. She was slung with gold chains, rhinestones, amethyst pyramids, antique fuses, papier-mâché and turquoise beads, leprechaun charms, Monopoly pieces, mouse skulls, sharks' teeth, gold fillings, pierced tektites, horseshoe magnets, ginseng and St. John the Conqueror roots, knit mojo bags, greasewood yonis and wax lingams, tiny flickering neon mandalas, brass bells, antique soapstone TV sets. . . .

He took her scented hand and kissed it. She turned the palm toward him and he leaped back with a startled sound.

An eye winked out of her palm.

She laughed at his surprise. "It's only a hologram, Alfredo. Nothing to fear."

It winked farewell when she took her hand away.

"It looks so real," he said.

"Ah, it's supposed to. But it's all illusion. Pierce the veil, remember? Don't take anything for granted."

"I try to keep it in mind," he said earnestly. "I'm always reminding myself that it's . . . it's all unreal. Is that it?"

"Yes, unreal. A dream, a dance. Maya."

He wondered. And all his thoughts of the audience—were they illusory too? What did he really know of the world beyond the rarefied realm in which he'd traveled? Nothing! Only what he'd picked up from the wires. And his programming choices were tailored, however unintentionally, by his mood, to suit his expectations. What evidence did he have that his audience was composed of isolated individuals without families of their own? Mightn't that "insight" simply reflect his own recent despair and the limited extent of his experience?

Throwing her hands over her head, the Seer spun a few quick steps of tarantella to catch his attention.

He froze, her captive prey.

She dropped her arms and came around the desk. "Tell me what worries you, Alfredo. I see fear knit up in your brow. There's a dark cloud over your crown chakra and clots in your solar plexus." Her face darkened slightly when she looked down at his groin. "Ugh. And there's something that looks like a hairball in your root chakra, bacon grease and steel wool—"

He couldn't keep from smiling when she said that.

"This needs immediate expert attention, a kundalini snaking of your plumbing. How could you have let it go so long?"

Her nimble fingers worked the snaps of his belt and trousers. She chanted under her breath. Bells rang as she lowered her head. The veils hid her activities from sight although he felt them well enough. He gasped, stumbled backward, and caught himself against the desk. The fog of mental chatter slowly parted. . . .

Suddenly Sandy streaked past the window—no more than ten feet away—waving into the room, his mouth going slack as he saw his father and the Seer. He lost his balance, tumbled from the board, but the wave carried him on.

"Good God," Alfredo said.

"So patriarchal," said the Seer, raising her head to scowl at him. "No wonder you have such problems."

"No, not that. My son."

"He worries you? Well, rest your mind." She straightened, pressed against him. A rodent tooth pricked him through his undershirt. "We need to activate the full kundalini. Spawning snakes."

"Not—not now," he said, peering out the window. Sandy swam away, one arm over his board. Alfredo hitched up his trousers and cleared his throat. He couldn't get his suspenders snug again; with a curse he ripped them off and hurled them into a document shredder.

The Seer sat down in his chair, lifted a tiny mirror on a chain around her neck, and checked her mouth. "Well," she said, "perhaps a little business is what you need. I've been looking where I can, you know, but I haven't seen a thing."

Alfredo came around to the conversation slowly. "Looking for the baby?"

"Of course the baby, who do you think? You see what

happens when you only disturb the slumbering serpents without waking them fully? Your head is full of condensed seed. You need to circulate the *chi,* draw it down again to the bronze vessel. Or else give up alchemy."

Alfredo sighed and sat on a corner of the desk. "So, then. No news."

"I told you not to expect too much. Even if the kidnappers were to trumpet their plans on the wireways, the chances of hearing it . . . you of all people should know how much info passes through us every day. We're bathed in it. Trying to fish out one tiny bit of truth about your granddaughter is like . . . like trying to get a one-eyed turtle to slip into a dog collar in an ocean the size of the universe."

Alfredo stared at her. "I'm sorry?"

She dismissed his confusion with a brisk gesture. "Old Buddhist proverb meaning great difficulty! Finding a needle in a haystack is nothing compared to this. I'm bombarded with misleading information; the wires buzz with speculation, rumors. Overload! No one knows a thing, Alfredo. If they did, I'd know it too. And right away *you* would know."

He clasped her hand. "Thank you, Seer."

"I don't need your thanks, Alfredo. You're an old friend. Just cross my palms with credit."

He nodded. "I'll make the usual transfer. And you won't give up?"

"Not till that turtle's on a leash." She rose. "You know you can call on me anytime. And be sure to tune in to the show some afternoon. It would be nice to have a gentleman in the audience for a change."

"You know I can't pick it up from in here," he said. "But . . . I'll take an afternoon off especially for you."

"You're a dear." She kissed him on the cheek and started out, but turned back before she reached the door. "Oh, Alfredo. I almost forgot. There's a rumor spreading . . . about this building."

"What kind of rumor?"

"Hard to say. I tapped a coded line, I think. But you may have inherited the corporation's karma."

"Great." He shook his head. "I've been thinking I should get out of here. Go back to Hollywood."

"Look into your heart, Alfredo. If you can't find an answer there, I'll ask around the networks and see if there's an opening."

"Thank you, Seer."

"*Ciao*. And have a nice day."

The door closed behind her. Alfredo turned to look back at the sea, and saw Sandy surfing at a more discreet distance. Alfredo watched him for a while, letting his mind clear. He was about to return to his work, trying to remember what he'd been up to, when he saw movement out on the water, something approaching from the shore.

He touched the magnifier on the window and felt a moment's terror when he saw what was coming. The fear passed quickly, and in its place was only resignation.

Signs and omens besieged him. He didn't have to look into his heart to interpret them.

It was time to sell the seascraper. Get out of business. Now.

The water was choppy, drab, and freezing, but Sandy hardly felt it in his insulated suit. A pretty good break swept off the northwest corner of the seascraper. He sat astride his bright green turbo-hyperflex board, counting the swells, working out the pattern of decent waves, reentering the necessary trance.

It wasn't any of his business what Dad did. He was only human. Was he supposed to stay celibate for the rest of his life because an accident had taken his mate?

I am here not to judge, but to surf.

He put down his head, knelt close to the board, and shoved his hands underwater. Tiny, powerful wrist-propellers kicked in, pulling him into the slurping hollow of a wave. He'd found the prop-gloves in a supply room; the underwater maintenance crew used them when they went down to scrape windows.

The wave grabbed him. He gripped the sides of the board, jerked his knees up under him, and got cleanly to his feet.

Yeah!

He shot past a row of windows. This was the weirdest break he'd ever seen. Secretaries stopped typing; execs paused with coffee squibs at their lips. Sandy waved, feeling better than zoned now, feeling alive and in the moment. None of that squashy desk-sitting for him, oh no. Several of the employees waved back. He couldn't hear them, but they seemed to be cheering as he surfed past desks, potted ferns, macrame hangers, monitor screens, job interviewees, janitors. All stared after him with admiration and green envy in their eyes. . . .

Gun that board!

He was getting too far ahead of the wave, losing power, falling into slop. There was a mean snarl to the breakers out here. If he didn't get over the lip or pull out in time, he got nailed. Deep water wasn't necessarily a cushion. He feared getting whacked against the seascraper.

He wiggled his way back over the crest, just ahead of the flattening tube, and found himself riding a herd of white and green steeds, surveying his private sea. He seemed to be floating right up into the sky, arms extended for balance, Jessie Christ himself in a lime green wet suit. Maybe he'd do all right in a corp after all, if this was how he got to spend his days.

Then a whole 'nother weirdness intervened to drag him back to earth, or at least to ocean. Take a guess.

Sandy slipped from the precarious safety of his board, came up sputtering with the taste of oil and iodine in his mouth. He dog-paddled, waiting for the board to home in, circle back, and pick him up. Then he clambered on quickly, got to his knees, and looked east to the coast.

Boats.

Not the usual commuter crowd of water taxis and ferrycraft. Too early in the day for that. These sped and bounced recklessly over the waves; something about them made him think, "Pirates." Maybe it was the cannons they carried.

Sandy dipped his arms in the water and aimed south, skizzing along the eastern face of the 'scraper. The water was all dimples and bumps, rising and falling. He kept low, hidden from most of the boats. He couldn't have seen more than a fraction of the flotilla. The whine of many motors, the shouts of passengers, carried out to him on the seaward wind.

Ominous forebodings oppressed him. One lone surfer against a whole fleet of pirates? Another battle for the history shows.

He pressed the intercom button in the nose of the board. "Corny? Hey, Corny, you there?"

The speaker crackled; water buzzed and danced on it. "Yes, Sandy?"

"Have you taken a look at the coast recently?"

"I have."

"Why didn't you tell me what's going on?"

"We're not certain what is going on. I'm waiting for orders from your father."

"How about at least giving me a warning? I can't see anything down here, Cornball. Bring the sling around and haul me up quick."

Schools of silver fish darted randomly beneath him, scattering like drops of mercury near the face of the building. Sandy looked east again, shading his eyes. Here came the boats, ripping up the water, maybe doing permanent damage. He gazed straight up and saw Cornelius working the crane, swinging the boom over the edge, lowering the sling. By the time it hit the water, Sandy was ready to give up the board and dive. The boats sounded like water hornets about to sting. He grabbed the sling, hooked it to the snag in his wet suit, and clicked the board on to a separate catch. Instantly he started to rise, twirling.

From midair, in the eastward-facing arcs of his spin, he saw fifty or sixty small to medium boats, some with long silver cannons in the prows, all of them crammed with passengers. As they approached the seascraper, they split up like minnows surrounding a log.

Cornelius pulled Sandy onto the roof. A crack team of sealmen—building security—poured up from the parking garage and stripped off their clothes, revealing oily, dark fur. Their lean, muscular torsos were crisscrossed by harnesses holding holsters and knife sheaths.

He'd watched them performing calisthenics on the rooftop in the mornings, singing anthems, but he'd never seen them in action. For a moment he worried about the people in the boats.

"You going in with 'em, Corny?"

Cornelius shuddered, eyeing the water with distaste. "I can't swim."

Sandy shook his head. "And you call yourself a seal?"

"An exile."

The leader of the sealmen barked an order and they all leaped over the side. Sandy jumped to the low wall and watched them dive. Graceful brown bodies sliced into the water, rippled along beneath the surface. The sight was breathtaking, despite the nautical menace.

But what exactly were the boats threatening?

As if in response to his thoughts, the boats settled down. After the engines quieted, the passengers began to unfurl huge sail-like banners. At first they were a mass of wrinkles, but then the wind caught them and snapped them open.

Sandy read the bold words aloud: "WIRES FOR WORKERS! BROADCASTS ARE BROADENING! IF YOU'RE NOT LIVE, YOU'RE DEAD!" He looked at Cornelius in bewilderment.

"Now hear this!" came an amplified voice. A man stood up in the prow of the largest boat; there were speakers taped to his hips and a mike at his lips. "The time has come for workers to share in the wires. Eight hours of deadtime is a daily crime—worse than murder. It cuts you off from the world!"

This was true in a way, though Sandy had doubts about its illegality. Office buildings were partially excluded from the net. Computer and communication links were allowed, but commercial broadcasts were jammed except in emergency tests, when shrill, bone-jangling alarms were allowed to paralyze everyone. It wasn't effective to allow employees to space in on their favorite programs while they were supposed to be working. Who could concentrate on two or more worlds at once? The office receded from consciousness as more compelling subjects filled the mind. Work suffered, poor thing. Some companies had invested in a mild form of random sensory stimulation—a kind of full-body Muzak—but this had been linked to an increase in nervous disorders. Wire silence was safer.

The man in the boat kept ranting: "We come to sanctify our challenge with a sacrifice! Together, we have the power to stop you corporate tyrants. Against us, you are nothing!"

"Is he talking to me?" Sandy asked.

In the next instant, a series of closely spaced blasts shook the air, frightening gulls from perches on the edge of the tower. Smoke streamers burst from the cannons, trailing fire and ashes. Sandy panicked, nearly leaping for the safety of the sealman-filled sea. But the smoke announced nothing more lethal than itself; it didn't even stink. The air above the boats turned black, impenetrable, while the building itself remained untouched. He waited for the wind to wisp away the clouds, but it was dense stuff. As they waited to see what the demonstrators were up to, the silence grew.

Finally, a few at a time, the boats bobbed out of the murk.

Empty now. There was no sign of the protesters. The sealie shock-troops dog-paddled in place, in lieu of any more decisive action.

"Where'd they go?" Sandy screamed down at the head seal.

"Down!" the sealman shouted back.

Sandy bolted for the elevator. It dropped a few moments, then stopped to allow his father to board.

"Did you see?" Alfredo asked.

"Some of it," Sandy said.

The elevator continued to fall.

Alfredo shook his head; actually, his whole body was shaking. "I never had enemies till now."

"They're not your enemies," Sandy said. "They're your fans. You didn't set the seascraper policies."

"I—I just want to be loved."

"We all do," Sandy said.

"My public . . ."

"I know. That's them out there."

The doors opened on a dark, hushed corridor. Down the hall, a crowd pressed up to a broad window, all staring out into the luminous green water. Space was made for Sandy and Alfredo.

Outside, the demonstrators were sinking past in slow motion. Now Sandy saw what had been hidden from him on the surface. Each protestor was wrapped in chains, draped with heavy weights. Around his ankle a boy no older than Ferdi wore a manacle attached to a length of chain that was fastened to the sort of double-barbed anchor Sandy had seen only in tattoos and Popeye cartoons. Most of the drowners were Sandy's age or younger. He marveled in a horrified way at their selfless dedication, their youthful devotion to such a foolish, fatal cause. With mouths and eyes wide open, they calmly and deliberately drowned for the right to bear wires. He wondered what programs they were experiencing in these last precious viewing moments; he hoped the shows were good ones.

They could be watching me, he thought. In reruns, but me all the same. Maybe I should be out there with them, putting my life on the line for the wires. Hell, those same kids made me rich and famous. What did I ever do for them? Sure, we had a few laughs, shed a few tears. Big deal.

Did I ever die for anybody?

He had plenty of time to think such thoughts. The protestors sank so goddamned slowly.

Sandy's breath fogged the glass. How ironic that he should be wasting it on a windowpane, taunting the drowners with the nearness of so much oxygen. Not that they noticed. Their eyes were fixed on some other scene.

"Sandy," his father croaked, breaking him out of his trance. Alfredo sounded sick. "We have to go deeper. We have to . . . to witness this. They're doing it for us—as well as to us."

The elevator carried them much, much deeper this time. Work in the depths went on as usual; no one had yet received word from above, though phones were starting to buzz. With the arrival of the Figueroas, hands froze in midmotion, conversations broke off. The floor manager left her platform and approached with a broad smile. Father and son ignored her, going straight to a window. Sandy peered into the dark water.

"Good afternoon," the manager said. "Is this a surprise inspection?"

Alfredo silenced her with a gesture. There were shapes out there, Sandy thought, but it was too dark to be certain.

Suddenly a lantern ignited beyond the glass, lighting the drowned features of a dark-skinned woman. No life remained in her eyes. Sparkles glinted on the chains that dragged her down. The spotlight was her own, and it lit a long plastic banner that slowly unfurled in the water above her, pulled taut by the weight of her descent. The banner read: VOTE YES ON PROP. 5,997!

Other lamps began to flicker on here and there, above and below, and other banners sprouted and streamed like kelp throughout the surrounding sea. The whole floor crowded to the glass. Sandy backed away, irrationally fearing that the windows would shatter and sweep them out to join the dead . . . or sweep the dead right in.

Alfredo's fingers closed on Sandy's arm. "I can't take any more. They're all . . . all like children to me."

They are your children, Sandy thought. You were a father to most of them. Which makes them my brothers and sisters. Some of them might even be me. Right now, as they die, as the brain blacks out, while wires carry a last little spark of life . . . they could be dreaming that they're good old Sandy Figueroa—dying. Poor Sandy. Poor everyone.

Minutes later, when they joined Cornelius on the roof, they found the security sealmen gathering the protestors' boats before they could drift.

"Let's get out of here, Corny," Sandy said. "You want a ride, Dad?"

Alfredo shook his head. "I think I'll be heading for home. Hollywood. I want to straighten out . . . a few things. Sandy, I . . . I don't want you taking over here. It's not our line of work. You know, I'm not even sure what this company does; but I do know it's not worth . . . this." He made a futile, cramped gesture at the waves. "I'm going to sell—no—*give* it away. To the families of these people, if they have any."

Finally, he bowed his head and wept.

Sandy turned away. He didn't know what to think or feel. No models existed for this scenario. Probably not even Danny Bonaduce, as bad as things got, had ever seen anything like it.

Cornelius steered landward, unspeaking, in the mint green Jaguaero, leaving Sandy the peace he needed to sort through his thoughts. At first he couldn't find any at all. His soul felt like a lidless eye. Shock had laid him open to a barrage of marrow-bursting wire shows—explosive sounds, morbid colors, and what was worse, the cloying NutraSweet-ness of public therapy channels, which tormented him with inappropriately mild advice and tranquil images. "Love yourself. Love your neighbor. Let Dr. McNguyen show you how...."

News shows clamored about the sudden rash of suicide squads offing themselves all over the state. He shut them out and tuned to a peace station, whose signal was a mellow brass gong that hummed unvaryingly but achieved intense harmonics behind his eyes. Every cell began to vibrate. Maybe he needed a nap.

Cornelius cleared his throat. "Would it be appropriate to ask where we're going?"

"Mm." Sandy opened his eyes, saw rooftops, swimming pools, stunted nut trees. They had come farther than he'd realized. "SacraDelta?" he said.

"The Reverend Governor?"

"Just an aimless drive, okay?"

Corny gained altitude, avoiding the low local air traffic, banking southeast.

The SacraDelta complex occupied the heart of the Franchise. Once a distinct entity, the amorphous capital was still one of the seediest districts in the state. The glittering dome of the Capitol Mall crowned a transparent mountain, a meshwork matrix of transport tubes, metalworks, and lock-to-fit office quondos where civil servants could be seen in the process of shredding paper and hair, or engaging in coffee-break quickies in windowed vending lounges. At the golden pinnacle, a tapering spire marked the headquarters of Thaxter Halfjest. Cornelius looked at Sandy questioningly, but he shook his head.

They swerved away from the bureaucratic fantasia, skimming over crowded alleys. He could lose himself down there in the dives and skids, but what he really needed now was someone to talk to. He needed a friend, someone who understood the ambivalence he felt toward wires.

"Look there," Cornelius said. "I believe that's Rancho Navarro-Valdez coming up below."

"So it is," he said, not wanting to rebuke Cornelius for this blatant ploy to cheer him. "What a coincidence. I was just thinking of Dyad."

This bald, weed-colored spot in the midst of the dense-packed Franchise was occupied by a few old Spanish-style houses. Sandy had visited the *hacienda* a number of times when Raimundo's family held parties for California's notables. Today, no other air traffic crossed over the region; in fact, most cars seemed to be going out of their way to avoid it.

"Why don't we, uh, drop in on Raimundo and Dyad?"

Cornelius headed straight in. Sandy waited for someone to come on the radio and question their identity.

He was still waiting when two silver needles lofted from the ground below. Twin plumes of cloud grew behind them, leaning in the direction of the Jaguaero, like tentacles feeling for them.

"Look out!"

Cornelius pulled the car straight up, spinning away from the ranch, and just in time. Rockets exploded where they had been. Shock waves cuffed the car like an irate parent's hand.

Sandy laughed nervously, leaning toward the radio. "Yo! Rancho Navarro-Valdez, you almost hit us! I'm an old friend of the family."

" 'Tate your name and biddinet," said a voice with a slight speech impediment.

This was no time to hedge. "Santiago Figueroa. I've come to pay my respects to, uh, Mrs. Navarro-Valdez."

"You hab no appoinmin." It was not a question.

"This was sort of a spur-of-the-moment thing."

"All vititor mut be clear by Raimundo Navarro-Valdez. He it away on biddinet."

"Look, would you please just tell Dyad that Sandy wants to see her?"

"Only de matter of de howt may grant permitton for entry. Crott our airtpate again and your vehicew wiw be detroyed."

"Tufferin' tuccatat," Sandy whispered.

He signaled Corny to keep circling Rancho Navarro-Valdez just outside the proscribed area. The *hacienda* buildings looked white as teeth in the center of the dry, dusty land. He thought of Dyad, a hostage in her husband's house.

"My only friend in the world," he said, "and I can't even drop in to say hi."

He studied the far-off towers of SacraDelta with new interest. "All right. Thaxter it is. But let's catch him at home. I can't handle the mall right now."

They pulled away from the ranch. Behind them, another explosion filled the sky—a parting shot. The radio had transmitted Sandy's lisping imitation.

East of the government's magic mountain, north of Rancho Navarro-Valdez, was an estate that looked like a green and leafy carnival in contrast to the dirty gridwork of suburbs surrounding it. Aircars darted up and down at this spot, like bees that had found a bottomless throat of nectar. Sandy didn't fear getting shot at here. Thaxter welcomed all comers.

Cornelius dropped the car into a crowded parking tower and took one of two spaces reserved for Figueroas. That's what fame and fortune bring, Sandy thought wryly. Parking spaces across the land. And a mass of fanatics willing to die so they can squirt in your shorts on company time.

Sandy and the sealman strolled across a lawn of spongy hybrid dichondra that gave off unpredictable odors when crushed underfoot. One step smelled like roses, the next reeked of garlic; they padded through an olfactory jungle of lilac and roast beef, rosemary, lemon verbena, and rum. Mercifully, fresh air kept the scents from growing too thick and confused, otherwise he would surely have grown ill from the nauseous mix. They climbed a flight of broad, golden steps through clouds of hot cocoa and fried onions.

The customary crowd milled throughout the lower stories of the house. Some hovered in dim lobbies, murmuring more softly than the music, others danced in bright ballrooms. Children chased up and down the stairs. A haughty Spaniel bitch hung on the arm of a Lab in black leather. (Thax was genetically liberal—had to be in a state whose teegee population grew by 5 percent every year.) The very same party had gone on without relief for as long as Sandy could remember. Many of the guests hoped to be glimpsed by Thaxter Halfjest, to interact with him, however briefly, and thus become part of his perpetual broadcast.

Naturally, Thaxter couldn't play host all the time. He was rarely seen in his own home. Most guests knew their roles and performed them smoothly; in this self-contained society, they intersected with the outer world mainly through gossip and the catering crew. Conversations recirculated endlessly, like the indoor waterways that flowed up the walls and down the stairs—a delicate, entirely artificial cycle that could never have survived in the real world.

Sandy asked after the RevGov and was referred to a transgenic butler. The tuxedoed figure stood stiffly in a corner of the ballroom, bearing a covered hors d'oeuvre tray. His face was a purplish mass of wrinkles and soft pouches, perpetually dribbling on the silver dome that provided essential protection for the canapés. The teegee watched Sandy through clusters of bright blue and red carbuncles, something like a scallop's eyes. Thaxter had been toying with aquatic designs, but not wanting to impinge on patent rights, he had settled on something less mammalian than the sealman. Sandy wasn't sure where the original genes could have come from. Cornelius seemed peculiarly disturbed.

"Excuse us," Sandy said. "Is Thaxter at home?"

The butler's mouth proved an unwelcome sight. Instead of teeth, it featured a fused beak and a parrot's livid tongue. And instead of English, what it emitted was a series of cackles and sputters, accompanied by some distinctly rancid brine.

"I'd like to see him if he is."

"*Krrrawww,*" the butler said, inclining his head with the air of someone being as helpful as he could be under the circumstances.

"Could you maybe point out someone who might know?"

"*Krrrawww.*"

"Tan, dude. Thanks."

They wandered the upper halls, listening at doors until Sandy heard the distinct singsong of Halfjest's voice, forever proposing solutions to problems no one else had noticed. Sandy knocked softly and leaned in.

A teegee guard with a face worse than the butler's tried to slam the door on Sandy, but the commotion caught the attention of Thaxter Halfjest, embroiled in argument with a small group at the far end of an opulent chamber. Halfjest beckoned to Sandy and the purple guard opened the door the rest of the way. He was part seacow, Sandy realized. A slug with a spine.

"Sandy, my boy!" cried Thaxter with his arms spread wide, ever the showman. Cornelius folded his arms and remained near the door, just within earshot. "I'm sure you remember Mario Vespucci."

Sandy nearly tripped on the end of an impossibly long trailing robe of red velvet edged with sable. Its source was an enormous man with a beaked nose nearly as bright as his vestments. The Pope of Las Vegas.

"Santiago, great to see you," said the pope. "How long's it been, eh? Five years? Ten?"

Sandy remembered to bow and kiss the proffered diamond ring. As he did, he was able to read the inscription around the band: CLASS OF '00.

"Your Holiness," he said. "I believe it was the 'Figueroa Family Christmas Spectacular.'"

"Ah, yes. I floated in to bestow a special gift-tax dispensation." He nudged Sandy discreetly, lowering his voice as if to keep secrets from his entourage. "Now I'm traveling incognito. That tightwad Scot in the White House wants to tax all electronic memos that pass between the states. Can you believe that? Taxing the business of politics! Bloody McBeth!"

"Mario," Halfjest pleaded, "calm yourself down. Find

your alpha! It's not good for the cardiovascular system to get so excited."

"Mine's solid plastic," the pope said, thumping his chest.

Sandy wondered how anyone could hide the Pope of Las Vegas, especially in Halfjest's society hothouse. "It's not much of a disguise, Your Holiness," he pointed out.

"I suppose not, but it doesn't have to be." Vespucci pointed at the ceiling. "Like a god, I drop from the sky. Like Superman, I leap home again in a single bound." He winked. "No one's the wiser. You're out of the redwoods, I hear."

Sandy shook his head. "Haven't gotten high in weeks."

"Did I ask for a confession?" He threw up his fatty hands. "It's the curse of my profession. Everybody wants to spill his guts!"

Sandy shrugged. "Sorry."

The pope leaned closer. "You're not by any chance a sender these days, are you? If you are, I'll have to ask you to edit this meeting out of your life."

"I'm strictly RO. But what about Thaxter?"

The RevGov grinned, took Sandy's elbow confidingly. "I've acquired a new special-effects device, straight from the Livermore Livewire Labs. It fabricates new scenes out of old sensations, and blends them into my broadcast seamlessly whenever I wish. That's what my adorable audience is living at the moment."

"You're kidding. You mean you're feeding your receivers canned reality?"

"I prefer to think of it as synthetic."

"But why, Thax? What's going on?"

"You heard the pope. McBeth wants to tax our intercourse . . . so to speak. (He'll be doing that too, I don't doubt.) He wants to know *everything* that goes on. Getting a wee bit paranoid, I'm afraid."

"And here you are talking about him behind his back," Sandy said.

"He's driven us to it. There's no privacy anymore!"

"When did you ever have privacy?"

Thaxter bowed slightly, smiling. "That's different. I was alone with my audience, whom I trust. But McBeth is pressing for presidential censure. He's anal in all the worst ways. He wants everything I experience to pass through the White House before public release. That goes against everything I stand for. California isn't beholden to those tiny zipperdown New England minds. I'm not standing for it."

"So there really *is* a conspiracy against McBeth."

"There is now, perhaps, a teeny one, but he brought it on himself. Not that I ever trusted the man. He still won't let himself be wired, despite all the petitions. I can't understand that mentality. He's completely backward! The man gets all his news from flatscreens. He's out of touch. He has something wicked to hide—he and all his neopuritan cronies."

The pope made a pooh-poohing gesture. "It's the last gasp of the old guard, Thaxter, why don't you believe me? After this, the revolution."

"I think it's already started," Sandy said. "A bunch of kamikazes just went after Dad's seascraper in protest of—"

"Yes, yes, I know all about it," said Thaxter, "and I say well done! They have my full support."

These words amazed Sandy. "Your support? But they're—fanatics! Kids! And they're killing themselves!"

Thaxter shrugged. "Which is what any devotee does in an impossible situation. Their selfless act illuminates a shameful corner of our society—the wage slaves cut off from life for eight hours a day, six days a week. I expected a benefit from this action, Sandy. It will lend momentum to the special election on Proposition fifty-nine-ninety-seven—to ban those awful office scramblers throughout California."

"I'm afraid you just lost yourself a whole fleet of voters."

Halfjest seemed unconcerned. "Plenty more where they came from. Besides, my stats show they were mainly too young to vote."

There was no flexing Thax on this point. Sandy gave up.

"Speaking of getting cut off, I just tried dropping in on Dyad."

"Oh, bad idea! Don't even try." Thaxter's face darkened; he looked almost enraged for a moment.

"I won't do it again. Somebody took a shot at me."

"Ooh, that girl—I don't understand her. Those so-called Castilians—another regressive faction—are moving the whole operation down to the South American Republic. She's probably with Raimundo in Baja by now. Those people won't be happy till they've found a time machine to carry them back to the Dark Ages. She had her wires completely removed, can you believe it? That's a dangerous operation! I've never felt so cut off from her."

"Mexico?" Sandy said. Great. Now I'll never see her.

"She's broken my heart," said Halfjest.

"I hate to break this up—" said the pope.

"Sorry, Father."

"—but I have a mass to lead this evening at Caesar's Coliseum, before the gladiatorial gambling games."

"So, Father," Sandy said, "you must know the answer to that old question, 'Does God play dice?'"

"Does he play? My boy, he's one of our best customers. We comp him to a suite, drinks, girls, you name it." The pope let out a great laugh. "It's worth the investment, believe me. The old boy never fails to lose his shirt!"

Thaxter clucked and shook his head. "How pathetic. A god who gambles? Don't you two agree it's time for some new divinities?"

5

Seersuckers

The Seer raged, raged at her studio audience. She had to *grab* their attention. They lived in her flesh, but the sight of it bored them. They preferred the veil to the face beneath it. They craved the illusions she cooked up for them, preferring insubstantial fantasies to solid food. And they loved it best when she insulted them for their bad taste.

"It's criminal, the mental degeneration I see here!" she cried. "Am I the only one who still has a mind of her own? Let's talk concepts, let's talk eons of time. You're devolving. You'll be blind and white as cave fish soon, your bodies will shrivel up, your eyes will cloud over, you'll be nothing but a bunch of body-temp insulation for your wires."

The audience laughed in tentative agreement.

"Oh, Shiva!" she cried in mock exasperation. "Do you even hear what I'm saying?"

Pulses of acknowledgment lit up the tall response boards along the walls, like lightning flashing in stained-glass windows. She noted the boards with satisfaction.

"I see that some of you are still breathing. But how much of this is *really* getting through?"

Fewer flickers this time. She glanced at the ratings monitor to make sure that the audience was still with her; they were too self-conscious to give their all just yet. She signaled her thruput man with a pinching gesture: *Peel me a few off the top.*

Her vision darkened. Her wires began to warm and purr. She slid sideways into the astral realm, sailing the pure ether of information, skimming the Akashic records.

Shadows filled the studio, blotting out the audience, the tech-crews, the walls of equipment. Her normal sight was displaced by a fly's-eye view, a composite of signals skimmed from the vast population of her audience. RO was a misnomer; most people never thought of the fact that they were all potential senders. Wires were wires, if you knew which switches to throw. They had been designed that way, with the distant goal of continuous two-way operation, just as the telephone companies had provided early push-button phones with symbol keys that no one used for years. It was all a matter of opening their eyes and using them as her own.

She looked out at dingy living rooms with stuccoplast walls; she leaned against splintered doorframes, stroked mangy dogs, squatted in an alley as her guts heaved.

"I'm disappointed in you," she said, closing her fingers to constrict thruput to a more manageable stream. "I mean, you people, you people . . . my God, you have no respect. Someone out there right now, yes you, shitting in a back street. Yeah, I see you—damn right I do! You ever stop to think that's disrespectful? You don't find me shitting on the program, do you? You don't tune in to find that kind of stuff going on. We all know it happens, we're adults here, but do I shove your faces in it? How would you like me to treat you with that disrespect? You're so tied up in me that each and every one of you would crap your pants or your reclining chair or your kitchenette, wherever the hell you are. If you want me to take care of your bowel movements for you, all right, I'll do it. But get this, people. *I'm not going to wipe your collective ass!*"

She completely closed the gap between her fingers and the signal window shut. Herself again, free of the leeches, she faced her equipment, her crew, and the restless studio audience.

"It's time to do a little skimming," she said.

The ratings monitors hummed as the audience grew. All over the state, people who'd tuned in with half a mind now got completely snagged. She was scooping receivers from a hundred competitors for this, her most popular segment.

Nobody outdid the Seer at her job. No one else had her particular talent for illusion weaving.

She gave the newcomers time to settle in.

"We're going through the fire today, folks. Anybody doesn't like it, tune out now. I'm warning you so that you can pretend to be responsible, free-willed adults capable of making your own decisions. The fire is painful. It's the fire of truth. You're not going to like this. Well, a few of you might, but I think by and large you're going to find it very unpleasant."

The ratings increased steadily. As usual.

"In fact, I think you're going to hate it. It's going to *hurt* you!" The lack of response infuriated her. "I mean, people, why do you put up with this every day? This has got to be the worst experience of your day. Why do so many of you sign on for the ride? For a few bits of throwaway enlightenment? What's it worth? You want out of here, people, you want to forget about me for good. Tune in on someone else, someone calm, someone who takes things for granted and never looks too deep. Tune in on *yourselves*."

There. She had them now—she'd hit a nerve. Even the studio audience looked angry, gnashing to get into her. She didn't want so much as a dribble of thruput at the moment. She stoked the hostility to an almost unmanageable level. That's showmanship. That's suspense!

"You don't like to hear that, do you? You don't like to be told to think for yourselves. It goes right against the grain. It rubs against all the training and habits that you think are nature itself. Well let me tell you something, people. You don't know the first thing about nature. If you did, you wouldn't live the way you do. You're the first of your kind—the prime degenerates, the first true two-dimensionals, the most devolved ever. You remember TV? Kind of a curiosity now, but your grandparents may talk about it. Those were the days, right? TV worked the brain cells and the muscles, too. With TV, you had a choice. You could shut it off. You could reach right out and change a channel just like that, of your own free will; you could look at a dozen different things. But *you* had to *decide* to *do* it. You couldn't be wishy-washy. And those images . . . nothing but flat pictures on a box: you had to use your imagination, your experience, your knowledge of the world to pretend they were real, that those flat little things were living, breathing, life-sized people. All that was healthy! That was the peak of our evolution! That was exactly the sort of thing our sun and planet and minds and bodies evolved a hundred billion years to achieve: TV watching. We were built for it, people. It didn't involve invasive technology; it didn't mean growing polynerves. Nope. It was natural, stimulating, healthy."

She paused. The audience was peaking. Time to fly.

"But things have changed since then, folks. Things have definitely changed."

She held up both hands, flicked her fingers wide open, and the techs went to work.

In an instant, they routed her out of the main signal and sealed her into a safe, muffled pocket of consciousness so that she wouldn't lose any personality or suffer psychic erosion in the flow of raw traffic. All the time, thruput was rising. With the Seer out of the way, it snapped up to full. She couldn't conduct the signal herself; her mind would have disintegrated in the blast like a dirt clod dipped in a torrent.

Darkness filled the room, filled her mind, rushed out through the airways, and filled her audience. It was intense, total as system death, but it lasted only an instant. Then the equipment came up to full and started the mind-numbing shriek of sensory feedback, the fire through which she daily dragged her fans.

All the receivers who tapped into the Seer were suddenly turned into senders, their signals thoroughly mixed and sent out again. Her audience, for a painful moment, was able to look through all its eyes at once. The fire was too much for most of them, so many solipsists sitting at home nursing on wires, thinking themselves the center of the world and liking it that way. Now a blinding light dawned in their heads. Democracy. They experienced the reality of a vast population, knew at firsthand that their cherished ego was nothing but an illusion made of silken self-deception. They saw that even solitude was an artifice, requiring the construction of incredibly elaborate barriers. They were little more than motes in a dust storm of humanity. Not only were they not the center of the universe, but the universe had no center.

Oh, if they could only have harnessed this power to govern themselves. That was the *promise* of the wires. But no ordinary politician had found a way to do this without going mad. It remained the domain of "magic"—or art, which is how she secretly thought of it. She was a weaver of the wired world's dreams.

Eyes within eyes within eyes; nerves inside of nerves. Each signal cannibalized itself and amplified along the axis of pain. Fine distinctions broke down to gross generalizations. The Seer kept silent but her flesh began to howl. The feedback's siren call reached her even in the sanctum of her signal cocoon. She couldn't resist the pure power of an audience, and this was that power distilled to its ultimate. Two hundred proof. The purity of broadcast consciousness climbed an infinitely steep curve, tugging her along.

She hit the floor without feeling it, bringing the audience

down with her. She went into convulsions, swallowing the white heat. She exploded, sailed out in every direction at once, fragmented into exactly as many particles as there were people in her audience. She felt she was all of them.

Hands grabbed her; a hard rubber pad was jammed between her teeth; her arms were strapped down to the sides of the throne. The crew, bless them, gave her release. She could truly ride the wires now, let her body fall away, leave the audience numb and trembling while she found new things for them to chew when they came back to their old selves, cleansed and purified by the fire, ready for the visions that she wove.

Free.

Floating in radiant darkness.

Seeing . . .

She saw wires. Wires running everywhere. Wires in the shape of human beings, wires like nerve schematics suspended in space, wires of all colors sending and receiving, receiving and sending, three-dimensional antennae of lovely, fractal complexity held in place by the faint sheen of a flesh-and-blood matrix that seemed almost ugly compared to the pristine wires.

Around the wires, energizing the darkness, spreading out through space, she saw a glow of divine electromagnetism. Polarities reversed, setting compass needles swinging, betraying true north. All the plasmic roads led to Power and the Flow.

Where the current tends I see the current trends.

Voices. In the distance.

The staccato chatter of binary conversation, an on-again: off-again ideology, fell uninterpreted through what remained of her conscious mind. It slipped down between the widening cracks in her subconscious and encountered her own wires, which drank the clamor thirstily. Turgor in her polynerves, a subtle, satisfying expansion. Data rose from the wires like steam. She leaned over the vent, the fuming fissure in the floor of her subconscious, as if she were a Delphic oracle receiving psychoactive vapors. Dreams filled her soul. Visions and voices came at last.

—no longer look into the eyes or through the eyes, but by the legerdemain of will swim through the eyes, head and arms and legs, to explore the curve of vision. I see around myself as the mother who bore me once saw round the corners of time. I have broken the wall—

—and I desire you as you owe me any love, that you suffer me to enjoy him. If you accuse me of unnaturalness in that I yield not to your request, I am also to condemn you of unkindness, in that—

—in the soffits of the six windows is a beautiful chorus of angels, busts in medallions, altogether twenty-four, making music, censing—

—this string zero one seven this—

—man, the woman, the children at the aerial table resting on a miracle that seeks its definition—

Raw traffic. The Flow from which she drank. Meaningless, even to the Seer. Her skill was that of spinning colorful strands from this woolly haze; her talent was for weaving these separate strands into a living fabric.

It was pure gossip, stray rumors and innuendo that, combined, seemed integral parts of a secret that was hers alone to reveal.

She shuttled in darkness, hands on the enormous invisible loom. Intuition inspired her. She hardly saw what was in her hands; she gathered the strands and wove them. This was something no one else could do. There was pure pleasure in seeing what emerged from the chaos:

A narrow band of stars obscured by tumbling blackness.

Dogmen slipping down metal stairs.

A girl's smile blazing like a weapon.

Almost ready.

A complete thought, an idea cribbed from the wire-borne cosmos, floated before her, still furled, like a crumpled tapestry. She grasped it by metaphorical corners and shook it out to see the whole picture.

And dropped the cloth, screaming.

She fled back to consciousness, groped her way blindly into flesh again, pulled her body on like a clammy wetsuit. Heart pounding, tongue thick in her throat, she spit out the rubber pacifier and opened her eyes.

Terrified.

The audience waited for her words. Waited for the oracle to speak, to illuminate them, to bring some bright speculation to their dreary lives. To give purpose to their passage through the fire.

She didn't know what to say.

There was no way to tell them what she'd seen. Not that it was unclear. She could describe it, yes—she simply didn't dare.

If what she knew were true, and if, being truth, she revealed it, she would die. And while much of what she wove was pure deception, enough to make her doubt what she'd just seen, some part of it always came true, and that was enough to keep her silent.

For the first time in her life, the Seer feared the wires. Feared what they had told her. Feared that they might speak again. Feared what they could do.

Her audience waited.

She had to tell them something. Anything. She must distract them.

She rose and faced them. Raised her arms.

An expectant hush. Walls shining with lights.

Tell them anything.

She threw back her head, closed her eyes, groped. . . .

Screamed, sybillic:

"*Elvis lives!*"

After each broadcast, the Seer gave private consultations. She kept a regular schedule for paying clients, but in order to accrue good karma she always took three needy visitors at no charge. Today, on her way out of the studio, she told the scheduling computer to cancel all her appointments.

When she peered into the waiting room to dismiss her charity cases, she found three people already selected. One was an overly familiar face, a woman who came every time her son ran off to join a cult. She was a pain in the neck; the Seer felt no qualms about dismissing her. The next was slightly more desperate, a man whose skin had a soft, rotten look, as if it were a mushroom ready to burst and scatter spores.

"You need a doctor, not advice," she said. "I could get in trouble telling you anything else."

"No meditations? Nothing to help me relax?" he pleaded.

She raised a warning finger. "I give you one little white-light mantric affirmation and the AMA's all over me like a jar of leeches. Forget it."

He slunk out of the room, leaving a damp patch of mold on his seat.

The last visitor, sitting quietly behind the door, made her hesitate.

Clothed entirely in black, even the eyes invisible, this one sat stiffly upright in the chair, bearing a black-swathed bundle.

"Excuse me," the Seer said. "You're a Daughter of Kali, aren't you?"

The figure inclined her head. "Greetings, Seer, most divine."

An older woman, the Seer realized. The Kali sect fascinated her. Even after the events of the afternoon broadcast, she was reluctant to let go of this one. The Daughters were a recent order, a curious new sprout from the occult mulch, and notoriously secretive.

"This is quite a rare occasion," she said. "I've never seen a Daughter of Kali in public. You weren't in the audience, were you?"

The Daughter shook her head. "My vows do not permit it."

"You must have urgent business to have come out of the Holy City at all." She decided that she couldn't resist this opportunity. "Why don't you come into my office?"

Her office was another studio, a small one that hadn't been used in thirty years. It was jammed with equipment, mostly inoperable except for blinking lights and tremulous needles; it was all for show. She remembered too late that it would probably offend the Daughter. Many occupants of the Holy City had forsworn all contact with modern technology—in particular the wires, which were anathema to the more fanatical sects.

But if wires made the Daughter of Kali uncomfortable, she didn't show it. She rocked the black bundle gently while it made a cooing noise. The Seer suddenly realized that the Daughter held a child. A Daughter's daughter. Odd . . . she'd thought they were celibate. They were definitely opposed to sex with men: Y-chromosome contamination. This must be a parthenogenetic child. Or perhaps the Daughter had gotten herself into some more old-fashioned kind of trouble. The Seer repressed a smile. No wonder she needed advice!

"How can I help you?" she asked.

"I came to show you this," said the Daughter, holding out the child. The veil fell away from the infant's face.

The Seer gasped, gazing at a remarkable visage. The baby's eyes shone like gold coins, new-minted, bright. The hair was short and straight, as orange as the skin. A girl child.

"That's a Figueroa," she whispered.

The Daughter snatched her back. "What?"

"This must . . . this *is* the Figueroa child. The one missing since the bicentennial. How did she come to you?"

Wait until I tell Alfredo she fell in my lap! Alfredo, my sweet secret lover . . . you'll thank me for this in kisses and credit.

"We found her on our doorstep," the Daughter said slyly,

as if suspicious of Figueroas and bicentennials alike. "An offering to Kali, made in the night."

"This is incredible. Don't you realize—? But no, you wouldn't. I'll tell you, this child has been sought far and wide. Only someone in your isolation could have missed the news. Her poor mother will be delighted, to say the least."

The Daughter made a sound like a growl. "The only mother she'll ever know is our dark goddess, Kali."

"She has a mother of flesh and blood, and a family. I happen to know them rather well."

The Daughter of Kali drew back indignantly. "If that's the case, then I've wasted my time. Take her then, return her to the parents. I'll have nothing more to do with such a polluted child."

She offered the infant again, not like a gift but like a thing to be disposed of. The Seer sensed a great coldness in the woman; one little reason and she was ready to surrender the child. In that case, it was just as well to save the infant from her "tender" care.

The black-wrapped bundle was lighter than the Seer had expected. She kept her fingers at the base of the head, to support the strangely heavy skull, but it didn't seem necessary. The infant was remarkably strong. She lifted her head and stared up at the Seer.

"There, little darling," she started to say.

But the Seer choked on her words.

Her tongue began to swell in her throat; her pulse hammered on the anvils of her ears. The child's golden eyes held hers riveted, hanging before her like twin suns while the rest of the world went up in flames. She felt her body ravaged from within, the polynerves writhing like a nest of earwigs suddenly exposed, stinging and thrashing inside her.

A sharp, searing field of energy thrust repeatedly into her ribs and skull, stabbing her with electric knives.

Golden eyes . . .

A monster!

The little freak who couldn't form a syllable was playing the Seer's wires like a practiced tech, drawing power from the rest of the studio, flipping on circuits that should have stayed off.

Sender, receiver, the Seer lost track of what she was. She felt a sly, invasive presence, totally foreign to her experience, like a hand that snatched up the tangle of her body's nerves and squeezed them together, crying, "This is what wires are for!" As if she had wasted them all her life . . .

"What—what—"

She gasped, unable to speak, hardly able to breathe.

A surge began to oscillate from one end of her body to the other, slow at first but building, peaking very near her heart. She tried to drop the child but her fingers would not obey; her palms were scorching.

"*Take—her—back!*"

The Daughter of Kali did not move. "I thought you wanted her."

The Seer went deaf and blind. She felt more isolated than she ever had in the astral of the wires. There seemed no escape from this place, and no sense in returning to her body, not as it was now.

Visions fluttered in. For a moment she saw the cloth she'd woven and then dropped. A final strand of knowledge joined the tapestry, forming a black border around it, a frame to set it apart from everything else. A slim bit of knowledge, but crucial:

Her fearful vision was true.

But she had failed to foresee this part of it. There must be other aspects she had overlooked—and that gave her a last glint of hope. There might be ways out of this . . . not for her but for everyone else. Or maybe not.

The weight of the child was lifted from her hands, but it came too late to benefit her. The nervous rhythm of her heart was out of control. That vital organ ceased to beat with any regularity and now shivered all over like a bag of worms.

Fibrillation is a far from painless death, but the Seer didn't really mind. It was good that her last sensations should be so . . . *intense*. Pain helped demarcate the boundary between realms. She wondered which death prayers best suited her mood. Tibetan, Egyptian, or something more modern? *Om mani padme Anubis Jesus Hermes almotherofgodhuuuuu—*

6
Poppies Will Make Them Sleep

The great California deserts had drowned beneath a waterless sea of homes. The Mojave was no more, although the sun still remembered it, and glared nostalgically down on shopping-mall cactus roof-gardens and air-conditioning maintenance crews with the same lack of mercy it had shown the prior hard-baked earth and yucca plants, junipers, and jackrabbits. Yucca and juniper still grew there, though mainly now in bonsai pots, keeping the roof-bound cacti company. Jackrabbits, horned toads, and defanged rattlesnakes retained nearly invulnerable niches as household pets. And there were new things under the sun as well. The coyoodle, a clever hybrid of toy poodle and native coyote, was popular among the spry septuagenarians who comprised so much of the erstwhile desert's populace.

But one thing the old desert had had in plenty, and which now was nowhere to be seen, was land itself. Houses sat on concrete shelves that once had been hills of sere, majestic tone: mineral black, rust orange, coppery green. All such subtle colors were now generalized, homogenized, democratized into brash pastels. Instead of gravelly soil, one walked on soiled gravel. The land was veined with driveways and highways; it suffocated under a heavy coat of parking lots crowded with vehicular homes. In fact, the pavement drank up so much desert sun that excess heat had to be siphoned off and sold to chillier climes. Winter snow—in fact any precipitation at all—was almost unheard of.

The desert was hardly hospitable to humanity, but that had never stopped developers before. Death Valley Estates, the favorite mockery of a generation of famous-name architects during its planning and construction, now featured many of the same names on its ten-year waiting list for homes. A similar list held applicants for membership in the Devil's Golf Course Country Club, although the wait was not nearly so long: players dropped dead at the rate of two or three a week in the summer heat. (The rate was much higher for caddies.)

For all that, it was a mercifully cool day when Poppy Figueroa, Clarence Starko, and a one-man sensory crew named Chick Woola ended their drive through the cluttered Mojave at the gates of a tiny resort.

The spot was as isolated as any vacationer could wish, being situated at the far brink of a played-out gravel quarry half full of green brine and spanned by a dangerous narrow bridge. Woola, doubling as driver of the studio van, hesitated before crossing. Clarry looked across the gulf and saw clusters of drab hemispherical and cubical lock-to-fit quondos scattered among rusted scraps of abandoned machines and factory buildings. The little hutches were windowless, devoid of ornament or appeal. Gravel dust swirled in the lanes. The only sign of life was a row of hunchbacked palm trees, their fronds a startling shade of crimson.

A sign on the bridge gave the name of the settlement:

BLEEDING PALMS
—A Martyr's Place—

It didn't appear on many maps.

"I don't like the looks of this," Woola the senseman said.

"You kidding?" Clarry said. "This is beautiful stuff. Beautiful." But he was slurping up baccorish like it was spaghetti.

He tried to sound positive, but inwardly he was probably more anxious than Poppy. And for good reason. Foul luck had brought them here; bad rumors that could bring him real trouble.

Two days ago, Poppy's message service had fielded an anonymous five-word blip: "I know where she is." The tag bore this address in the middle of nowhere—or the next thing to it.

Clarry had been monitoring her mail, but not carefully enough. He would have destroyed it before it ruined him, but it slipped past. No one was supposed to know the baby's whereabouts. Not even *he* knew that, and he was closer to the deal than anybody except the old witch-bitch who'd set it up. If he could have gotten in touch with her, he'd have asked her advice, though he hated her more than ever now that the danger to himself had deepened. Unfortunately, Clarry had no idea how to reach her; he didn't know who she was or where she lived. Once the job was done, the goods delivered, there'd been no more messages or visitations. Until this one. Someone else was talking now. Maybe one of her own people, turned traitor.

He rode alone with his fears, hardly sensing Poppy beside him—as if his anguish were any match for hers. No one could help him, no one could hear his warnings. There was no help either of them could offer the other.

Poppy was dragging him deeper in the shit all the time. Because she trusted him, not knowing that he'd put her there in the first place. Poor Poppy. Poor Clarry.

So there was no turning back, not for any of them. Especially not for Clarry. No, sir. He had to find out who was talking and exactly what they knew, if anything. See if he was implicated.

The bridge trembled under the weight of the van. Clarry stared down at the murky water. Grotesquely smooth, slick salt pillars poked up like stiff drowned fingers from gelatinous puffs of silky, fluorescent, lime green moss.

"What a scene," Poppy whispered, leaning out the half-open window to look. A shudder passed through her, registered as a dance of lights and needles on the wireboard. It *was* beautiful stuff, Clarry admitted inwardly. Truly morbid. Under other circumstances he would have appreciated its dramatic possibilities. Anyone who lived out here must be twisted, sick. He only prayed it was all a deception, a false lead, some nutty hermit thinking he'd divined an answer to the mystery show. That was exactly what they needed for "Poppy on the Run": more bizarre distractions on the ever more twisted trail of the Figueroa baby, more weird illusions disguising the truth, clues leading nowhere. False tracks could save Clarry's skin and the show's ratings at the same time—as if there were any difference between the two.

Woola parked the van near the trunk of one scabrous palm tree and shut off the engine. The scarlet fronds scraped and clacked overhead like hermit-crab claws in a dry breeze. The sound summed up the desolation of the place. Clarry gulped another time-release antidepressant, swallowing it dry except for the tobacco juice already in his mouth.

Poppy got out and Woola took her seat. Clarry craned over the meters to check signal quality.

"You be careful," he called after her.

She glanced back and gave him a brave little smile. She looked terrible.

Clarry wished he could go along with her—go *instead* of her—but he didn't figure in the show. He was strictly a wire-puller, behind the scenes. Anyway, through the wires, riding in her skin, he knew everything the moment she knew it. Everything but her thoughts.

Right now she was bearing him along toward a little quondo with a sign above the door reading OFFICE.

"Intense," said Woola.

"*Sh*."

A bell jingled absurdly as Poppy closed the office door behind her. The place was empty, walls bare except for an old lunar calendar years out of date. The only light came from a dingy lens mounted in the middle of the domed ceiling. At least she thought it was a lens: it could have been a dirty skylight. After a few moments, her eyes adjusted to the dimness and she went to the plastic counter looking for a bell she could ring for service.

Instead she discovered a man curled up on the floor behind the counter. A ragged terry-cloth bathrobe covered most of his head but left his ancient gray legs exposed. Dead, she thought. Then he muttered, "No vacancy."

Nothing moved but his lips, between the folds of terry cloth.

"I . . . I'm looking for someone."

"Oh, wow. Do I look like someone? Wow, with my luck I probably do."

"I got an invitation to Number Six."

"We don't allow visitors. Punishment only. And one meal a day. Like, whoa. You're not here to punish anyone, are you?"

"No. I mean—"

"Wow, like, that's too bad. You . . . you wouldn't have any idea how to go about it, I guess? I mean, to, to really hurt someone . . . not just physically, but their feelings too, like, you wouldn't know how to do that, would you? I mean, like, wow, that would be just . . ." The man seemed to be working himself into action.

"I can find it myself," she said, eager to put him at ease; and he subsided.

"Sure. Leave me here. I mean, obviously I can take care of myself. No problem here, no sir. I've got nice clothes, a comfy place to sleep. Like, sure, you just run along. I don't need any attention."

"Yeah," she said. "Like, wow."

Outside, she shaded her eyes with a hand, avoiding sight of the van. With somewhat more ominous feelings, she headed into the shadows of ruined machinery. In the distance, heat shimmered over a craggy range of hills covered with what looked like factory-made spit bubbles: the newest form of quondominium. Polyhedral, they locked together into cozy, instant neighborhoods, infectious to the earth and spreading. She wondered how much longer Bleeding Palms could maintain its dreary isolation.

The heat was dizzying. Putting out her hand, she leaned against the side of a tall, silo-like building. The corrugated sheet metal was incongruously cold, and flaking away into rust. A beetle touched briefly on her knuckle and buzzed off. She closed her eyes, felt the wires deep within, imagined them humming away with a life of their own, parallel to her life but separate, inhuman. It was reassuring to know that every bit of this was being recorded, right down to this very moment . . . and this one . . . and this . . . not in broken pieces as she experienced them, but continuously, creating an illusion of a fluid, unified reality. This moment would never be lost, no matter what happened to her later. Clarry was getting it all on ice.

She felt, lately, that something terrible was coming. Nothing as bad as what had happened already, of course; only a neat way of tying things up. "Things" being her life, which had ended, really, on the night she lost the baby. That had been the climax of Poppy's story. After that, she might as well skip to the end.

That's what she was doing now. Skipping. From moment to moment to moment, the good parts all behind her, a few loose ends to tie up before slipping out of the wires. Time to start another story.

This desert trek was a false lead, and she knew it.

She didn't want to be pessimistic, but she knew there would be no easy solution to the mystery. No hard solution, either. Her audience would gradually come to realize that Calafia wasn't going to reappear. The "gimmick" would soon lose its appeal. People hated unsolved mysteries in a wire show. There's no suspense in knowing that you'll never know a thing.

Like her, they would soon give up wondering. Give up hope. Perhaps that was why she felt so calm now, so detached. She was readying her audience—though they couldn't know it—for a huge disappointment.

Her thoughts meshed with the feel of rust beneath her abraded fingertips. I'm flaking away, too, she thought.

She swallowed a dry mouthful, gravel dust gritting between her teeth. Clarry must be wondering what she was up to. Oh, well, he could cut this part later.

Lifting her eyes, she saw Number Six. It was a cracked dome like the crown of a long-buried skull, baked and blistered by the sun. The door, ajar, looked as if it would never shut again. Cold in winter, an oven in summer. Some poor soul's home, that broken head. The brain all withered inside it . . .

She went forward, laid a hand on the warped wood, and gave the door a gentle push. A lizard scurried out between her feet. She put her head through the opening. Was that singing she heard?

". . . Tum-tum-tumbleweeds . . ."

"Hello?"

She stepped inside, and felt a cold pulse pass through her, an electric tingle that caught her up short for a moment then vanished. A fleeting sensation, but one she had felt before, going into office buildings during business hours.

Her signal was being jammed or scrambled. As long as she stood inside this room, she could neither send nor receive. Suddenly, her isolation magnified, she felt afraid.

* * *

As Poppy stepped into the hut, Clarry stayed with her. He wished he could work her manually, like a remote human camera—turn this way, now that, zoom in, fall back. He wasn't content seeing only what she saw, doing only what she did. But that was wires for you.

The tiny dome was full of branches, pale and scraggly lumps of dead vegetation. A thin little voice wailing an off-key tune told him what he was seeing: "Tumbling . . . with the tumbling tumbleweeds . . ."

Tumbleweeds, yes. Their branches scraped at Poppy's hands, snagged her clothes. Across the room, at the far curve of the dome, he saw the face of the terrible singer drowning in the dry weedy clumps. Her skin was white as sun-bleached bone; her gray hair drifted like a winter cloud, tangled in the tumbleweeds. When she saw Poppy, she started to rise, and half a dozen weeds leaped toward her, dragged up like marionettes by the strands of her hair.

Clarry felt physically relieved. There would be no clues here, only madness and senility. Nothing to give him away.

"Tumbling, tumbling, tumbleweeds," the old woman piped.

"Hello," Poppy said. "Are you the one I'm suppose to meet?"

"Meet? Oh, yes. There's not much time. I need help with the garden. Everything's forgotten how to bloom."

Poppy made an attempt to get closer, but the weeds were much too dense.

"I'm Poppy," she said. "Poppy Figueroa?"

"Poppies? Poppies will make them sleep!" The frail voice grew almost musical, though out of tune. "You can remind them how. Once they were everywhere, just like the tum-tum-tumbling tumbleweeds. I loved to look at them. They covered the hills and the green valleys, a mist of lovely colors. Poppies were the state flower, you know. Now there's nothing but the tumbling tumbleweed."

The hag turned toward Poppy, involuntarily drawing the

weeds into bunches around her midriff. She scooped them closer still, as if gathering a flock of desiccated children to her breast. "Tumbling, tumbling . . ."

"Did you send me a message?" Poppy asked. "About my daughter? Was that you?"

"Poppy!" the old woman barked, her eyes turning bright and alive. But the spell passed like a cloud's shadow.

The woman sank down in her crackling throne; the tumbleweeds buoyed her up. Her dry weeping wended through the thin branches. Abruptly she lurched forward, causing the tumbleweeds in her hair to leap forcefully free of the other weeds that snared them. They sprang almost to the ceiling as she flailed her hands. Her fingers were covered with lacerations, scabbed with old blood; her gingham dress was in rags.

"I was there when you lost her," the woman intoned. "I was there. And I know where she is, yes, I know."

Clarry's fingers twitched on the wireboard. Crazy old bat, why didn't she come right out and say it? Why torment him like this?

"And where is that?" Poppy asked.

"McBeth took her! His gods! Bad dogs—bad dogs! Shouldn't talk like that to their masters. But you should have paid your taxes."

Clarry sighed, slumping over the board with relief.

"Oh dear God," Poppy murmured. "That's the show, old woman. That was only a show—it wasn't life."

"So? Not life? You think I don't know what's real?"

"I'm sure you—"

"I know what I know, you know!"

Clarry withdrew almost completely from Poppy, monitoring the session with a fraction of his attention, ignoring the crone's babble and Poppy's polite responses. After coming all this way, she might as well talk to the hag. It would provide some light amusement once he pared it down to a few good lines.

Relieved, he began to laugh at all his fears. Woola was

laughing too, but for different reasons: because the old gal was whacked. She didn't know the truth. Maybe only one person knew the whole truth.

And it sure wasn't Clarry.

Poppy hesitated at the threshold as the cold pulse of the signal-jammer faded. Should she go back out, back into Clarry's reach?

What would he think, cut off abruptly? If there was any chance of danger to her, he'd come running within seconds.

It occurred to her that whoever had brought her here had not, perhaps, wanted their encounter recorded. Clarry wouldn't like that, though.

Relaxing, she peered about at the dimness of the dome. It was empty, swept clean, unfurnished except for a small table in the center. On the table was a generic prismascreen holovision set, the cheapest kind imaginable. As she approached, it came to life, as though it had been waiting for her.

She found herself looking at Clarry Starko inside the prism. He sat in what she recognized as the cluttered editing room in his Hollywood quondo, seated at his old Sens8 deck. He stared right at her, out of the screen. He looked different, his hair shorter than he kept it now, and he was wearing a moustache. This was Clarry as he'd looked when she first met him, when he'd approached her about doing the spin-off.

That thought was painful. She'd been planning the pregnancy then, full of anticipation, seeing every offer that came her way as an omen of good fortune, bringing security for herself and the child.

Well, she was no Seer, that much was proven.

The POV camera moved toward Clarry, startling him. The end of a baccorish rope fell out of his mouth. "Who are you?" he said to the domed room, to her. "How'd you get in here?"

The voice that answered, out of sight on the screen, was cool and refined, electronically smoothed until it retained no human edges, nothing to distinguish it: "That doesn't matter, Mr. Starko. I've come to make you an offer."

Clarry gave his visitor—and incidentally the camera, the hut, Poppy—a long look before answering.

"What kind of offer?" he said at last.

"I want to stage a scene, with you producing. It will make your name and seal your fame."

"Yeah? One scene? How can you be so sure of that?"

"The great directors take great risks—especially today, when every stunt has already been accomplished. The audience is bored. To partake of history, you must take part in history. I am offering you a chance to record a historic moment as it is happening. To participate in its creation, according to your abilities. You may not interfere with it as it takes shape, but you are free to do what you wish with the crystals you procure. I will manage everything except the production; that remains properly your jurisdiction."

Poppy bent closer to the screen. The hologram had perfect focus, infinite depth of field. The camera must have been worn as a pendant, small and inconspicuous. Such instruments were commonly used for filming the simultaneous flatscreen and holo versions of wire-show programs, so that the wired actors—and the audience living through them—did not have to avoid looking at cameras that might otherwise have shattered the reality of their programs. She examined the black glass windows behind Clarry, and in them she barely made out the invisible speaker's reflections: a shape cloaked in blackness, faceless, tall. No wonder Clarry looked so baffled—his visitor was hardly even human.

"You're an actress, aren't you?" Clarry said, turning on his enthusiasm now, but sarcastically. "Some old-timer. You want me to stage your comeback, like Gloria Swanson in that old strip-flicker, *77 Sunset Boulevard*. You want to break into wires cause nobody watches flatscreen flicks these days. But why come to me?"

"I have no desire to recapture my past, Mr. Starko. I wish only to change the future."

"Like how?"

"First, let me show you how I intend to win your loyalty." As the camera wearer approached Clarry's editing board, the room swam and curved around the lens's eye, dissolving at the edges. Poppy saw a black-gloved hand press the eject button on the Sens8 editor, and a cube of recording crystal slid out of the slot. The hand dropped a black ice cube into the player, then pressed the start button.

Clarry's room, and the desert hut, abruptly filled with screaming. Poppy clutched the fabric of her blouse, feeling feverish. In the prism, Clarry backed away from the deck, then lurched forward to shut it off; but the black-gloved hand stopped him. The signal was obviously feeding through his wires. Poppy couldn't feel it at this remove—thank God for that—but his whole body shook with it.

"What—where'd you get it?" Clarry gasped.

The black hand relented and switched off the deck. "You recognize it?"

"It's a snuff cube. You—you could be executed just for carrying it!"

"Yes, because it's authentic. But how did you know? It's quality snuff—you can feel yourself being sliced limb from limb, while at the same time you're the one doing the slicing. It can be synthesized, fabricated legally, but not on a black-market snuff-cube's zero budget. This is the real thing, the work of a talented but penniless wirist . . . as I'm sure you recall."

He was pale, his forehead beaded with sweat. "You had no right switching me in there without warning."

"It can't be too surprising, Mr. Starko. You recognized it, didn't you?"

He didn't answer. He stared at her—stared straight at Poppy, it seemed—without speaking.

"Why is it, Mr. Starko, that male artists feel obliged to

spray blood everywhere, to bathe an audience in grue? Is it because you fear blood? Because you envy women the power of menstruation? Blood is the carrier of life and death, isn't that it? Aren't those the powers you wish you could master? The things that truly terrify you and make you feel helpless and weak?"

"I don't know what you're talking about."

"I'm talking about darkness and mystery . . . about death and blood and the grave, Mr. Starko. You have some familiarity with it, don't you, acquired in the underworld of this little hell we call Hollywood? I know that's where you came from, the source from which your roots perhaps still drink. You never studied in the studio schools; you weren't born to rich snobs or wire stars. You had a *practical* schooling in the wires. Snuff shows. The blackest of black-market media. You've come a long way since then, Mr. Starko, but that *is* what got you where you are."

"What do you want?" His voice was hard now. He didn't look frightened anymore; this was business. "If you're thinking of blackmailing me with that crystal, you don't know me like you think you do. I may work in Hollywood, but I'm not what you'd call rich. Go after the ones who make those snuffs if you want money—the ones who bring in street trash and twistheads—the ones who really excel at blackmail and threats to get people like me to work for them. Unless, that is, those kind of people make you nervous."

"I don't want money, Mr. Starko. You're forgetting what I said. I want your artistry, your help with a little scene I've cooked up. In return, no one has to know what name Clarry Starko went by when he made his little underground extravaganzas. No one has to know how he financed his first pop-rated wire shows."

Poppy had the feeling a long pause was cut here. Clarry's face changed too abruptly.

"A scene, huh?" he said. "What kind of scene?"

The camera swam very close to him. The woman's voice

sounded abnormally loud for the whispering of confidences. The syllables ringing in Poppy's head cleared it of misconceptions, hammering out her ignorance in a few short snatches of dialogue.

As she listened, as a younger Clarry stared, the woman in black described the scene that Poppy was to play on the eve of the bicentennial. She described it in intimate detail, with a skilled grasp of exactly how and what the wires could carry; she described the scene almost precisely as it finally had been enacted.

The mysterious station wagon.

The kidnapping.

Poppy stood unmoving in the empty desert dome, paralyzed by horror and the unwilling recognition that Clarry had always been her enemy.

"And . . . and what happens to the baby?" Clarry asked when she was finished explaining the crime.

"That's none of your concern."

"No? And what about Poppy Figueroa?"

"What do you care? You don't know her any better than you knew the one in here." She taped the black cube, still in the deck.

"What makes you think she'll go for it?"

"I believe she will, if you pitch the proposal as I instruct. She's an actress. An out-of-work actress, too young to believe her career is over, despite the recent trauma in her life. She'll jump for the part."

"And how do you know *I'll* go for it?"

The black hand reached out once again and switched on the Sens8. Clarry stiffened, moaned, his eyes popping.

"I think I can convince you," said the voice.

The generic prismascreen in the quondo hut went dark.

Poppy waited for another sign, something else from the holoset. She thought of Clarry sitting in the van watching this exchange through her eyes. Why hadn't he come running long ago?

Oh. Yes. Now she remembered. Her signal was jammed. He'd been getting nothing but static since she came inside. But that alone should have drawn him minutes ago. Maybe he was lost among the domes. Maybe he was right behind her.

The thought drove her out of the dome in a panic. She didn't want him to see the holovision. She didn't want him asking what she'd seen.

She stood bathed in sunlight, her back to the door, trembling. When she thought she could support herself, she stumbled away through the shadows of silos and factory buildings. She thought she was heading away from the office and the men, toward what remained of the desert, but suddenly she came out of the shadows and saw the van ahead of her. Clarry, behind the smoked glass, was just sitting there.

Sitting and watching. And knowing all the time where her baby had gone.

Seeing her, he opened the side door and leaned out. "What a bust, huh? Doubt we can use much of that."

Her feet carried her forward unintentionally.

The bloodred palms seemed to wobble, melting upward in the heat. Poppy didn't say a thing. She knew—as if the woman in black had told her directly—that she must not speak a word of what she had seen. But that would be easy. The silence of the desert was immense; how simple to join herself to it. Far away she heard a grim pounding, as of huge hammers falling against the earth. She hardly recognized her heartbeat.

She touched the hot metal side of the van, felt the caked dust beneath her fingers, all at a great distance. The palm shadows crabbed at her own; she pulled free of their dim ectoplasm, walking out into sunlight again, past the van, away from Clarry and the things he knew or didn't know. Wondering if the whole show was an illusion; wondering what illusion Clarry had seen. It might have been lies, all of it. But she would never dare ask him if it were true or real—would she?

Sunlight crashed on green water in the quarry below. Scummy fingers tugged at her wires. Drowned things called her name.

"Poppy?"

A hand on her shoulder.

"Get away from there, it's dangerous. The cliff could crumble right out from under you."

She blinked at Clarry but couldn't quite see him. His eyes were blotted out by afterimages of the sun.

"Dizzy," she murmured.

"It's hotter than it's been all day. Let's get back to the van. It's cooler."

Not as cool as the green brine full of fingers, she thought. She shrugged his hand from her shoulder.

Getting back into the van with him was perhaps the hardest thing she'd ever done.

After they ate dinner at a Lo/Ox Health-Junk Shak, Clarry decided to stay in the desert for the night. He took three rooms in a motel on old Interstate 40—the 40-Winx—giving Poppy and Chick Woola their own rooms and taking one for himself where he could set up his portable editor with a link to the central Sens8 deck in the van. Poppy was distant all through dinner. He looked up a few times to see her watching him, but when he asked what was on her mind, she only shrugged. She said she was tired and went into her room without adding anything more.

He supposed the whole thing with the baby still bothered her. For him, it was hard to imagine why, and her continuing grief often caught him by surprise. It wasn't like she'd gotten a chance to know it; there was no one to miss or mourn for. The episode was months behind them now. But then women were funny that way. And today it had all been dug up fresh again, leading to enormous disappointment.

For himself, he felt mainly relief.

Clarry called up the afternoon's recording, reentering the dark interior of the dome at Bleeding Palms. His concentration sharpened to a single point: the hyperaware trance he always entered when he edited, the closest thing to the edgy, focused buzz he'd used to derive from the drugs that had made him such a perfect, soulless wireman for the Ho-Wood horror masters. But better than a drug high, it was reliable and rewarding. He hardly chewed rope when the work went well.

The clustered tumbleweeds rasped his hands, the old woman with skin white as bleach sang her feeble song. There wasn't much he could do to salvage the scene except trim it into a short, smooth segment made up of the best bits of conversation.

To his sharpened senses, the recording quality seemed really poor, as if he had a bad link with the central deck. He punched it up again, trying a new line, but it wasn't any better.

Which meant . . .

It wasn't a bad connection, it was the recording itself. The whole scene in the dome had a thin, grainy feel, like a cheap bootleg copied and recopied so many times that bits and pieces of the flow had started dropping out, leaving holes in sound and smell, glitches that undermined the impression of reality, plateaus where there should have been sharp peaks. Less than subliminal snatches of other recordings leaked in at odd moments, creating a bad-tasting synesthesia.

But that didn't make any sense. There weren't any recordings under this one. He was working direct from the master, a fresh cube.

It must be the link after all.

He decided to go out to the van and work on the regular deck, where he could at least run a diagnostic to pin down the source of the fuzz.

He knocked on Chick's door. Woola opened it slowly and

peered out. A strange blond kid lay unconscious on the bed, silver vial halves in his hands, his makeup smeared, his temples bruised. Clarry vaguely remembered him hanging out in the parking lot.

"I'm going out," Clarry said. "Sorry to bother you."

The van sat in a lot alongside the road. At night, heavy surface traffic roared through the desert, mainly trucktrains rushing freight through the Franchise. The little van shook in the turbulent slipstream of every leviathan that passed. He felt less safe than usual in his editor's womb.

He fired up the Sens8 masterdeck and phased himself into the editing channels, holding on to a few at once, separate strings to be spliced or woven at will. It was best working with a few POVs to give the audience a choice of conduits. But today's session featured only Poppy. It was tediously simple. So why all the distortion?

He checked the cube. It was clean and shiny. He cleaned the slot and started the player again. Then he set off walking through the noonday heat, away from the shade of the corroded metal wall where Poppy had leaned for a minute or so, thinking about God knows what. Here came the dome. Quality was fine. It looked like the problem was with the link, all right. Then she stepped inside.

"Tumbling . . ."

There it went again, instant fuzz, right in the master.

Now that he thought about it, there had been a kind of thin strangeness to the whole event, even at the time. During real time it seemed insignificant; but when he slowed it for editing and examined every instant, the poor quality became obvious. It eroded his sense of reality.

In the dome now, he heard the whimsical old windbag and Poppy's hellos.

"Back up," he said, and the Sens8 complied.

Poppy backed out the door.

"Freeze it."

There. The instant the signal quality deteriorated matched perfectly with her step across the threshold.

Coincidence?

He hung in the moment, hung with one foot in midair, halfway into the dome. Behind Poppy was desert, hot and clear, as real as though he were living it himself. Ahead of her was haze. A veil. Like a bad, an amateurish splicing job.

He backed up still farther, pressing a thin, translucent wedge of time between Poppy and the dome's interior. He could see into the room quite clearly now; it was no more than a flash in Poppy's eyes, but that was enough.

The dome was empty.

No tumbleweeds. No cackling hag.

Empty except for a table and a holovision set.

"Twisted shit," he muttered.

He slipped his grip on time and advanced slowly, watching the veil fall, watching tumbleweeds emerging from the gloom along with the old hag. Once you caught on, it all looked incredibly fake. He couldn't believe he'd fallen for it. But then, he'd been concentrating on other things, hoping to see something like this . . . a false lead that would let him sigh with relief. He'd been lulled, suckered by wishfulness as much as by special effects. Shit.

All that time, while he thought she was humoring some old biddy, she'd actually been watching HV, seeing God knows what.

What had really gone on in there? Why hadn't she said a thing about it?

Bad feelings. Very pale ideas were coming to him now, like the bloated white bellies of dead fish bobbing to the surface of his mind after some explosion or poisoning in the depths.

The message that had summoned them here was no madwoman's fan letter. It was the work of someone devious. Someone who knew both Poppy and Clarry, and how their minds worked.

Clarry had heard of a new special-effects device, a reality

synthesizer, that could do something like this, but it was in the prototype stage—nobody in his circles had ever even seen one. Whoever sent the message to Poppy had inside power—in Ho-wood or its R & D labs.

Only one person had all that *and* the baby.

That old bitch in black.

What sort of game was she pulling now? Double-cross, turnbacks, screwing with her own plot the way she'd screwed with Clarry's head.

She'd blackmailed him, now she was turning him in. He knew he was right. She was setting him up.

He'd better to talk to Poppy, find out exactly what she'd seen, even if it meant (God!) confessing his own role. If he confessed, then he might gain some kind of protection when the bitch in black forked him over to the cops.

He had to find out what she knew. To do that, he might have to tell her everything.

Clarry didn't bother to switch off the deck. He went straight back to his room to calm himself with a tranq. As he choked it down, he glanced at the portable deck and saw that Poppy was still on-line, not actively recording but simply running a current through the master deck. Standard operating procedure: the deck stayed tuned in to her constantly, in case anything happened that was worthy of the show.

He shrugged off his normal professional qualms about getting inside her without permission. Just a peek, to figure out where she was at so he could work out the best way to approach her.

Predictably enough, she was rolling around in bed, weeping.

Keeping wired to her, in RO mode, he went down the hall to her door and pounded on it, hearing the knocking through both sets of ears. Poppy pulled the pillow over her head and incidentally over his own. He tried mentally to push her off the bed, as if he could jerk her around by her wires. It was an exercise in pure frustration.

"Hey, Poppy," he said, pitching his voice low, confidential. "Come out here a sec, would you?"

She lay still, and he lay there inside her, frozen by the sound of his voice. She was afraid of him; her muscles felt rigid.

"Poppy, it's me. I've got to ask you something. Come on, wake up, this is important."

He was about to give up on it, ready to convince the manager to let him in—"I think she overdosed in there"—when he felt her stir and get unsteadily to her feet. She'd been hitting the vial again; her temples burned where she'd held the twist halves in place too long. Woozy. No wonder she wasn't moving in a hurry. It made him feel a little better; maybe she wasn't really avoiding him. Maybe she was only twisted.

The door opened. He stood face-to-face with himself. He blinked out of her eyes an instant before feedback kicked in, the blossoming nerve-scream cut off long before it peaked. He took her by the elbow.

"Come on, we gotta talk."

She tried pulling away. "Wha—"

"Outside, Poppy. Seriously, we have to talk. It's more private outside."

She wore only a thin gown, but the night was warm. He hurried her toward the van, and in bare feet she kept stumbling. "Clarry, stop it, you're hurting me."

He let go. She moved away, wide awake now, watching him distrustfully.

She knows, he realized. That look of hers says everything. Somehow, in that dome, she had learned the truth.

"Poppy," he said, and stopped short. What came next? The words didn't exactly flow from this point onward.

"I'm going back to bed."

He flipped into her, felt gravel digging into her heels, the wind streaming around her legs. A truck thundered past.

"Poppy, I know what happened in the dome."

She stiffened. Backed off.

"No," he said. "Don't run—we gotta talk."

"Stay away from me!"

Again he wasted effort trying to control her, to mentally push or pull her toward him. He couldn't help it—he had confused their bodies. But his desperation seemed to have the opposite effect. She moved away. Turned to run.

"Poppy! Tell me what happened!"

Goddamn it.

He headed after her, caught between her form and his. She was in pain, but her fear—which he couldn't touch through the wires—must have been far stronger. She ran like hell, past the van, out of the motel lot, along the roadside. Monster trucks howled past as if the night were a hungry throat sucking them down, taillights dwindling, dopplered sirens stretching out thin in the distance.

Through her eyes it all came on as a blur. She was crying.

"Poppy, come back! We gotta talk! I'll try to explain—I'll tell you everything, I swear. Just tell me what you know!"

Through her wires, he couldn't hear himself anymore. The traffic was too loud. She was getting away from him, except for her wires.

He told himself that he could catch her, hold her, make her listen. He had shoes, after all, and she was barefoot.

He took off running.

Just ahead, she seemed to be dodging in and out of the shifting lights—but that was an illusion. It was the lights that moved, not Poppy. She stood still now, a calm silhouette. He couldn't tell which way she faced until he saw himself come running toward her out of the night, caught in the glare of headlights. Then, superimposed on that, he saw her face from his own eyes.

"Poppy," he said.

He felt her gasp, heard the intake of breath.

He reached—

She darted away, spinning into a gap, finding a momentary

vacancy in the steady traffic. She traversed one lane in poised stillness, like a dancer. Three more broad lanes to go, all of them dark and empty for the moment, deep as valleys.

Then lights came roaring up. The darkness turned into a deadly river, a lightstream that carried them both away. The bright mountain came roaring out of nowhere, out of everywhere, and the merest corner of it snagged her, but that was enough.

Clarry felt everything, every brutal bit of the impact. It drew him in even as it wiped her out. He was one facet of a three-lobed scream, sharing it with Poppy and the brakes of the truck. He heard the storm of sound through two sets of ears . . . and then through only one pair, because Poppy's had failed. Her polynerves were senseless. In the van, on the masterdeck, the needles fell still, the wires went dead. The river of traffic stopped in midstream—but only for Poppy.

As for Clarry, he kept walking on down the dark road that started where the wires ended. Walked and wondered if he'd ever find his way back to the place where Poppy lay in brightness and in blood.

7
Trauma in Tinsel-Town

The advantage of alcohol, however old-fashioned, over other drugs was its excellence for suppressing conscious awareness of the constant seethe of wire shows. With enough of it ingested, even the basic subconscious processes could be poisoned and sabotaged sufficiently so that no part of one's anatomy remained attuned to the wires.

Sandy had not quite reached that point, or else he had passed it and was on his way back to bodily sentience. Whatever the cause, he found himself regaining consciousness in a muddle of Poppies. He grumbled and turned away from her faces wherever they appeared. He didn't wish to be disturbed by any member of his family in his present state. But she kept pressing in: Poppy with the Newsbodies, Poppy in old clips with the family, Poppy in ever present and increasing danger, Poppy in . . . the hospital? He didn't remember that episode: it must be a late development in "Poppy on the Run." That stupid, tawdry show. If only he could shut it off, shut down the signals completely—shut the mouth that was thundering his name.

He woke, then, in the shallows of Thaxter Halfjest's palatial carp pond. He could still hear ominous echoes of his name, following him from wasted sleep. He lifted his head from a pebbly shore and gazed across a shimmer of lily pads and colored aquatic lights to find Cornelius, shirtless, sitting up to his distinctly human nipples in the center of the pool. The sealman's whiskers moved rhythmically as he sang a seal's lullaby. A floating snifter bobbed beside him, anchored to a fountainhead; it was filled to the waterline with Drambuie.

Suddenly Cornelius's hands plunged forward and engaged in a brief, silent struggle beneath the waters. An instant later he brought a fat blue-spotted coy into the air. Fish and sealman regarded one another with strikingly similar expressions: both pop-eyed and bewhiskered, both with gaping mouths. Cornelius bared his pin-sharp teeth, preparing to bite the carp in two.

"Corny, no!"

Startled, Cornelius dropped the coy. He blinked at Sandy, vaguely perturbed, and dragged a wet wrist across his mouth.

"We're guests here," Sandy said.

"It's a great help with a hangover, sir."

"Aw, Corny. Oh, Christ." Sandy's own hangover, in its inimitable way, made its presence known. If he'd thought biting a live carp would stop the pain, he might have considered it. He sank back down with a moan and stared up at the moss-bearded chandeliers. "How did I get here?"

"I carried you. I thought you would find fresh water refreshing."

He sloshed some of the tepid stuff over his face and soaked clothes. "Did you hear someone calling my name or was that a dream?"

Cornelius gestured at a speaker above the pool. "I believe the Reverend Governor summoned you."

"I wonder what he wants." Sandy scratched his belly

through his shirt. "Corny, when was the last time I slept in a bed?"

"Actually slept?"

"What do you mean by that?"

"As opposed to sharing a mattress or other, slightly padded surface for the purpose of sexual congress?"

"Jeez, now I *know* you were hatched in a tube."

"You haven't actually *slept* in a bed since we left the seascraper—which was one week ago. May I remind you that I have relinquished my own nocturnal comfort to accompany you on this reckless descent into debauch."

"No one forced you."

"No, I did it for my own peace of mind. You are my friend, and I would be remiss to leave you to your own devices."

"Admit it, you're getting royally tanned."

Cornelius considered this and eventually gave a reluctant nod. "It is preferable to the cramped schedules of the seascraper, being an existence perhaps more akin to the lazy sun-worshiping lifestyle of my sealie ancestors."

Sandy shook his head. "The workaday world is not for us, Corny. We must take it as we find it. Ride the lurchy surf of reality. Ooh . . . my head."

He rose unsteadily and extended a hand to his companion. "Come on, Corny, sushi time."

"If it's all the same to you, I think I'll stick with oatmeal this morning. Since I can't have fish that's truly fresh . . ."

"There must be a lobster tank around somewhere."

Footsteps rang suddenly in the marble corridors near the poolside. Thaxter Halfjest appeared, hurrying toward the water's edge with his arms spread wide. The greeting was his usual, but his face was weirdly pale and drawn. "Sandy, my boy! There you are! I wasn't sure if you were still with us. Someone *said* they had sex with you last night, but you know the stories people tell."

"What's up, Thax?"

The RevGov let his arms fall.

"I have terrible news. Poppy is at Welby-Kildare in intensive care. Your father's hiring a professional care staff to bring her home, but that will take time. You really should get down there, Sandy."

Sandy walked dripping from the pool, remembering his "dreams." "My God. That's why her face is plastered all over the wires. What happened?"

"I'll get the car," said Cornelius. He rushed from the room, leaving wet footprints on the slick floor.

"An accident, I gather. You'd better put on dry clothes. I'll have a bundle sent out to the garage, if you'll tell me your size."

But Sandy's discomfort seemed trivial to him now. Even his headache receded. "No thanks, Thax, I'll dry on the way. Hey, Corny! Wait for me!"

Sandy hadn't been home in over a year but Hollywood was the same as ever, the whole foul bowl of humanity swimming in a psychedelic rainbow soup. Smog-scrubbing aerophytes, released in the 'Teens to metabolize the Basin's lethal hydrocarbons, had scoured the sky cleaner than a dog's dish; but their byproducts had also covered the region with a multicolored film that never completely washed away, lending new accuracy to the old nicknomen Tinsel-Town. Everywhere you looked, toxic glitter and sequins sparkled in the afternoon sun. The fine sheen of gilt tended to flake off in one's hand, filling the streets and powdering clothes with polychromatic dandruff, getting all over everything. In a windstorm, the LA Basin resembled a decorative paperweight—shaken, not stirred.

Cornelius steered above hills dry and wrinkled as a crone's backside, passing over teetering quondotels dwarfed and shadowed by perilously stacked freeways. He circled over the spiny khaki expanse of the Princess Zsa Zsa Memorial Cactus Preserve, finally becoming involved in a jet jam just east of the Beverly Canyon.

In an area as congested as the Basin, local traffic controls and personal aircar anticollision devices led to an annoying condition best known as Puppy Magnet Syndrome. It was virtually impossible to collide with another jet, thanks to the many safeguards in effect; midair fender-plunges were a thing of the past. Two cars flying straight at each other would swerve automatically just before collision, like the north poles of two magnets brought together (as demonstrated by the antics of the traditional black-and-white magnetized Scotty-dog pups that have thrilled so many generations of children). With three or more cars involved, the ballet of avoidance became more complex. And when hundreds or thousands or even dozens of cars converged on a single destination, an enormous bubble of canceled confusion—spherical gridlock—was the result, a sphere of empty territory from which all cars repelled each other simultaneously, so that none could enter the desired zone. The only thing to do in such an instance was to sit and wait and let the computers sort it out.

The more popular the attraction, the longer the wait. And today the Welby-Kildare Hospital—under the sponsorship of Dr. McNguyen—was extremely busy. Siren-packing ambulances took priority, sending repulsed cars spinning from their path as they zigzagged in and down to the emergency roosts.

As he orbited in abeyance, awaiting an opening, Sandy regarded the smoky abyss of the Beverly Canyon, a gift from the San Andreas Fault line to real estate developers of the twenty-first century. The Canyon's polished inner walls were glitzy with windows, balconies, hanging gardens. The Figueroa home, several miles up the crack, sat on the most exclusive stretch of the famous verge, invisible from here, mainly because it was blocked by floating advertisements.

A huge, luminous fly-through hologram billboard materialized ahead of them. Sandy stared at it first in annoyance, then in envy.

The image showed seven people, each representing a different race, and of widely varying ages. Bold titles flickered around them, sending loud synchronized blasts of sound into Sandy's wires:

> Forget About Ozzie and Harriet!
> Brush Off the Bradys!
> Who Needs the Bundys?
> Screw All Murgatroyds and Figueroas!
> None of Them Had a Seventh of What We've Got!
> The First Family That Really Represents You!
> Folks You Can Count On!
> And We're Coming Right Now . . .
> To Work Our Magic—
> **THE MAGYK 7**

Our replacements, Sandy thought bitterly. They keep trying to fill that void. After a suitable period of mourning—thirty days—Hollywood had started right up again trying to re-create the formula. They were still trying, but so far it had never quite worked out.

He almost missed the tag line:

> We Can't Promise Some of Us Won't Die—
> We're Not Immortal!
> But We Won't Give Up the Show
> And Let You Down!

Sandy saw Corny's fingers tighten on the wheel, and was positive the sealman tried to aim the car right at the middle of the big dad's head; but the computer had just given them clearance, and they were heading down.

The hospital lobbies and corridors were crammed with scads of Poppy-fen, mobs of women (and not a few men) in hysterics, their orange-implanted eyes blurry with tears, their faces torn and devastated. Unfortunately, most of them recognized Sandy and Cornelius, and came rushing: "Sandy! Oh my brother! Corny, help me! Help me! I'm cut off—I'm dying—where am I?—My baby—where's my baby—please—please—an autograph . . . ?"

Fortunately, a troop of security guards spotted the problem and moved between Sandy and the faux Poppies.

"She's this way, Mr. Figueroa, in the Daktari-Howser Wing," said one young fellow. "It's a plesh to accompany you. I lost my virginity to Dyad through you, sir. Nice piece, that. I think you handled her just as I would have, only . . . well . . . I'd have liked it immensely if you could have held off ejaculating just a wee bit longer. Always wanted to tell you that, sir. But this really is a ple—AACK—!"

"Thanks, Corny," Sandy said.

The Poppies were not the only wire-fen in evidence. One waiting room they passed was filled with people saying in unison, "Go ahead, Dr. McNguyen, you can level with me. It—it's terminal, isn't it?" They could have been tuned to any number of shows—or commercials. A few young kids hopped by on clumsy chicken-foot grafts, in emulation of the ever popular Rooster Man.

Intensive care proved to be a circular room with a perimeter of sealed, sanitized transparent chambers surrounding it. Sandy pushed through a crowd of doctors, nurses, and medical programmers, spotting his father in one of the clear rooms. He rapped on the glass until Alfredo nodded for him to come in.

A nurse stopped him at the airlock. "I'm sorry, we don't allow anyone but family members inside."

"I'm her brother," Sandy said.

"No." She indicated Cornelius. "I meant him."

The sealman stiffened.

"But he's part of the family," Sandy protested.

"We wouldn't let the family *dog* in either."

"That's all right," Cornelius said coldly. "I can see her well enough through the glass."

Sandy glared at the nurse, a curse on his lips, but he figured it was hospital policy, however tortuous. He passed through the airlock. In the halfway chamber, a violet light purged him of microscopic hitchhikers, then a bell chimed and the inner door opened.

"Sandy," his father said. "I'm glad you made it. She's . . . in a coma."

A cat's cradle held Poppy in careful suspension. She was swathed in skinplast with pins protruding from every part of her body, like needles in an acupuncturist's training manikin. The head of each pin bore a tiny bead of emerald light, all of them blinking—at times randomly, at times phasing into sequence.

The only bits of flesh he could see were her eyelids, half-shut, the merest orange crescents visible beneath them. She hardly seemed to be breathing.

"When did it happen?"

"Last night. She was in the Mojave working on her series. She was hit by a truck."

"An accident?"

Alfredo hesitated. "Nobody knows precisely what happened—or why. Starko was there, but the way he tells it, well . . . I'm not so sure."

Sandy swallowed.

Neither of them wanted to speculate openly, but Sandy couldn't help seeing the obvious. Poppy had been broken by her baby's disappearance. Taking too many drugs to control her mood. The last time he'd spoken with her, she had seemed to be loitering far beyond her usual zones . . . defeated.

"What's the point of living?" she had said, just a throwaway line, another sob among many. People always said those things in moments of misery. It was a standard wire-show plaint. It hadn't registered as realism until now.

Too late.

If there was anything accidental about the incident, it was probably the fact of her survival.

Sandy bowed his head, wishing he could hear a heartbeat, anything, to know that she lived. The blinking pins made her look like some kind of alien insect in a hanging chrysalis.

"I'm sorry," he whispered. "I should have been there for you, Poppy. I should have kept in touch, so you'd've had someone to call. I should have helped you find your . . . my niece."

Not so much as a tremor of understanding ran through her eyelids. His own eyes began to tear with the effort of looking at her; the blinking green needles dizzied him. Alfredo's hand closed on his shoulder.

"I can't stay here," Sandy said.

"Will you meet me at the house, son? Mir and Ferdi are there. I'd like us all to be together right now. I've made arrangements to bring Poppy home as soon as she's stable. It'll be good for her if we're all there when she wakes up."

"When is that supposed to happen?"

Alfredo stared at the transparent wall as if it were made of brick. He didn't answer. A commotion passed through the outer ward, but it was already dying down. Cornelius came out of the crowd and stood near the glass, looking brisk and efficient.

Sandy squeezed his father's arm. "I'll see you at home."

Cornelius joined him outside the airlock. "How is she, sir?"

"In a coma. God, Corny, I've been so pale and selfish. So fucking tawdry . . ."

Sandy stumbled, but Cornelius caught him. Sandy's shoes were squeaky with water.

"Let's get out of here. Get home."

"The canyon house?"

"Where else?"

The Figueroa house, so full of memories, lay beneath them now, a felicitous nightmare of conflicting architectural styles—Bauhaus, Victorian, SoCal Freestyle, Spanish colonial. Somehow it all worked in spite of itself. Sandy loved the place, with its confusion of slate and skylights and red tile roofs, merloned towers and gable windows, in places both maudlin and stark. It lay couched in cactus and flowering succulents, birds of paradise peering everywhere, purple jacaranda blossoms fluttering across the balconies and off into the warm depths of the canyon, frozen red oceans of bougainvillea spilling over the brink. If only this homecoming weren't such a sad affair.

Sandy saw a group of tourists at the outer gates, pointing out the descending car. "I see we're in the news again," he said. "I'm surprised the hospital wasn't mobbed."

"When you were in with Poppy, a man came through the ward selling bootleg copies of her surgery cubes."

"Hey-Seuss! Where'd he go?"

"I sent him to the emergency room with a broken finger."

Sandy opened his hatch and jumped out into a baking wind; bars of lime cloud lay in layers across a rainbow-sherbet sky. Cool shadows filled the house. Memories boiled up from the walls and floor, like reruns on a channel he couldn't change. All this stuff inside him ran much deeper than the wires.

Corny headed straight for the kitchen seafood-tank. Sandy heard splashing and laughter at the back of the house. He walked toward the indoor pool. Poking his head into the bright room of rippling light, he saw Miranda leaping nude from the high-dive into a pool full of naked men, while a plump balding old guy he vaguely remembered as a pestering pitch-man stood at the edge of the poolside, waiting till she surfaced to rattle off more of his sure-fire ideas:

"It's a natch, Mirry! We'll hook the little boys of all ages! 'Lolita Versus Megalon'! With your looks and Jap special effects—"

It took Sandy a few seconds to get control of himself. His first urge—suppressed—was to scream at them all to get out, to berate his sister for frolicking in the face of a tragedy. But she didn't live by his rules. She would only laugh and tell the stranger to ignore her stodgy older brother. *It's my house as much as yours, Sandy.* Poppy's condition was only another odd development in the life she had mistaken for a wire show.

He fled the noise and laughter. Halfway down the hall, he was surprised by Ferdinand, who came padding toward him dripping wet, also nude, and eating a gooey sandwich.

"Hey, bro, water's just right. Bunch of studleys out there, eager to please. You coming in?"

"No, uh . . . thanks, Ferdi. How have you and Miranda been doing in your search for Calafia?"

"Cala-who? Oh, that? We gave up. I mean, come on, what's she to us? Poppy can worry about her own show. Between you and me, Mir and I've got a project in development. 'Child Bride'! It's really a vehicle for her, but there's this whole incest angle that no other show's really pursued, and I'm pretty sure I'll play the part of her husband—"

"Sounds like new territory for you," Sandy said, and shuffled past him.

Kids, he told himself. They're just kids. You can't expect any more out of them. . . .

Out in the living area, he found another stranger, a black man, looking out into the chasm where pigeon-gulls circled and pecked each other into flocks of bloody feathers. He looked vaguely familiar. He was nibbling on a string of brown chewing-rope that led into his pocket, and spitting frayed bits into the abyss.

The man saw Sandy and put out his hand. "Santiago?"

"Have we met?"

"Not in person, but I've heard lots about you. Used to follow your show faithfully. I'm Clarence Starko. Clarry."

Sandy shook his hand. "Poppy's wireman? You . . . you were there when . . . ?"

Clarry shivered. "I was there. I was with her till your Dad showed up. He was nice enough to invite me over here till we got some news on her."

"No news," Sandy said, shaking his head. He walked to the glass and looked down into the shadows. "What really happened last night?"

"Oh, man. That. It was the worst thing ever happened to me. Poppy was really depressed. We'd got this false lead about the baby, you know? Went all the way out there on a wild goose ride. You can imagine how she felt, her hopes all up and everything, and then a big zee, total bust. It's like her spirit finally broke. That's all the show's been about anymore. Poppy's quest. We were even gonna change the title."

"She was depressed?"

Clarry nodded, spat over the balcony. "Something about the desert made it worse. Even got to me. She seemed tired so I got us some motel space, and I thought she'd gone right to sleep. But I'm sitting there at the editor, looking out the window, and all of a sudden I see her outside, walking toward the road, this busy-as-hell highway, kind of like she's in a trance. I thought she might be sleepwalking, so I went after her." He shook his head. "I wish she had been asleep, so I could have woken her up and brought her in again. But she was wide awake. She stared at me when I asked what she was doing. Stared and said, 'Don't try to stop me, Clarry.'"

Sandy went cold. "Suicide," he whispered.

"I did try, though—of course I did. But she went crazy. Tore away, went running down the highway. I was so close to catching up with her . . . so close . . . when she threw herself out in front of a truck. Just like that. I thought it was all over."

Starko stood silent for a moment, looking at his feet, shaking his head. His hands opened and closed on empty air. Several inches of baccorish slithered into his mouth.

"She wasn't quite dead," he said after a while. "The trucker called for help. Turned out to be a mobile hospital on the road nearby. If it had been a mile farther off, she wouldn't have survived at all."

"I'm not so sure she did survive," Sandy said.

"Yeah. I know what you mean."

Sandy suddenly had a chilling thought. "She wasn't recording when it happened, was she?"

"No. We were on standby, but none of it's on ice."

"I just thought, if it was recorded, and if that crystal got out . . ."

Clarry nodded. "The ghouls would eat it up, you're right. But you don't have to worry about that."

"You were there for the kidnapping, too, weren't you?"

The man looked startled. "Yeah. Of course I was. I produced that show. I've been there for everything. Poor Poppy."

"Do you still have the master cube?"

"Sure. Why?"

"I'd like to go over it myself. See, I had the sense when I finally felt the broadcast that it had been edited. There was a kind of . . . *thin* quality to it. Synthetic. I used to do some of the editing on our old show, so those things kind of leap out at me. You must know what I'm talking about."

Clarry Starko shifted from foot to foot, chewing his rope. "Maybe. Yeah. The cops grabbed that master and kept it quite a while. You're saying somebody screwed with the image?"

"Maybe the cops," Sandy said.

"Now why would they do that? What could *they* be hiding?"

"I don't know," Sandy said. "It's just a funny feeling I had that the whole scene wasn't real."

Clarry shook his head. "I never had the heart to watch it again, but now you've got me interested. The Sens8 in my van has a long memory; the original recording's still in there—I always keep them in case something happens to the master cube. We could dupe a new crystal and play it against the cube I gave the cops, see if there are any changes."

"When could you get it?"

Starko was already heading for the door. "Right now. I'm parked up top."

* * *

Clarry unwrapped a blank cube and downloaded the original kidnapping sequence from the deck in the van. As he sat tapping his fingers on the master that had gone to the cops, gobbling baccorish, he thought about Sandy. Her brother. How similar they were. He didn't want to let him down; that would be like shoveling dirt over Poppy, burying her alive. He couldn't undo his betrayal, but maybe he could help straighten things out. It was like an unexpected second chance.

Besides, that bitch in black was trying to set him up somehow, he was sure of it. If he worked fast, maybe he could stop her. Which meant finding her. She'd held the advantage right from the start, breaking in with those snuff jobs he'd done on his way up from the gutter, those crystals he wished he'd never agreed to record—not that he'd had any choice at the time. It'd been blackmail then, too; his addictions had betrayed him, held him captive on a daily basis.

Not that—and it was hard to admit it now—there hadn't been a little hate in his heart back then, motivating him. Hate of the system, which had nailed a white-as-rice family to the top of the ratings in a state where whites had been a distinct minority for years. The Spanish surname Figueroa couldn't disguise the fact that they were white, white, white. There were ethnic family programs, but they seemed to succeed in spite of the support they *didn't* receive, and their wholesome, untroubled life-styles, so out of touch with ghetto and barrio realities, seemed even more artificial than the Figueroas'. Consequently they never gathered any loyal following or touched any deeper nerve. So, yes, he'd done his part in the kidnapping mainly because of the knife held to his throat . . . but there had been a darker spot of delight in him at first. Until he got to know Poppy as a person, and not as a symbol of his frustrations. And then his sense of being out of control had begun steadily to worsen. . . .

Well, now was time to take back control. Get the bitch

where she lived. Make some of his own moves for a change, instead of just jumping whenever anyone poked him.

He went back into the house with a cube in each hand. Sandy showed him a huge console in the den. It was an elaborate system, with whole panels of function keys Clarry had never seen before. Sandy dropped the cubes into twin player slots.

"One thing," Sandy said. "Don't say a word about this to my father, all right? I don't want him getting his hopes up."

"Sure thing."

"Thanks, man. If Poppy trusted you, I guess I can."

The thought of Poppy's trust was like a dagger. Clarry forced a smile. He had a mouthful of rope juice and wasn't sure where to spit it. Sandy made him nervous. He swallowed.

"Sure thing," Clarry said again.

"Okay, now lead me through it. The police cube first. The broadcast I saw."

Clarry bent over the console, already feeling a professional envy. What a system! Finding exactly the spot he wanted was as easy as drawing a breath. It came bleeding up from his wires, pervading him, a scene frozen in time.

Here's where I went too far, he thought. Past the point of no return.

For a moment he felt an inexplicable panic. He was afraid to feel it again, to relive it.

But the panic was not entirely his own. Some was Poppy's, wire-borne, as the scene started moving.

Night. Vertigo. He stared down at the crowds, hearing the sounds of pursuit. A wagon stalled below.

Now, came a soft, subvocal cue, just like one of his own thoughts, but in a girl's soft voice. Poppy's voice.

He hugged a small body close to his breast for a fleeting instant. The baby. *Which I never even got to hold or touch, except for patting Poppy's belly.*

Before he could appreciate Calafia, he let go of her.

He watched the soundless fall, saw the swaddled infant plunge into the bed of the station wagon, saw the car start forward into traffic. A pang came from somewhere deeper than the wires. He'd lost something of himself in that instant—something irretrievable.

"Back up," Sandy said from outside the scene.

The image blurred and held. Then the wagon rolled back into place, the child fell upward into Poppy's arms, the crowd babbled like a group of maniacs drowning in reverse.

It all started again.

Panic. The child falling. The wagon moving.

Full stop. Reverse. The wagon moved backward, the child tumbled up toward his/her outstretched hands. Froze in midair.

"Okay," Sandy said. "Call up the other copy, same point."

It took only seconds to match the two scenes. Clarry focused on the baby, fixing her at the same point of her fall in both versions. Both channels held simultaneously. He was Poppy twice over now, Clarry inside of Poppy inside of Poppy inside of Clarry. An embodied echo. Both versions of Poppy were identical. He saw no discrepancy in the baby, either.

But down below, in the street, it was another story.

Sandy said it first: "Something's wrong."

"The wagons," Clarry said. "They're completely different. Look at that—different color, model, everything. The driver's different, too. There's no wood paneling in the original."

Suddenly it was obvious. The master crystal had been altered—but how? And by whom? The police wouldn't tamper with it. This was their only clue to tracking down the vehicle.

Unless they—or someone with access to evidence—hadn't wanted the vehicle to be found.

In the master cube that the cops had seized and returned, the driver was a tall white man with thinning hair. In the original recording just now taken from the van deck, the driver was a huddled figure wrapped in black.

The wagon in the cops' cube was white with fake wood paneling along the sides, the one in the original, black and bare-sided—like the wagon he'd arranged for the substitution. If he had watched the sequence after getting the master back, he would have noticed the change immediately. But he'd never bothered. And the police had been looking for a white wagon driven by a white man.

If they were looking at all.

"All right," Sandy said, "isolate the wagon from the original image." He spoke to the computer rather than Clarry. "I want to know where those things come from. Where are they used? That's an old gas burner. They're not even legal anymore except . . . oh, shit. Except in the Holy City."

He stammered this out just as the computer completed its analysis: "Gas wagons are currently illegal in California. The only area exempt from emission restrictions, for constitutional reasons, is district CL-37, the so-called Holy City."

In place of the kidnapping scene, Clarry now found himself hovering above a map of California. The Holy City was marked out by red tints in the middle of the Frange, just south of Snozay, where the bicentennial sequence had been taped.

"The Holy City," Clarry murmured.

"It fits," said Sandy. "Most of the sects in there are pretty primitive. I'll bet that's where the wagon came from—and where it went with my niece."

"Jay Cee," Clarry said. "But who's crazy enough to go in there after it? Where do we start?"

"I know just where to start," Sandy said. "And maybe you can help me."

Sandy's enthusiasm was contagious. And he did want to catch up that bitch in her own net. He could do this—he could help undo his errors.

"Yeah, Sandy, sure. What's your idea?"

"I used to be a sender. I've still got the wires for it. I'll flip the switch and do it again, but on a closed circuit this time. I'll pay you whatever you ask to stay at the receiver and monitor my progress. One guy alone in there shouldn't attract too much attention."

Clarry let out a low whistle. "You're going into the Holy City?"

Sandy nodded. "Going in *live*."

8
Kalifornia, Here I Come

As Sandy huddled down behind a pile of metal scrap, his nose an inch from wet cement that reeked of oil and garbage, he had the sense, illusory, that he could feel his polynerves. Unless there were another cause for all the chills that racked him.

Fear, maybe?

Nah.

He raised himself on his elbows and looked over the scrap heap, but he couldn't see a thing. Too dark. The absence of noise worried him more than that of light. The Holy City was suddenly quieter than a librarian's tomb.

A minute ago, he'd been sure he was being followed, and now there was nothing to suggest that the forbidden zone was even occupied. Two obvious explanations occurred to him: either he'd shaken his pursuers and they'd gone off somewhere else entirely, or else they were waiting out there, waiting with all the patience of skilled trackers, until he betrayed himself with some stupid action.

Some stupid little thing like snagging his cuff on a bit of

burred metal, which pulled the whole tortious scrap heap down on him.

Sandy managed not to cry out, but the wreckage had a voice of its own. The parts clanked and clamored down on him. In seconds, he was half buried in the stuff; he lay pinned with only his arms slightly free.

The pile settled into a new, more stable position. Sandy gave up on silence. With a groan he stretched forward, grabbed hold of a handy post, and started to haul himself out from under the scrap.

"Leggo my leg."

The post shook off his hand. Sandy looked up but still couldn't see anything, not so much as a silhouette. He had to admit it was all pretty dramatic. Clarry might make good use of it someday, despite the dark picture. Part of his deal with the wireman was that when all this was over, Starko could mix it into a package and sell broadcast rights for whatever he could get.

In that final cut, this voice would sound great booming out of the darkness. It suggested a big, somewhat oafish character. He waited for it to say something else.

"Who are you?" it said.

Sandy groaned, shifting his weight to pull out of the slag. He freed his legs and started to rise, but something shoved him back again.

"Don't move. I said, who are you?"

"Slack off, I'm not bothering you."

"You're messing up my stoop. You got five seconds to tell me who you are, then I throw you to the Holy Rollers. It's time for the midnight patrol."

The Holy Rollers. Sandy didn't know them, but he knew he never wanted to.

"My name's Sandy," he said. "I'm looking for a church."

The voice laughed.

"You came to the right place," said the voice. "Any church in particular?"

"Is . . . is there any difference?"

Now the voice crowed. "You must be new around here."

In the distance Sandy heard what sounded like wolves howling, along with a continuous clatter he couldn't identify. Firecrackers, maybe. Or dull thunder.

"Okay, newboy. I'll let you come inside until they pass, then you gotta keep moving. My lama is in heavy meditation; I'm supposed to keep up the banishing rites nonstop. He wouldn't like it if he caught me bringing strangers in. Evil influences, you know. So keep quiet, okay?"

"Sure," Sandy said. Anything to avoid the Holy Rollers.

A hand took hold of him and helped him to his feet; he was pulled stumbling through debris he couldn't see and up a short flight of steps.

"Quiet, now. Not a word."

Sandy nodded, pointless though the gesture seemed. He had the feeling this guy could see him in the dark. It made Sandy wish he'd brought along night-spex. His original logic was that by seeming defenseless he would attract the pity of some compassionate religious group, which would have the pleasure of adopting him as one of their own.

The wolf howls were closer now. He heard *yip-yip-yip-*ing, eerie cries echoing between the invisible buildings, and a softer sound nearby that might have been someone sobbing or mumbling or tunelessly speaking the words to a song.

Suddenly a gong clanged in his ear. Sandy dropped to the ground. A horn began to wail a ghostly reveille, then broke off abruptly as the deep voice of his unseen benefactor started declaiming mystic threats against a background of eerie humming:

"Ho, demons! You're treading on thin ice around here. Whoa now, I'll tell you, some fuzzy-faced evil guy with three eyes came around last night and he didn't live to regret it!"

Sandy sat up, hugging his knees. The horn wailed again, cymbals crashed. Out in the street, the clatter was incredible.

The Holy Rollers were right on top of them. He made out words in their wailing:

"Hallelujah! *Awoo-oo-oo!*"

"Glory be! Glory Hallelujah!"

"We're comin', Lord! We're countin' on your radiant mercy, Lord! You just show us the way to the trespassin' unbeliever—we'll make him sorry he was ever born to your glorious light!"

"Mercy! Oh, have mercy! I feel you, Lord!"

Meanwhile, Sandy's companion let up on the trumpet and continued with his own impassioned cries:

"Now hear this! All demons must evacuate this area immediately or suffer eternal punishments. Any demon remaining within the proximity of my voice in five seconds is going to have his eyes boiled in his head, his own tongue eaten for dessert, and his genitals lopped off and stuck on a stake as an example to others. That's five seconds and counting! One . . . two . . . three . . ."

"Lord, you's beautiful as they come!"

"Hallelujah!"

"*Awoo-woo-woo!*"

". . . three and a half . . ."

"Guide us, Lord! Show us the way!"

"I smell a sinner!"

"I smell dinner!"

"Show yourself, sinner-dinner! Let yourself be purged from the sight of God!"

"Four . . . four and a half . . ."

The cries went fading down the avenue, along with the unholy clamor of their passing. It sounded like they were dragging something that scraped on the street and made a terrible din. If only the light had been better. He wondered what Clarry made of all this, way out there somewhere in the profane Franchise, living out of his van, plugged into monitors. Cornelius was with him, too. The sealman had begged Sandy not to go, then finally had sworn to stay at Starko's side until Sandy was safe at home again with little Calafia in his arms.

"Four and three-quarters . . ."

"*Awoo-oo-oo!*"

"Five! That's it. All you demons who hung around are dead meat now. Come on, show yourselves."

Sandy cleared his throat, making the least possible sound.

"I see nobody challenged me. That was pretty smart of them."

Sandy felt his hand being taken. He stood up and was guided carefully back outside, down the steps, and into the street.

"I wish one of those demons would stick around someday. I could do with a little excitement."

"Good act," Sandy said. "I'm not surprised they took off. You're a scary dude."

"Dude? Well, I never—get out of here! Go on! Get moving or you'll get the demon treatment yourself!"

"Sorry, uh, ma'am," he said, hurrying off through the scrap that had buried him a few minutes before.

"Ma'am?" the voice cried after him. "You are the most insulting—I should have thrown you to the Rollers!"

He moved down the street, dragging his hands along the faces of buildings. It was hard going, but he got better at sensing obstacles without actually running into them. Even so, he finally decided to wait for daylight before going on. He slipped inside the next open doorway and huddled in a corner with his insulated jacket pulled tight around him. It offered minimal protection against the chill of the night, but he was exhausted. Within minutes he jerked back from a hypnagogic demon, and then sank instantly the rest of the way into sleep.

He didn't remember his dreams, and wires couldn't record them.

"Wake up and show your mark."

"Maybe he's a deaf-'n'-dumb, Reb. Poke him."

Sandy's eyes opened on a gray and dismal scene. He was too groggy to avoid the boot toe that jabbed him in the ribs. Three figures in cowled cloaks fenced him into the doorway. Steady drizzle had dampened the cloaks, making them look limp and heavy. The trio didn't seem to be in very good moods.

"G'morning," Sandy said. "You don't have to kick me, you know. I was waking up anyway."

"I said show your mark," said the middle boy, the one called Reb. All three were teenage boys, but this one, the tallest, looked like the leader. He turned to his right-hand man and said, "You do it, Zev."

Zev grabbed Sandy's left hand and pulled it closer, palm up. They stared at the skin as if measuring his lifeline. Then Reb looked into Sandy's eyes and laughed.

"He ain't got one," said Zev.

"One what?" Sandy asked.

"A mark that says what sect you're with," said Reb.

"Hey, Reb, maybe he's with the No-Mark Sect!"

The boys all laughed.

"Is that a crime?" Sandy asked.

They looked at each other. "Might be," said Reb. "But it's good luck for us. We get a commission on any hunk of fresh god-bait we pick up."

"God-bait?" Sandy said.

"Grab him," Reb said, standing back.

The other two stooped and grabbed Sandy by either arm. He was bigger than either of them, but he didn't think resistance was a good idea. This was more or less what he wanted, right?

Rain hit his face as they dragged him into the street.

"I'm coming, I'm coming, guys. Don't go so rough."

They didn't seem to hear him. Reb walked ahead, sloshing through puddles, every now and then turning to make sure the rest were following.

"What's this about a mark?" Sandy called to him. "If I

need one I'll be happy to get it. I don't want to break any rules. I'm new around here."

"Obviously," Reb called over his shoulder. "Don't worry—as soon as we figure out where to sell you, you'll get one. The Wandering Jews run the best placement service in Holy City. Course, you might not get out much after that. Depends on where you end up."

As they walked on, Sandy saw the Holy City revealed by daylight. He saw people in the buildings, people on the sidewalks, people staring down from old freeway overpasses as the Jews led their captive through the streets. Some had shaved heads with red rings painted on their pates like targets; some apparently never cut their hair and wore it like veils across their faces. Some went naked, others were wrapped in lengths of rusty wire or coaxial cable. One old man with a six-foot beard leaned from a shattered window and harangued the Jews as they passed. Reb stopped to lob a brick at the guy. He hit his mark.

"Don't proselytize, Rapunzel!" he shouted.

The old man looked humbled . . . or simply stunned.

"Oy vey," Reb said as they walked on. "You can't tell this was ever America. Religious freedom went right out the window when no one was looking."

"What about my freedom?" Sandy asked boldly.

Reb shrugged. "You should have held on to it tighter. Don't worry, you'll do all right. We have some good regular customers. Like the Church of Christ, Nuclear Scientist. They're pretty interesting. Claim they can split the Holy Trinity to produce safe, clean energy efficiently. They need research subjects. You want to donate your immortal soul to a power company?"

"I'd rather keep it in one piece."

"Maybe you'd make a good Ignostic. That's the Siblings of the Otiose Order. They study all the things God can't be bothered with. You could have a rewarding spiritual career counting balls of lint."

"Do you by any chance know of a church that drives cars? I mean, those old gas wagons?"

Reb looked at him with apparent disbelief. "Drives 'em? No. Fixes 'em? Yeah. You want to join the Celestial Mechanics?" He tipped back his head and laughed at the concrete underbelly of an overpass. His laughter woke a flock of bats. "No one ever *asked* to join the Mechs. They pay pretty good, though, and you look like the sort of guy they'd like to convert."

"What kind is that?" Sandy asked.

Reb looked at his Wandering Jews, and the other two joined him in laughing. They all spoke at once:

"Nosy."

"Curious."

"A fool."

Sandy grinned despite himself. "That's me."

The Celestial Mechanics, having agreed on a price that Sandy thought slightly embarrassing (free upgrades and a year's service on the Jews' solar skateboards), gave him a pair of ochre temple overalls and an empty toolbox. They conducted him to one of three deep rectangular pits in the floor of their outer shrine.

"Acolytes sleep here," he was told.

Apparently he was the temple's only acolyte. He climbed down into the pit and found a wad of old oily rags.

"What's this?" he asked the priest who stood smoking a pipe at the edge of the pit.

"That's your bed," said the priest.

Reb had introduced the little black man as the Grand High Grease Monkey, but a name tag sewn in cursive on the pocket of his monastic overalls referred to him more cozily as "Bob."

Sandy considered the rags. At least he wouldn't have to share them.

"What about my mark?" he asked, holding up his hand. "Do I get one of those?"

"After you've been here a while, your fingernails will identify you."

Sandy sighed and kicked the lid of the toolbox. "It's empty."

"Patience, acolyte. With every initiation you will receive a handy new tool. This evening your education begins with the Rite of the Wrench. Now I'll leave you to settle yourself and prepare for the undertaking ahead of you. Change into your overalls."

When "Bob" was gone, Sandy clambered out of the pit and went to the open door of the outer sanctum. It overlooked a fenced parking lot; the street lay beyond. He'd been aware for some time of the growing sound of wolf howls that signaled the approach of the Holy Rollers. He heard their hallelujahs as he reached the gate; they thundered into sight.

The rattling roar that accompanied their passage was in fact the sound of roller skates. The Holy Rollers were unremarkable in appearance except for their manner of transportation; they were far more fearsome, more impressive, by night. Nothing but a bunch of little old ladies on skates. Hardly the sort to raise one's hackles.

Or so he thought until he noticed that their blackened, leathery purses were handbags made from human heads, which they clutched and swung by the hair. And their bibles were bound in a soft-looking, whitish leather. . . .

Then they were gone, leaving him breathless. He fought the urge to scurry back to the pit for cover. A sturdy cyclone fence protected the temple. He was safe. He could consider himself fortunate for having evaded them last night.

"Starko," he whispered, "you following this? I think I got lucky. The Celestial Mechanics should know where to find any old gas wagons. I'm gonna play along with them, go through these initiations, make some friends—and then start snooping."

A toolbox rattled behind him. He turned to see smiling "Bob" returning with several other mechanics, both men and women.

"Acolyte, are you ready to receive instruction in the use of the Wrench?"

Sandy bowed his head. "I am ready, O Master. Consider my mind an empty toolbox, waiting to be filled."

Clarry's van was a rat's nest of sushi packs, empty soy squirts, and coffee bulbs. The cuspidor was constantly brimming. After a while, he had stopped noticing Cornelius's unusual body odor—a sort of musty, wet-dog smell—and found it easy to treat him simply as another assistant, explaining the operations of the deck, teaching him the rudiments of editing. Cornelius did all the tasks manually, by visual controls, since he wasn't wired. Even so, he was the fastest learner Clarry had ever met.

"You're a natural at this, Cornelius. You sure you never ran a deck before? Because you could be good. I mean really good."

"Never. I wasn't allowed near the Figueroa decks."

"Shame. Cause you've really got the touch, my—uh—man."

The sealie seemed flattered. "Thank you, sir. I do enjoy creative work."

Amazingly, they shared the confined quarters without driving each other crazy, perhaps because they were so different. Roommates of similar personalities—or species—often proved incompatible. But the man and the seal couldn't have been less alike. Clarry and Corny.

Whenever Clarry sagged at his post, Cornelius took over. Not that there was much for him to do. The recording process was largely automated. Corny practiced and worked on various editing/production assignments Clarry gave him for his own amusement. They agreed that at least one of them would cover the deck at all times, in case Sandy got in trouble or made his big find. Sandy wore a subcutaneous tracer by which they could track his progress through the Holy City or find him in an emergency. He hadn't moved in weeks, however. Not since joining the Mechs.

At first they shared the van more or less continuously, but as the days wore on with little in the way of progress or revelation, they began to work in shifts. Clarry would check into a sleeping lot for a few hours, perhaps take a walk or go shopping to stretch his legs, and then come back to give Cornelius a break. He didn't know how the sealman spent his free time, and he didn't ask.

Sometimes, for the sake of variety, they drove the van to new locations. They got to know the outskirts of the Holy City fairly well, particularly those areas with good food. Clarry looked for Creole cooking and could compare the merits of various gumbo recipes for hours. Cornelius lived on a strict diet of raw fish with the occasional bowl of oatmeal or miso soup thrown in.

The work was tedious to Clarry, mindless monitoring, but it served a useful purpose. It made him feel that he was doing something to help Poppy. He couldn't talk to Cornelius about it, of course. The sealman's motives seemed purely sentimental. Sandy was his best friend.

Faithful as a dog, Clarry thought of the sealman.

Which made him kind of jealous. He'd never really had much in the way of friends.

As the weeks passed, Sandy's palms and fingernails turned from pink to permanent gray with grease and oil; his tan forearms grew grimy and scarred.

It was a tough temple in which he'd found himself, and his training took all his attention. After several days any thought of his real mission was absorbed and all but occulted by his spiritual education. They were unexpectedly happy days. He had never used his hands before, and the work gave him pleasure, a sense of accomplishment. Of *reality*. Only at night, in the mere ten or twenty seconds before he dropped into exhausted slumber, did he think briefly of the child, Calafia, who had been stirred up from his father's and sister's cells. She was the product of incest in the purest sense. But there had been no physical conjunction of father and daughter: only the chromosomes had lain together, arms entwined like the sleeves of unraveled sweaters.

In a sense, Calafia had been cobbled together out of spare parts.

Sandy's new surroundings affected his sensibilities. His mentors considered him a bright pupil; but then, he was the only pupil. They encouraged him to ask whatever he liked, as long as it referred to mechanics. Eventually he tried to steer these lessons toward broader subjects, such as the other sects in the Holy City, with particular reference to their means of transportation. They called this comparative religion.

His toolbox filled swiftly. Each day saw the addition of a larger ratchet to his collection. His biceps grew from carrying the heavy box.

To the Celestial Mechanics, these were not simply tools—they were keys to unlocking the secrets of science, of technology, of progress. They felt that much practical knowledge had been lost through disuse, and that the old ways should be—at the very least—remembered, practiced, and preserved. Someday, they hinted apocalyptically, man might need to live again without wires and computers and automated everything. In such a situation, the Celestial Mechanics were prepared to play a leading role. It would be valuable then to have a deep understanding of what they referred to reverently as "Moving Parts."

"Everything moves," an unusually solemn "Bob" told him one evening, waxing enthusiastic as he described ever larger orbits with his hands. "The planet hurtles through space, the moon swings around the planet, the earth circles the sun, the solar system is caught in the slow rotation of the galactic disk, which in turn expands forever, moving out among all the other galaxies like a cloud of steam. Imagine if you could harness all that energy, that cosmic steam, and use it to power a huge machine. Imagine if the expansion of the universe were able to drive enormous pistons. Maybe it does. Imagine numerous universes all linked together, some of us expanding while others are contracting, one set of pistons pushing up, another coming down. Who could possibly know the use of that inconceivable engine? Does it propel a locomotive or a lawnmower?"

"Good question," said Sandy, who wondered what either of these *l*-words referred to as he swung his legs in the pit. "You think I could ever get to work on an old internal combustion engine someday?"

"I don't see why not."

"You know what I'd really like to see?"

"Bob" knelt down beside him, engulfing him in clouds of pipe smoke. "What's that, my son?"

"One of those old gasoline things."

"Bob" shook his head sadly. "It's rare to find them running these days, but we do get them in from time to time."

Sandy brightened. "Yeah? You mean, I could work on one?"

"Might be. A few sects keep them, and they're always breaking down."

"How many would you say are in the Holy City?"

"Oh, I couldn't even guess. Not many. You see them in the streets. I've also seen them parked in churchyards when I go in to fix generators and things like that. There must be a hundred or so. It's not impossible that you could have a chance to work on one with your own hands, if that's what you'd really like."

Sandy shrugged.

"Just remember, Santiago, those are things of the past. The future machines lie elsewhere. It's true that you're an acolyte, but in a sense so are we all. While we preserve the past—and honor our origins—we owe our allegiance to the future, to the developing machine."

Sandy's spirits sank. A hundred or so. The Holy City was full of gas wagons, too many to track down. He nodded as if acknowledging "Bob's" words, but his thoughts wandered off.

"Santiago, do you have a moment?"

He came out of his reverie. "Uh, sure. I was just about to go to sleep, that's all."

"There's something I'd like to show you. Something I think you're ready to appreciate. It will explain what I've been saying about our purpose, our ultimate goals. Come on, if you're interested."

Sandy got up and followed "Bob" into the grimy corridors of the temple, through the main cathedral with its hydraulic presses and battery cases stacked in pyramids. Beyond was a door through which he never had passed. He'd thought it must be an especially sacred place because of the expressions on the faces of those going in and out: they always looked as though they'd gazed into the heart of some ineffable mystery. Despite himself, he was excited to see whatever sat beyond that door.

Several Mechanics were at work in the inner sanctum, even at this late hour. For a moment their bodies obscured the object of their attentions, but then they noticed Sandy and, smiling and nodding, moved aside to let the machine stand naked and majestic before him.

It stood upright like a person, headless but otherwise human, except for the fact that it had four arms. It was beyond doubt the most beautiful machine he had ever seen. The body was tall, the shoulders half a foot higher than his own. It was a three-dimensional webwork of wires and polished struts, a spider sculpture. His eyes traced the trails of nerve and sinew, muscle and organ fiber, all of it replaced or rendered in metal, flexible plastic, and ceramic. In place of the heart and lungs was an opaque cocoon, a hollow region that looked like the arachnid master of that android web.

"A robot?" he asked.

"Yes and no. It's entirely dependent on human will. It will have a polynerve link to its operator, but its own nerves are superconductors. It will amplify the human will, allowing performance of the most delicate operations—as well as those requiring great strength. This is the ultimate aim of technology, as we see it now—to extend and refine human creativity, not to replace it."

Sandy stepped closer to the gleaming headless figure. One of the legs was encased in a transparent sheath. The Mechanics were in the process of covering the entire skeletal body in this same tough, invisible stuff. Except for that and the head it was apparently almost finished.

"None of us here need wires for what we do," "Bob" went on, rapt in the presence of the construct. "Others, outside the Holy City, have become overly dependent on them. But someday a balance will be struck—that's evolution for you. And this machine, or others to come, will certainly play a role in that progression."

"It looks almost finished," he said.

"It lacks only a few days of work. That's why I thought you should see it. Soon it will be out of our hands, delivered to its owners. As an acolyte, you should be aware of this beautiful machine. You may never see another like it. Or . . . you may be building other versions of it someday."

"It is beautiful," Sandy said. But it frightened him as well, reminding him of the polynerves that pierced every part of his anatomy. This thing of metal made a mockery of flesh. The hands alone were so intricate, so precisely machined, that his own fingers looked clumsy and crude by comparison . . . except perhaps for the perfect wires living inside his flesh.

"I see the wires as a tremendous force for democracy someday, after the bumps and kinks are ironed out. I prefer to hold off on wires of my own until—well, probably for my lifetime."

"In other words, all of us are like test pilots right now."

"Yes, that's right. And especially the ones who control this."

The other Mechanics couldn't seem to keep their hands off the body. They eyed Sandy jealously. When he stepped away they closed in again with their tools, busily shaping the crystal skin to fit the robot form, constantly touching the body, touching it, touching—as if it were a holy relic.

"What do you think?" "Bob" asked as they left the inner sanctum.

"Very nice," he said. But he hoped he wouldn't have to see it again.

"My secret dream," "Bob" confided as Sandy once more lowered himself into the sleeping pit. "Do you want to hear it?"

"Sure. But if you tell it, will it come true?"

"Bob" grinned down at him. "Once there was a great man—not a mechanic, but still a great man—named Martin Luther King. He noticed that mankind had built machines that could carry us into the deep-sea trenches, or all the way out into space, but for all our advances, we still couldn't treat each other decently as human beings. And this gave me an idea. What if we could build vehicles for ourselves, suits or special bodies, that would help us travel through the social realm, the world of human relationships, that most treacherous of all frontiers . . . carry us safely and humanely, with collision avoidance and emotional guidance controls. Imagine? Machines that allowed us to be real human beings? Maybe, between the wires and computers and body augmentation and gene tailoring, some combination of all these things, we can create a new technology to do this. Of course, the programming would be tricky at first, but I believe it could be done. And then maybe, someday far beyond that, when it's all become second nature, we could shed the machinery and just . . . just be ourselves. Not that one can ever shed a submarine or a space suit and expect to survive. Who knows what interpersonal realms we might have entered by then: strange places we can hardly picture now.

"Anyway, that's my dream, Sandy. Sandy? Oh . . . well . . . you sleep then. And Cog bless you."

An alarm woke Cornelius in his rented sleeping box. He roused himself, gulped down the last few prawns that swam in an aerated saltwater Thermos, then let himself out onto the catwalk. The airy, ten-story sleeping garage lacked walls, floors, or ceilings; it was nothing but girders and beams with cubbies bolted to them, joined by meshwork ramps and stairs.

It was nearly dusk. Clarence would be hungry. He stopped at a stand to buy jambalaya and Cajun popcorn. The smell of spicy food turned his stomach, so he held the bag out to one side as he hurried to work. Waste of good shellfish . . .

The van was parked on a corner in a desolate neighborhood, at the edge of a nightmarish landscape where the earth, poisoned by industrial waste, had been treated with soil cleaners that had reacted unpredictably with the toxins, forming huge billowing mushroom and elephant shapes, all gray-green, soft and slimy looking, though they were dry, slippery, and solid as polished marble. This eerie jungle separated the nonsectarian Frange from the Holy City.

As soon as he spotted the van, Cornelius hesitated. It was moving, rocking violently. Only one thing could account for such activity. Cornelius sank back into the shadows out of sight, setting the food aside, prepared to wait. He must have dialed up a satisfaction service. Clarence was only human, after all, and like most humans, he talked about sex constantly but did nothing about it. Cornelius supposed he had finally worked himself into a passion. Maybe now he would stop talking about it for a while.

Cornelius was ready to walk off in the other direction when the motion ceased and the side panel opened.

Two dogs got out, a male Lab mix and some sort of Spaniel with her hair done up in a beehive. The male carried a large metal case slung over his shoulder, something electronic.

The dogs looked both ways but missed Cornelius, who felt an increased need for invisibility. He didn't even peek for a moment. When he convinced himself to look again, they were walking down the sidewalk in the other direction. Turning a corner, they vanished.

It was nearly dark, the shadows offering plenty of protection in the deserted street. Still, a terror of exposure filled his limbs with ice. When he finally roused himself, he moved toward the van with a stiff, rapid gait, his whole body trembling.

The door was ajar. He pulled it open and crept in.

Clarence slumped over the console. The needles flickered wildly; Cornelius had never seen them like that. Some had actually fallen dead.

Dead . . .

Blood pooled around Clarence Starko. It ran out from under his cheek, over the deck, trickled down his arms, and pattered on the garbage that littered the floor. His eyes were open but he didn't blink. He didn't see Cornelius or anything else. Redundantly, his murderers had wound the baccorish rope several times tightly around Clarry's neck; one end was still clenched between his bloodied teeth.

But what mattered more to Cornelius was the behavior of the needles. The Sens8 was out of action. Sandy had been cut off.

Unless—

He hunted around the interior, finally spotting and snatching up a small plastic case that looked like a hand computer. It had been kicked under a cabinet. On the screen, a luminous map showed a blinking dot—the seeker they used to follow Sandy's progress. Happily, it was intact.

Cornelius felt nothing but gratitude.

Then it occurred to him that whoever had done this to Clarence might be coming back.

Or . . .

They might be going after Sandy, now that they knew what he was up to.

Cornelius hopped out of the van, locked the door from the inside, and slid it shut. Tinted windows hid the massacre from sight. He tucked the seeker in his pocket, looking both ways to make sure that he was unobserved.

Across the street, the forest of slick deformities loomed up like something vomited from the floor of the sea.

Despite his fear of the ocean, Cornelius hurried into it.

As it turned out, Sandy did see the robot again, and not too long after his first view of it. "Bob" decided to bring him along with the delivery and installation crew.

A team of five embarked on a cold night through the Holy City. It was the first time that he had been out of the temple of the Celestial Mechanics since his initiation.

"It's time you got out into the world, Santiago. This is going to be a big part of your practice—lending your support to customers. Hand holding."

The robot was covered in shrouds and padding and strapped to a cart, which it was chiefly Sandy's responsibility to haul on foot through ever more decrepit sections of the Holy City. "Bob" and one of the other Mechanics carried weapons for reasons that weren't clear to Sandy until he heard the howling of the Holy Rollers, far away in the ruins.

"Okay," "Bob" said at last, motioning to Sandy. "You and I have to stay back here for the moment." He nodded to the other three, all women, and they went into a dark, recessed entryway in the face of one decrepit building. "Better they go ahead of us," he told his acolyte. "That way there's no confusion."

After a minute the Mechanics returned, followed by three figures entirely swathed in black. "Bob" tugged Sandy away from the cart, giving the others room to untie the bundled robot. The Mechanics lifted it onto their shoulders and headed into the shadows. As the three black figures started to follow, "Bob" cleared his throat and stopped them with a soft, "Excuse me?" They turned to stare at "Bob" and Sandy; their faces were hidden but their hostility was not.

"Might we come in?" "Bob" said tentatively. "I am the head Mechanic. I should make a few adjustments as part of the installation."

The three stared at him for a moment, a long moment, until one said, "What about him?" A woman's voice, fiery with mistrust.

Sandy touched his breast. *"Moi?"*

"He's my acolyte, an excellent pupil. This is part of his education, meaning no offense to any of your sect."

The three turned inward, conferred briefly, then the first one spoke again: "You, 'Bob,' may come inside if it is absolutely necessary for proper functioning of the construct. But your acolyte stays out here."

"Fine," Sandy muttered.

"Please, it's a cold night—he'll be no trouble."

Sandy said softly, "Hey, 'Bob,' I'm fine."

"If he could just wait in your lobby," "Bob" pleaded.

Half a minute passed in silence, the Mechanics waiting with their burden, the three in black seeming anxious to get inside. Finally, impatiently, two hurried back into the shadows. The third snapped, "He waits in the lobby then. No further."

"If it's not too much trouble," Sandy said under his breath. "Bob" silenced him with a look.

"Thank you very much," "Bob" called to the woman as she turned to go in. He caught Sandy by the elbow and whispered, "Careful here, Santiago. They're very easily offended by our kind."

"What kind might that be?"

". . . Men."

The lobby was a large chamber carpeted in ancient maroon pile, its darkness only slightly relieved by a few small candles. Stairs rose off into black heights, and the mouths of corridors yawned on either side. Sandy took a seat on a cement bench. The four Mechanics and the black-robed women vanished into one of the corridors. He heard their footsteps fading, then came a lull, and then a sudden, muffled commotion: voices and scuffling feet and whispers mixed together. Then, as if a door had fallen shut, this sound ended as abruptly as it had begun. He leaned against the wall and cleaned his fingernails.

Time passed slowly, or so it seemed. Much of his recent experience had been a waste of wire time. All of it was being recorded, every single moment of his machine-shop education squirted off to Clarry for viewing and editing.

Editing. That was Clarry's forte; and it would have been a luxury in real life. In the final version of Sandy's adventure, Clarry would undoubtedly cut this part, this sitting in a dark lobby. The four-armed robot would be good for a few incidental images, perhaps serving as a focus for Sandy's stint with the Celestial Mechanics. But most of his stay in the Holy City had so far proven dramatically fruitless.

Sandy could see it now: his first solo feature. It would start with him on his first night, hiding behind that pile of scrap, just before being discovered and evading the Rollers. Then the scene with the man or woman or whatever it had been. Then a few segments of Sandy wandering down dark, unfamiliar streets before finding a place to sleep. Cut to his rude awakening by the Wandering Jews, and a few scenes of his treatment at their hands. Reveal in glimpses the varied cults of the Holy City, suggesting a vast anarchic society too rich to be explored in more detail. Then, so as not to steep the poor wire audience in every bit of irrelevant byplay, the show would cut straight into the garage of the Celestial Mechanics, not to make too big a deal of it, but simply to introduce a few of the characters he'd met here in the Holy City. "Bob" would play a minor role. Funny to think of it that way, considering that he saw "Bob" almost every waking minute of his day. But once this program was edited, the Great Grease Monkey would be stripped down to a trivial part. He'd suggest Clarry leave in a few snatches of his training, then skip right to that dramatic night when the robot had been unveiled. And sure, they could even put in some of this very night, to show the fate of the robot. Wouldn't want to leave that loose end hanging. But Clarry would certainly cut this endless waiting.

If only he could cut it out now!

Too much of his search had proved to be nothing but incidental. He'd landed in a position from which it was impossible to investigate on his own, even if he'd known where to begin in a city full of roller-skating headhunters and the Ignostics only knew what else.

Sandy stood up, began to pace, and suddenly realized that he was alone, unattended, for the first time since the Wandering Jews nabbed him. Free to go!

He crept toward the door, waiting for someone to stop him. The woman priests, if they were watching, would probably be happy to see him leave. And "Bob" was somewhere else entirely. "Bob" was—

"Santiago! There you are!"

—right behind him.

He tensed, knowing that he wouldn't bolt for freedom. It was dark out there, dark and scary. Roaming randomly in a night full of religious predators wouldn't bring him any nearer to his goal.

He turned back to the corridors as "Bob" hurried toward him across the lobby.

"It works, Santiago! Wait until you see! It's coming this way—by the Central Gear and Mainspring, I'm ecstatic!"

He heard voices again, rising in exultation, coming closer. He heard laughter and song, all of it female.

Something glittered in the dark entryway as candlelight went flowing up and down the slender rods and wires of the transparent body. Its four arms clacked and whirred experimentally. The robot moved from the shadows with a steady, graceful stride, as if it had been born walking. Black-robed worshipers followed, holding back a few feet so as not to overwhelm it; it was none of their wills that powered or guided the thing.

Now the robot had a head, a brain, and a face of its own.

A small living face with bright orange eyes.

Sandy gasped and grabbed on to the door latch. He held on for his life and his sanity, both of which seemed to be floating away. He felt suspended, all doubts in abeyance. His awe was no less than that of the black sisters who surrounded their robot-borne baby.

Another step she took, and another, heading straight across the lobby, straight toward Sandy. An infant's head on a powerful metal frame; an infant's body hidden inside that breast; an infant's will compelling the construct to cross the room and stop before him. An infant's eyes, but not an infant's intellect.

The orange-eyed baby stared at him. Sixteen powerful transparent fingers rested on his shoulders in a gentle, terrifying grip. He felt a rush through his body, a powerful surge that registered not in his nerves but in his polynerves.

"I've been waiting for you," she said.

Sandy swallowed. "For me?"

The baby smiled. She had already cut her two front teeth. He had missed this milestone in his odd niece's life. Immediately he had the urge to miss every other event that might befall her.

He wanted to tear away, to run through that door and into

the night and keep running, risking everything, abandoning his search and all his work merely for the pleasure of an immediate escape from the specter of this mechanically augmented baby.

But he couldn't move. She held him not only in a metal grip, but in a mental one. He'd been harnessed in one easy motion, and his wires were now held like reins in her hands.

"Come with me," she said.

Divorced from his will, betrayed by his limbs, he followed.

PART THREE

9

The Meatpuppet Master

Kali hated wearing people. Flesh was icky—all blood and heat and fart sounds. But she was drawn to this one, sucked right in, her soul captured by his blood's gravity. Flesh was a magnet and she was iron. But she was iron with a will.

Unlike the Daughters, the man was vulnerable, just as the Seer had been. This time she would be more careful; she wouldn't interfere with his biocircuitry. Death was a power failure, no good to her. She had to control him without killing him. But she could do that now. It was better than having a pet puppy dog. And since she could get around on her own in the grown-up machine, the Daughters wouldn't be able to come up with any good reason for her not to have a pet.

"Pay the Grease Monkey," she told them. "We're keeping this one."

The High Priestess's expression was unreadable behind her veil, but another Daughter cried, "He's a man! Kali forbids it!"

She stamped her crystal-shod foot. "I *am* Kali."

No one could argue with that.

She sent the blond man into the dark corridor, ignoring the complaints of the Celestial Mechanics. The pipe-smoking priest started after his acolyte, but the Daughters reacted violently to any further intrusion by a male into their domain. Kali had judged them adequately. Their faith in her was almost as good as wires, which they lacked. They would defend her decision. Besides, they probably liked the idea of keeping a male as a pet. She might make him do tricks to entertain them.

She followed the man down the corridor, taking great delight in her long, smooth strides. She had always known that walking would be like this.

She steered him into the nursery ahead of her. Over Kali's crib was an intricate wooden mobile, a gift from the High Priestess that modeled the global genomic library. It pleased her to follow the twisted, entwined connections among all parts of creation, from prokaryotes to humans, and to situate herself somewhere outside of them all, observing.

"You were looking for me, weren't you?" she asked the man.

He backed into a corner and stared at her, trembling. The shivers were uneconomical, since he was quite warm already, so she stopped them. His eyes bulged. She made him blink but it didn't look right. She blinked him again, faster this time. It still wasn't natural, not like the Daughters' eyes. She tried not to think about it, leave it to him. A moment later he blinked on his own, and she was content. At least she didn't have to do everything for him.

"Y-yes," he said. "I—I—I—"

The stammer was unnecessary, a nervous misfiring. She fined-tuned his vocal apparatus, making him moan and babble for a few seconds. The next time he spoke it would be better.

She thought it would be amusing to look at herself through his eyes, but as soon as their eyes met—Kali looking into Kali—she felt the hint of a terrible pain running through her, so she made him avert his gaze. She continued by causing him to fold his knees and kneel reverently before her.

"What is your name?" she asked.

"Santiago Figueroa. You can call me Sandy."

She giggled at this.

"My name is Kalifornia," she said. "But you can call me Kali."

"Kali," he repeated. "I'm very glad to meet you."

His words came more easily now. He was relaxing. Santiago Figueroa seemed like a nice man. Suddenly she was full of happiness; she flexed her tiny muscles and the metal ones responded. The man cringed away from the motion of her four mighty arms.

"What's wrong?" she said. "Isn't this very pretty? It's my grown-up suit."

"Yes," he said, "it's lovely. But it's also very strong. I think you'd better be careful with it."

"Don't worry, it won't break."

"No, I mean . . . be careful you don't hurt anybody."

She crossed her glassy arms. "I won't if they behave themselves. Do you think I'm mean or something?"

"No, no, not at all." He laughed and showed her a very nice smile. She liked it so much that she fixed it there. After a moment she felt and saw him straining to get rid of it. His eyes twitched and he fumbled with his fingers at the corners of his mouth.

"What . . . what are you doing?" he asked, not daring to meet her eyes. "That hurts. A little bit, but it hurts."

She felt through his polynerves and didn't find anything like pain. "No it doesn't," she said. "It's a smile. It's very nice. It means you're happy."

"Oh, I'm happy, sure. I just think a slightly smaller smile is even nicer because it doesn't hurt so much."

She let the smile shrink a little, then let it go completely. She was tired of making him happy. Sweeping her four shiny hands over her shiny body, she said, "I got tired of grown-ups having all the power. Now I'm just like them in every way. No, I'm even better. The High Priestess can't tell me what to do. If it were up to her you'd be in a lot of trouble here. You don't have to worry though. I'll protect you."

Sandy bowed his head slightly. "Thank you, Kali. I appreciate that. You're right, I was looking for you. Everybody wants to know where you are."

"Who's everybody?"

"Your grandpa. Your mommy. Your other uncle and aunt."

"I don't have a mommy. I'm Kali."

"You do, though. Your mommy is my sister."

Kali thought about this for a moment, then put her lower pair of hands on her hips, half akimbo. "How can that be?"

"Can't you tell? Haven't you seen your pretty golden eyes? They're just like mine, Kali. Look here."

He put his fingers on his cheeks and she saw that he was right. His eyes were golden, just like hers. She had to withdraw from his eyes in order to look at him without the threat of feedback.

"Your mother's eyes are golden, too," he said. "Nobody else has eyes like ours."

"Is my mother a goddess?"

"No, you have a human mother. She's not very well, I'm afraid. Your grandpa wants to see you, too. He'll be happy to know that you're well."

"First I want some clothes so I can look like everyone else."

"Clothes?"

"I can't go around like this, can I?"

"I hadn't thought of that. We'll see what we can do. You're big, but not so big that we shouldn't be able to dress you. Those extra arms might be a problem though."

"A robe will do for now," she said. "Go get a blousy one."

"I don't know where—"

"I'll work you. Go on."

She marched him out of the nursery and up a flight of stairs. Daughters cowered on the steps; some shrank away, others stared at him with disgust. She made faces at them, then tightened his vocal cords so that he could say, in a little voice like her own, "I'm watching you! The man is my eyes." If they seemed to doubt it, she called them by name.

At the top of the stairs, in the laundry and wardrobe, she had Sandy pick out two of the special robes reserved for the High Priestess on ceremonial occasions. The laundress didn't say a word. As Sandy started back down the steps, a crowd gathered to block the way.

"Move!" she said him. "These are for Kali!"

The veiled High Priestess rushed up, grabbing at the robes. "Give me those," she cried. "They're mine."

Sandy caught her wrist. The Daughters gasped and the High Priestess screamed, trying to pull her hand away.

"Don't touch me!" she shrieked. "Don't ever touch me!"

"Let go of the robes," Sandy said.

"They're my robes—don't touch me!"

The priestess used her free hand to tear at his cheek with nails long and sharp as a cat's claws. Kali didn't feel it, but Sandy gasped. She forced him to keep his grip on the High Priestess while she struck him again and again, struck him until her fingers were bloody. Kali never let him move until the High Priestess had lapsed into panting, still held by Sandy, defeated.

"Kali speaks through me," he told her. "Kali sees through my eyes. And what she sees makes her very, very mad. You are selfish and mean. Kali wants these robes so she can be close to the Daughters; she doesn't want them to be frightened of her grown-up machine. You should want to give Kali what she wants. If you don't, she'll hurt you."

Sandy let go of the High Priestess. She retreated a few steps, rubbing her wrist with a bloody hand.

"You must never touch him again," said Kali through Sandy's mouth. "He is my uncle."

"I know who he is," the High Priestess shrieked. "He-Demon!"

"Get bandages and skin-glue. You hurt him, you make him better."

The High Priestess stared at Sandy a moment longer, then hurried away. The other Daughters let him pass. Back in the nursery, Kali looked at the wounds on Sandy's cheek, touching them lightly with a crystal finger. Tears trembled on his eyelids. She gave him a little smile to wear.

"It doesn't hurt," she said. "I turned off the nerves."

"I'm sorry, Kali, but you're wrong. It does hurt. You may have shut down the polynerves, but I have others you can't control. You can't feel them, but I can."

She thought about this, wondering if she should be upset with him. Maybe he couldn't help himself. He really was inferior.

"Well, you'll soon be fixed up. Now dress me."

"Yes, Kali."

"But don't get blood on anything."

"Yes, Kali."

They tied the robe around her collar, where it hung like a cape. The extra arms interfered with a proper fit. Clothes would have to be made especially for her.

As she dressed, admiring her appearance through Sandy's eyes, the door swung open to admit the High Priestess.

"Good," Kali said. "After you glue and bandage him, get drugs for his pain. Quick-as-can-be!"

The High Priestess bowed. "Yes, Kali, I thought you would want them. I brought them along."

She held up a black cylinder, Kali's needle. Seeing it, Kali grew suspicious: sometimes that needle brought death rather than mere cessation of pain.

"Wait," she said. "Bring it here."

The High Priestess bowed and walked toward Kali. "You wish to see the needle?"

"Yes," Kali said. "How do I know what's in there?"

"Simple enough," said the High Priestess. She buried the needle in Kali's neck.

The grown-up machine sputtered out of Kali's control. She tried reaching out for the traitorous High Priestess, but none of her augmented nerves would fire correctly. She spun away across the room and slammed into the wall. Darkness flooded her veins and then her brain, and she went down.

Sandy, like a puppet whose strings had been severed, dropped to the floor as the needle withdrew from Kali's carotid artery. He lay in a daze for several moments, hearing a clamor that gradually subsided when Kali slumped into unconsciousness.

"Can you move?" said the harsh voice of the High Priestess.

He was afraid to try, for fear of finding himself paralyzed. His limbs were under control now—his control. He pushed himself to a sitting position. The High Priestess extended a firm, horny hand to help him to his feet.

Kali lay in a sprawl of fabric and machinery, her little head thrown back, mouth and eyes slightly open, like any other child who has fallen asleep on her feet. He backed away from her, afraid she would wake and take control of him again. He had never known such a horrible sensation. In a life on the wires, he had felt almost every sensation it was possible to feel through polynerves, but never anything like that lack of self-control. Normally livewire sensations caused no movement of the limbs; they were isolated from one's motor activities by a current that inhibited medullary reticular formation neurons to suppress muscle signals.* As in REM sleep, you dreamed of running, but your legs never moved. But Kali had made him move. She had dreamed him into doing whatever she wanted, while he was awake and struggling for control.

"She'll sleep for a while," the High Priestess said. "In the

---

*If you want to get technical.

meantime, before she gets up, put this on. It interrupts her control of your wires."

She gave him a soft plastic object, contoured to fit behind one ear, and helped him fit it into place.

"Shouldn't you pull her out of that thing?" he asked, getting to his feet.

The woman in black, apparently unruffled by Kali's takeover, nodded and bent over the robot. She drew apart the robes, unsnapped a panel in the chest, opened the metal ribcage on silent hinges. Kali lay cradled within, her tiny arms and legs fit snug inside motor-amp devices, a rubber socket patched to her groin. As the High Priestess pulled out the jacks, Sandy gasped and bent closer.

"She—what is that?"

"Peripheral control cable."

He sighed. "I thought for a minute that 'she' was a 'he.' "

"A common mistake. You never saw her before, then? Not even in the design stage?"

He shook his head. "No, my father never—"

Sandy broke off, staring sideways at the High Priestess. She lifted Kali out of the robot and laid her down in the cradle, covering her with a black blanket.

"Who are you?" he said.

She chuckled, nodding. "Men are not allowed to gaze upon the Daughters of Kali. At least, that's the law. But I wrote the law, so what the hell."

She lifted her veil. In the dim room, it took him a moment to be sure of what he saw, though he had already begun to suspect as much.

Her face was pale, worn, but full of strength and character. It reminded him of Poppy, though sharpened and tempered by experience to an inner hardness that Poppy lacked, and never would have wanted. It wasn't Poppy's face, of course.

It was his mother's.

He put out a hand, not quite daring to touch her.

"Hello, Santiago." She caught his hand and pressed it to

her cheek. It was superficially a tender gesture, but her dark eyes remained cold and dry. This was not a role she felt comfortable with. "I never expected to see you again."

There was one rerun that Sandy never relived, though the master was an infinite loop forever playing in the back of his mind.

When he was seventeen . . .

With the Figueroa show at the peak of its popularity, the scenarists had gone scraping the bottom of the dramatic barrel for situations, mining myth and legend and pulp magazines. There was no setting or circumstance they wouldn't consider.

The family had dealt with almost every issue a family could face and still remain popular. Birth. Incest. Celibacy. Drugs. Asceticism. Schizophrenia. Holism. Failure. Success. Crime. Punishment. War. Peace. Gluttony. Bulimia. Basic human nature was ransacked daily for sitcom possibilities. Alfredo and Marjorie had decided to create the little Calafia to provide a few new situations; but the technology was still uncertain, an R & D dream. That was something for the future. While the family's creative consultants brainstormed, the Figueroas decided to take a vacation.

They enjoyed improv. Actually, it was what they did best. No matter how elaborately contrived the scenarios, they tried to avoid scripts, knowing that the best situations developed with the fluidity of reality and couldn't be forced or faked. Even so, they rarely invented a day from scratch, improvising everything from breakfast to dessert. Now they had the chance to create an entire month's adventure.

Marjorie suggested the moon.

Mars was more scenic, but it took a week to get there; the moon was a short hop away. Holo-brochures touted its world-class hotels, cosmopolitan population, great ethnic food, duty-free shopping, and low-grav recreation. It was all hype.

From the moment they landed, Sandy's disappointment knew no bounds—unlike the lunar living space. It was like a giant hamster warren, a habimall without exit doors. They could have been almost anywhere on Earth; even the reduced gravity, which was supposed to keep husbands from tiring while wives shopped, only succeeded in making everyone constipated. There was no hint of otherworldliness. The potentially awesome views from their hotel were spoiled by the sprawl of tektite-processing plants and Bova-Burger restaurants that surrounded the moonmall. Within three days, they exhausted the mall's possibilities. Sandy felt like a prisoner inside a vast J. C. Sears, a waking nightmare rendered even more awful by the unshakable conviction that at any moment he might float away.

Marjorie suggested a moonwalk. She hired a guide. Inside a day they were all dressed up in vacuum suits, riding out of town on an open-vac stumbler, an off-road vehicle named for its awkward manner of shifting between fat tires and hydraulic legs. It took hours to get into wilderness; man had been on the moon for nearly eighty years, after all—plenty of time to mess it up. What little "virgin" lunar surface remained was strictly in the form of limited preserves.

Once the industrial tracts fell behind, nothing marred the scenery except the treadmarks of lunebuggies, which scarred every slope and eroded every once-sharp crest in sight. No rain would ever fall to soften those tracks, no wind would ever blur them; they were etched forever in the surface of the moon, along with the usual graffiti, unless some tidy meteor might happen along and wipe them out.

Finally the Figueroas dismounted, entering a mare that could legally be traversed only on foot. At last, Sandy thought, they had found some peace and isolation, beyond the crowded malls and factories.

Still, it was a busy weekend. Small cars were dropping all around them, and other, more practiced campers—moon residents anticipating the rush—had already grabbed the best spots. Wherever they went, someone had gotten there ahead of them. And so they pressed on, Ferdinand and Miranda bounding ahead, Alfredo and Marjorie strolling close together. Neither Poppy nor Sandy could pretend much enthusiasm. Sandy kept thinking that the moon looked better from earth, and the earth did too. He tried to appreciate the rare view of his home among the stars, but adsats for soft drinks and sexual aids kept eclipsing North America. He always remembered a board that floated past, advertising the premiere of a local epic: FRIDAY NOON MEANS FEAR FOR LUNA!

They finally made camp in the hollow of Ubehebe III, a tiny crater that provided at least the illusion of lunar wilderness, if one discounted the litter cluttered at the bottom. Sandy went to sleep wishing they had stayed at home.

He woke to the sound of screaming.

It wasn't a sound in the usual sense. It carried only through the speakers in his helmet, and through his polynerves.

Disoriented at first, thinking it merely another complication in his insecure dreams, he didn't rise immediately. He found himself moving with another body, looking through other eyes, feeling thunder all around and through him. He started up with a shock, but this was no dream. He had tapped into his mother's wires and was feeling what she felt.

Marjorie huddled in a dark, narrow place, a thin wedge of stars above her. The whole moon seemed to be shaking. She put out her hands and touched rock on both sides. A cloud of black blotted out the stars, and a crushing weight closed down on her—squeezing Sandy out of her body, sending him bounding up the side of the crater, screaming.

His father reached the top of the bowl ahead of him, shouting for his wife. The guide meanwhile leaped aboard the little flying wedge that carried their luggage and rocketed out of the crater to a nearby scarp of steep lunar rock. Rocks were still sliding down when Sandy first sighted the place.

Avalanche.

Like one in a dream, a floating nightmare, he tried to run

but his panic pushed him too hard. He fell, tumbled in dust, came up screaming. His speakers carried sounds of wailing, the cries of his brother and sisters, Alfredo's shouting—but nothing from his mother. Marjorie's wires were dead. Cut off.

Afterward, they guessed she had gone for a solitary walk, sneaking past the guide, who'd warned them never to travel alone. She'd been deep in a narrow rock defile when some tremor—perhaps of her own making—had set off the rockslide that buried her. There was never the slightest hope of recovering the body. They planted a marker and held a funeral in that spot. The last episode of the Figueroa show was broadcast live from the foot of that talus slope, relayed to earth.

The Figueroas had faced everything they could face as a broadcast family. The death of pets and relatives.

But this death destroyed them—as an entertainment commodity, as a public institution, as a family.

Sandy still remembered feeling her die. He had never doubted that she lay buried beneath those rocks. He had been *there,* inside of her, in her wires, when it happened. He had tried to take comfort in the fact that her death was instantaneous, probably painless, though that was no real comfort at all.

He had felt all kinds of doubt in the last three years. Doubt of himself, doubt of humanity, doubt of the worth of the universe.

But he had never doubted his mother's death.

Now there was no doubt that she lived.

"It was a special effect," she said. "When we set off the avalanche, I was already miles away."

"We?"

"I had help. I couldn't have done that myself."

"Who?"

She blushed. "Your father was unfaithful to me, Sandy.

He'd had a mistress—that Seer slut, you know—for years before I found anyone who . . . well . . . understood me."

"But why? Why did you want us to think you were dead?"

"I had my reasons. I needed secrecy to continue my real work. Alf never dared to dream as I did. To him, Kali would be only a granddaughter. He couldn't—wouldn't see the possibilities. He was dragging me down, and using all of you to do it."

Sandy shook his head. He was numb. He felt as if he were still controlled by something outside of himself, as if even now Kali had some power over him. He looked over at the baby. Asleep, she looked purely angelic.

"Amazing, isn't she?" said Marjorie Figueroa. "A marvel of programming. Growing fast, too."

"You . . . you did it for her sake? You were planning back then to kidnap her?"

"Santiago, there's too much to explain. And I'm not going to tell it to you anyway. You shouldn't be involved in this."

He wondered that he felt no urge to embrace her, no need to weep or rejoice. Instead he found a coldness in his heart, matching the coldness he knew must be in hers. This was his inheritance.

"I'm already involved," he said. "We're all in it. This was cruelest to Poppy. She tried to kill herself because of it. No tricks that time, no false broadcasts—she almost died. She may never recover from that."

Marjorie's head fell forward. "I heard about Poppy. I'm sorry. I tried to let her know that the baby was all right. I was trying to warn her away from that man, Clarence Starko. She should never have trusted him. *He* was the one who betrayed her."

"Clarry?"

"I bought him off myself. I used him to arrange the kidnapping."

"And—and Poppy *knew*?"

"I tried to tell her. I thought it would help if she knew

something of the truth—though not all. Not nearly this much. How did you find me?"

"With Clarry's help. We tracked you from the original recording of the station wagon."

She looked puzzled. "That image should have been altered. I was told it had been."

"My God, who's working with you? That tape was changed when the police had it."

She turned away from him. "You shouldn't be here. Who else knows about this?"

He shrugged, knowing that he shouldn't tell her.

"You're not doing something foolish like broadcasting live, are you?"

"Only to Clarry," he said. "Not even Dad knows I'm here."

"Good. Because it's dangerous to be here. If anyone knew you'd found me, there would be trouble. I don't think I could protect you."

"Protect me from what?"

She looked back at the sleeping baby, then took Sandy by the arm. "Come with me. I don't know what she hears. Her wires never sleep, you see. She's constantly picking up things. You'd better pretend she's still controlling you."

They went into the corridor, surprising several Daughters who were watching the door. Sandy tried making his voice squeaky and small again, in imitation of Kali.

"Get away from there!" he said. "I see everything you do."

They scurried away. His mother, veiled and playing High Priestess again, led him through a large room with a stage at one end and row upon row of seats. A few Daughters sat frozen in their seats, watching mother and son pass. She took him up a narrow flight of stairs and into a tiny room with a window at one end. A candle in a glass jar sat flickering on the ledge. Sandy peered through the window and looked down on the huge chamber through which they had just passed.

"What is this place?" he asked. "An old church?"

"It was a movie theater. You wouldn't remember those. Here, it's time for the midnight show."

She flipped a switch on a black metal box, and a flood of light poured through the window. The far wall of the temple grew startlingly bright.

"Electricity is strictly forbidden in the temple; the Daughters think this light is generated by the power of Kali's spirit. Actually we have a hidden power line coming into the building. I need it to run the computer I'm using to program Kali. She has an incredible mind. Her human brain is merged with something of the machine. It's part polymatter, like the nerves. She's an amazing creature. The Daughters don't yet realize how amazing. They're easily impressed."

She stepped into the path of the light and began to make flickering gestures with her hands. Enormous shadows danced across the white screen, cowing the worshipers. Marjorie selected several bizarre, intricate figures cut from paper and mounted on thin sticks; with these she enacted a puppet show that was projected into the temple. As the shadows danced, she chuckled, but Sandy took little amusement from the performance. Finally, as if disgusted with herself, she shut off the light and leaned heavily against the projector stand, shaking her head.

"My poor Daughters," she said. "They're tragic cases, most of them. Brutalized as children, emotionally retarded . . . I give them shelter and kindness and something to believe in. I set up what I thought would be a suitable environment for Kali, you see. A goddess needs worshipers."

"Do *you* worship her?" he said.

She gave him a look of weary irony. "You think I should say no, but don't all grandmothers idolize their grandchildren? It's more than that, in my case. Kali is my life now. She *is* worthy of worship—or soon will be."

"Worship? She's just a baby."

"Just a baby? I'm afraid not. She's a potent tool. She has

the body of a child, yes, but she has the powers of a goddess and the heart of a network executive."

"The nets . . . are they behind this?"

"You already know too much, Santiago. Believe me, everything you learn puts you in greater danger."

He nodded, thinking he was beginning to understand. "She can control people, so she's one step ahead of the usual wire technology. She'll grow up believing she's a goddess, that she deserves her power by divine right."

"She does deserve it!"

"But she's a baby."

"She doesn't think of herself that way. In many respects, her mind already surpasses those of most adults."

"Does that give her the right to control them? I can't believe this was your idea. Did you come up with it, or did the nets approach you? Did they decide you were the best one to bring it off? They wouldn't dare approach Father with it, would they? Only you were ruthless enough to donate—sacrifice—your own flesh and blood for this. . . ."

She straightened and pulled the veil back over her face.

"I could throw you to the Daughters," she said. "They would tear you to pieces if I asked them."

"Go ahead. You already tore me up once, mother. On the moon. I wish you *had* died then. That was easier to swallow than this whole scheme."

"You never should have known about it," she said. "This knowledge was not meant for children."

"I would have learned eventually, wouldn't I? When Kali appeared? When she came to control us? How is that supposed to happen? Will she come creeping into our dreams, taking over gradually?"

Marjorie didn't answer. She seemed to be shaking, perhaps with anger. But Sandy's fury was at least the equal of her own. He started toward the door.

"Where are you going?" she said.

"I'm leaving."

He stalked out of the little room and down the stairs, pushing his way through the Daughters as he made his way back to the room where Kali slept. Behind him he heard his mother screaming: "Stop him! Stop him!"

They tried to block his way, but he made the baby voice again and they cleared out. Opening the door to the nursery, he saw the baby lying in her cradle. As he picked her up, her eyes flickered open.

She stared straight at him. "Uncle?" she said.

"Yes, Kali. I've come to take you home."

"Stop him!" came cries from the hallway. A few Daughters came timidly into the room, but no one moved until the High Priestess forced them aside.

She stood in front of Sandy, blocking the door. "What are you doing?"

He pulled the baby to his chest. "I'm taking her home, where she can grow up in a human place, like a normal child."

The Daughters gasped.

"That's right!" he shouted. "A normal child! That's all she is—or should be. She's no goddess, she's just a little baby."

"Kali," said Marjorie, coming no closer, "reach into him. Take control. You hear his blasphemy. He is a heretic. You must cast him out—disconnect him. You know how to do it, Kali. Those who disobey must be shut down."

Sandy laughed, although her words frightened him. No doubt Kali could shut him off, if her control of him were as complete as he feared. He laughed only because his mother had forgotten that he still wore the device that jammed Kali's signal.

Or did, until a tiny hand reached up behind his ear and snatched the thing away.

Packed away in her grown-up suit again, Kali stood in the center of the room, staring down at her uncle Sandy. He lay crumpled on the floor as though sleeping. When she reached out through the wires to live through him, she felt nothing at all. He was blank. She had edited him right out of reality.

"Good," said the High Priestess. "He's insane, you realize. He was sent by enemies to defy you."

Kali knelt and gently stroked his cheek. "Uncle," she whispered. She had loved the look of his orange eyes, the way he talked to her so kindly.

"You can still make him move, can't you, Kali?"

In reply, Sandy's limbs twitched and he jerked upright, getting clumsily to his feet. He banged around the room unsteadily, walking into walls, stumbling over the Daughters' long robes. They backed away, shrieking squeamishly, but secretly delighted. Kali found she could tweak his vision enough to keep him from walking into things. She let him wander aimlessly around the room, mouth slack, eyes staring, until she grew bored with him.

Something else caught her attention.

"What are those sounds?" she asked.

"Sounds?" said the High Priestess.

From somewhere nearby came a muffled boom and the sound of screaming, then a clatter of feet. Most of it was on the street, but some had begun to echo inside the temple. Kali heard breaking plastic that must have been the doors in the lobby.

The Daughters and the High Priestess rushed out of the room. Kali followed them down the hall toward the lobby, where they met a flood of frightened Daughters coming the other way.

"Men!" they cried. "Dogs and men!"

Kali smelled acrid smoke. The High Priestess turned, trying to push her back. "You must run and hide yourself, Kali. Come—the back way."

Kali was tired of being pushed around by grown-ups. She held her ground. "I want to see," she said.

"This isn't a game! Come along quick or you'll get hurt. They're looking for that man—your uncle."

"What do they want with him? Are they his friends? Are they my family?"

"You have no family apart from us, Kali. Now do as I say."

Kali laughed. "No. You must obey me."

She pushed the High Priestess out of her way. Over the heads of the daughters she saw a crowd of strangers filling the lobby, men in black suits and helmets, dogmen armed with weapons more lethal than fangs.

"He's back there!" the High Priestess shouted.

"Don't tell them," Kali said.

"I'll take you to him!"

"No!" Kali howled.

She sent her will across the lobby, reaching into the wires of the strangers. The dogs were not wired, but it was enough to control the men. She peered through two dozen eyes at once. They were fixed on her and on the High Priestess, who now screamed, "Come with me!"

Kali caused their weapons to rise. She knew how to make the men do what she wished while allowing them to use their own instincts for such details as aiming and firing. Every bolt found its target.

Kali was only inches from the High Priestess, but not a single shot marred her shiny new grown-up suit's surface.

The High Priestess fell at Kali's feet, fell in tatters of red and black; smoke rose from her charred and glistening torso. She writhed, staring up at Kali, her veils displaced.

Kali bent over to see if the High Priestess's eyes were orange. She had thought they might be, but they weren't. She lost interest.

Her mind returned to the soldiers or whatever they were. Everywhere she sent the men, the dogs were sure to follow. She kept a good grip on their wires.

The Daughters cowered in the lobby and the hall, their minds torn between Kali, the dead High Priestess, and the soldiers. She no longer trusted these women; they lacked wires, and faith was a flimsy thing by comparison.

It was time to leave the nest.

She sent out one last signal to her uncle Sandy, but she couldn't feel him anymore. He was shut down, probably for good, wrecked somehow. Edited out, the High Priestess had said.

Kali shrugged. She had more family out there somewhere.

"We go now," she told the soldiers, her escort.

They turned and went back the way they had come. Kali walked with them and within them, heading for a home she'd never seen.

10

Ba-Ha-Ha

Oblivious to his changing surroundings, Cornelius stared at the tiny map-screen in his hands, and particularly at the symbolic speck of light that represented Sandy. The Holy City ignored him as thoroughly as he ignored it. The question of whether teegees had souls was a sticky one; no one seemed interested in resolving it long enough to convert him. There were limits, even here. Besides, he already resembled some of the other wandering mystics, engaged in one-pointed contemplation of what could easily have been a prayer calculator.

Finally, in the murky dawn, he circled the same building twice. Sandy's blip was situated somewhere inside. He found an entryway of shattered plastic, stepped over and through the shards into a darkened foyer, and became the object of a myriad of frightened gazes. Black shapes huddled in the corners of the room like grounded bats, silent except for an infrequent whimper. None moved at his entrance.

Since they posed no apparent threat, he stepped gingerly through the congregation and into a long hall. He saw nothing but the light blinking in his palms.

Suddenly he bumped into someone.

"Excuse me," he said, brushing past.

Whoever it was made no reply, stumbling on toward the lobby. He glanced back at the figure silhouetted against the outer doors. When he looked down at the screen again, he saw the Sandy-blip getting away.

"Wait!" he cried, running back.

He caught Sandy in the lobby and pulled him outside, away from the pressure of woeful eyes.

"I'm glad to see you," said Cornelius. "I know you told me not to follow, but Clarence Starko was killed last night. I thought you also might be in danger. I hope I haven't interfered with anything critical."

Sandy smiled but made no reply. Cornelius thought perhaps the daylight dazzled him, though the rays were still so faint and gray that outdoors was little brighter than the dim lobby. It was just barely bright enough to show the drab, stained ocher of Sandy's outlandish overalls, on which his name was stitched as if for Corny's reassurance.

"I see you're well," Cornelius said, trying to convince them both. "You are well, aren't you?"

Still no answer.

Sandy swayed slightly, that faint smile fixed to his face, then turned a few degrees and brushed past Cornelius.

"Sandy? Santiago!"

Cornelius could no longer convince himself that Sandy was well, or in his right mind.

The search for Kali was a matter of secondary importance to Cornelius. If she was in the Holy City at all, she wouldn't be going anywhere in a hurry. She wasn't even old enough to crawl. The main thing, as ever, was to care for his friend.

The sealman slipped his arm through Sandy's elbow and guided him gently back the way he had come. After walking all night, he felt quite weary, but concern for Sandy gave him strength. He was to need every last erg of it on the way out.

Though Cornelius had traveled inconspicuously while on

his own, something about the sight of a man and a seal together attracted the attention of the Holy City's residents. Evangelists pestered them all day, slowing their progress. It was not until nightfall that they made swifter progress. Sandy's expression never changed throughout the harassment. He tagged along without complaining, although he could scarcely negotiate the cluttered streets. He stumbled constantly and would have fallen many times if Cornelius hadn't been there to catch him.

At last the streetlights began to flicker, and he knew they were reentering the world of electricity. He saw people strolling about in common clothes, no sign of self-inflicted torment on them, no extreme religious symbols visible.

Ahead, a blaze of lights announced the grand opening of a habimall. A brass band played salszydeko polkas. Balloons floated from concessions and apartment windows. Civilization.

Leading his stupefied charge by the wrist, Cornelius bought a paella platter and left Sandy guarding it at a round plastic table. Then he went to find out exactly where they were. His Jaguaero was in a terminal somewhere on the outskirts of the Holy City, and they were going to need it.

Hold tight. Hold tight. Hold tight, holdtight, holdtightholdtight, ooodlyhelp me Corny I got seafood, Mama!

    Shrimps and rice.

    (Cut-cut-cut the wires. Disconnectee, Mama.)

    Very nice. At twice the price.

    Hold tight. Think. Hold tight. Where am you? Why? Who are I?

    Welcome back to another episode of Riquard Wiglore, Media Surgeon?

    Me? Wiglore?

    Hold tight—

    —For another episode of "There You Are!" The livewire

show that takes you to exotic locales and proves that wherever you go, "There You Are!"

Shrimps and rice.

Who are you? Hot new star of "The Magyk 7"—not since Sandy Figueroa has a young man had such yearnings—hold tight.

Welcome back for another orgasmic hour in the nubile young body of Fawni Pornish.

Very nice. Oooh . . .

Hold tight.

Where?

Hollywood, California.

"Call a doctor! Somebody call a doctor!"

I don't need a doctor. I'm Doctor Wiglore.

I am—

"Sandy? Santiago, can you hear me?"

"This guy's out of his mind!"

California is a state of mind.

Regina Quatermaine, Ambisex Cop!

Kalifornia is a police state. She's my jailer.

Disconnect.

The wires.

Cut.

The wires.

(Hold tight.)

The wires.

Mexico . . .

"I've seen it before—he's a wire addict. This man needs a doctor—"

But I *am* a doctor.

And There You Are.

Cornelius returned to find Sandy at the center of a commotion, the star of a small-scale but energetic performance. He lay sprawled on the floor, staring at the ceiling, twitching and shaking. The sealman pushed through the crowd and knelt down beside him.

"Wire epilepsy," someone said.

"I heard about that. It could happen to any of us."

"Really? What channel is he on?"

"It's contagious?"

"Sandy," Cornelius said. "Sandy, can you hear me? What's happening?"

For a moment Sandy did seem to see him. His eyes widened, his shoulders hunched as though he were trying to vomit something out.

"What is it?" asked Cornelius.

"Wurrs . . ." Sandy gasped.

"Wires?"

"Kulli . . ."

"Calafia? Did you see her?"

Sandy's face turned red with the strain. Wherever he spoke from, it cost him tremendous energy to get his words this far. "Cut . . . wires . . . meh . . . Messico . . ."

"I'll get you home soon, Sandy."

"Messico . . . Messi . . ."

"Mexico?"

He remembered the conversation in Thaxter Halfjest's home. Dyad's wires had been disconnected; she was in Mexico now. Did Sandy want Cornelius to take him to Mexico to be disconnected?

Why?

"All right," Cornelius said. He slipped his arms under Sandy and lifted him up. "I'll take care of him," he told the crowd.

"Hey, aren't you—yeah, you are! You're uh . . . what's his name and . . . uh . . . remember those guys before the Magyk 7?"

"That's right! It is them! The Figaronis!"

Corny bowed. "We're here for the grand opening," he

said. "Now please excuse us—we're expected at a head shop." He moved off quickly.

He had never liked or trusted the wires, though they had made possible the Figueroa show—the happiest time of his life.

And if the wires were responsible for Sandy's condition? Obviously they should be disconnected. Removed.

Cornelius hadn't known such a thing was possible. Switched off, yes. But removed? They were an intricate tangle, spread everywhere. It must be very dangerous.

Could he trust Raimundo? There was no love between him and Sandy. Still, Raimundo must have had a trusted doctor perform the operation on Dyad. Cornelius would see to it that the same person treated Sandy. Dyad would help.

Mexico, then. It was settled. Settled, but far from finished.

Teegees were not permitted to cross the border either way without high-level permission or a six-month quarantine. The laws were strict. Mexico valued its humanimal labor—mostly Chihuahuas employed in offshore American plants—too highly to risk teegee epidemics. There was no way to get Sandy across by himself.

As he carried his friend through the crowd, the band thumped and blared. Suddenly a familiar face appeared out of the melee—a face he'd know anywhere. A face everyone knew. Soft plastex cheeks, shiny eyes, neutral hairstyle, a human with ridiculously regular androgynous features.

It was Newsbody 90, reporting on another grand opening.

Cornelius watched the 'caster drift through the crowd, shoving a toasted seadog through the mask's clammy lips, comfortable everywhere, known and loved by all, basking in the recognition.

Corny had never been so glad to find himself at a habimall grand opening. And he'd been stuck in more than one or two.

(Cut-cut-cut. Cut the wires—cut the wires.)

Dark night, midnight, lightning, thunder. Candles leap in

a drafty old stone-walled cell. A chill wind breathes on her bare, heavy breasts, whistles through the gaps in her long sharp teeth.

A baby wails. She snatches it up, clutching tiny feet in one fat hand, dangling it head downward over a silver tureen. Black figures dance and mutter around her; their song forms a smoky wreath of evil runes. The infant shrieks. Someone slips a knife into her hand.

(Cut-cut-cut-cut—)

"Hail, Satan!" she croaks. "Pour your dark power into the elixir of this child's lifeblood. When I bathe in the fresh blood, let the power come into me. Let it wash away the foul scars of age. . . ."

She raises the knife and lays it against the child's soft, white throat.

(Cut-cut-cut! Cut the throat—cut the throat—)

"*Just a minute, madam!*"

She hesitates. Her dark accomplices begin to blur and fade, their chants broken by this stranger's deep voice. Is it her lord and master, the Dark One, arriving early?

No. She sees a tall, silver-haired mortal wearing a white frock. He bears a bottle of bright red liquid, the exact shade of baby's blood.

"Who are you?" she cries.

"A visitor from another age, another channel of time. I've come in answer to your prayers. Why all this muss and fuss, this bloody spattering for the sake of a soft complexion? Can it be that you've never heard of Dr. Batori's Miracle Youth Formula?"

"What?" she says.

"This is truly a Dark Age. Madam, there's no further need to slaughter innocent babes to extract the essence time-honored for its wrinkle-removing properties. Now you can procure the same potion merely by opening a bottle. No gore, no chore."

"Are you mad?" she wails. "Baby's blood from a bottle?"

"It's the same substance you'd get by slitting that baby's throat, but whipped up in quantity in our patented marrow vats."

"But . . . does it work?"

"Does it work? Why, madam, you will see and feel the difference on the first application. Why not try it?"

She snatches the bottle from his rubber-gloved fingers, unscrews the cap, and fills her palm with warm, bottled blood. It smells real, it looks real, it even—she splashes her cheeks delightedly—tastes real!

"Why, madam, just look at yourself!"

The doctor holds up a mirror, and in its surface she sees her withered hag's face changing, the wrinkles and fat sloughing away beneath the slick red mask. Within moments she is young and maidenly again. Her belly feels tighter, her legs are slender and firm.

She wipes her face and, with an imperious gesture, dismisses her outmoded minions forever: "Begone! But not you, Doctor."

The silver-haired fellow bows becomingly. "Why, madam, don't you look delectable?"

He holds up the bottle, addressing her and the eyes, the nerves, the wires, the *Santiago* deep within:

"Dr. Batori's Magical Youth Formula. When you're ready to come in out of the Dark Ages! (By agreement with McNguyen Industries.)"

(Cut-please-cut-please-cut-please-cut.)

Allejandro Gutierrez, a border inspector for twenty years, was full of stories of the things he had seen. They had piled up in his head until he thought he would go crazy. His family was sick of hearing them; his California counterpart, in the inspection booth across the lane, had tales of his own to tell, and Allejandro could never finish a sentence without the other man cutting him off. He could speak for days of what he'd seen, but no one had ever asked him.

Until now.

It was a typical day at the border station. Private vehicles paused for Allejandro's inspection as they passed into Mexico. Grounded aircars, pedal vehicles, skateboarders, all jostled together in the broasting midday heat. Little boys threaded through the traffic selling sandals, shouting, "Chiclet—two dollars!" Waving plaster cobras and models of the spacebuses that were slapped together in the factory city that had once been Ensenada. It was busy, but not so busy that Allejandro couldn't make time to talk to his guests.

They had pulled up in a polished, mint green aircar, parked alongside the booth, and walked in looking like strange twins. *Another story,* was his first thought. Then his American partner across the way began jumping around and shrieking, "You're Newsbodies! You guys are from Channel Ninety, aren't you? Alex! Look! They're gonna make a star out of you!"

Journalists, yes, but odd ones. Allejandro invited them to stand in his booth and watch him at work. The tall Newsbody, whose tautly bulging mask covered a remarkably large nose, said Channel 90 had sent them to feel at first-hand the duties of a border guard. The other, shorter Newsbody said very little, though he sometimes sang catchy little songs and shouted what sounded like nonsense. The tall one said his partner was doing live commercials; it was all part of the program.

Allejandro was bursting with stories, yes, but all the traffic made it difficult to speak to the Newsbodies. He considered inviting them home after his shift, so he could really tell his stories properly. Meanwhile, as he searched cars, he shouted his stories over his shoulder to the men in their masks. They seemed anxious, or at least the tall one did; Allejandro suspected that the assignment bored them. He started to tell them about the time the poison-oak topiary robots that patrolled the desert stretches to the east had gone out of control and come crashing into Sandego—but then the big one distinctly yawned under his mask. How could he convince them that the job was full of dangers and surprises?

Here came a car full of nuns. Damn.

Allejandro tipped his cap to let them pass, but his American counterpart, having little respect for the Catholic Church, made them stop and get out of the car. The vehicle was air-conditioned and the nuns, of course, were dressed in very heavy black clothing. It was disgraceful, making them stand out in the heat.

Suddenly the American guard backed out of the car with a bag of red powder that wasn't dried chili. Allejandro let out a shout to warn the Newsbodies.

By then the nuns were firing at the booths, and at Allejandro himself, producing guns from their black robes, plucking fire-knives out of their wimples. Allejandro crawled into his booth and called for help. Sirens began to wail. He heard the nuns' car screech away into the dense Tijuana traffic.

The tall Newsbody pulled his babbling partner out the door, heading for their car.

"Where are you going?" Allejandro cried.

"Where there's a fast-breaking story, it's our duty to follow!"

Allejandro watched them drive past the booth into Tijuana, feeling numb and disappointed, his moment of stardom already fading. Just before the traffic closed around them, the green car leaped upward and sailed into the smoke above the city.

They should have stuck around, he thought. Heard his stories. Those nuns were nothing compared to other things he'd seen.

We now return to our regularly scheduled commercial, featuring Chas Tatty as Klarabell La Honda, Porcy Jones as Tryque Trombalos, and introducing Eloi Killian Shemhamphorasch as Blorg.

Below, the pocked and cratered surface of a blue moon:

"Think it's safe to land, Trych?"

"I don't know, Klarabell. We'd better ask Blorg."

Blorg, warily, hungrily, watches them approach. Blorg starves for manflesh. The cage is sturdy. Blorg knows it will not be fed unless it cooperates.

"Blorg, is it safe to land?"

"It looks hungry, Klarabell."

"Well, feed it."

"I'm not going to feed it. Look what happened last time. That's Glanz's leg in there. You feed it."

"I'm not going to feed it."

Says Blorg, "You no feed, I no tell."

"Look, Blorg, we don't have any more human flesh for you. Our larders are a little low. If you eat more of us, that's it. This ship doesn't fly itself. We have to land and look for food. There might be an old colony supply ship down there, with maybe a few survivors left over for you."

Blorg turns its backs on them.

"It's useless. It'll never tell us."

"Hey, I know! Why don't we try giving it some of Those New Cheesy Chewy Beefy Superstrings?"

"It won't eat that. It wants real meat."

"But they're a real meat-synthetic, in a fun new shape. Blorg might like them."

Later.

"Mm. Blorg like Superstrings better than manflesh. Blorg happy. Blorg say safe to land, but no supply ship. Blorg say go to nearest superstore and buy more of Those New Cheesy Chewy Beefy Superstrings."

"Wow, Blorg! You're okay!"

(Please. Cut. Wires.)

Sandy moaned in the backseat, eyes half open but still far from waking. He stirred and thrashed and shouted, "Blorg quite satisfied!" He tore at his Newsbody 90 mask and began to chew on the lips.

Cornelius prayed they weren't too late.

Beneath them, the life had been stripped from the land. He looked down on brown desolation, sparse vegetation. Once-bright plastic signs lay toppled in the cactus-choked parking lots of ghost malls. Here and there, a figure hunched atop a plodding mule raised a trail of dust that the wind blurred. He couldn't understand why Raimundo had chosen Baja California for his home. According to the navigator, the car was fewer than three miles from the Navarro homestead, but there was no sign of inhabitable land.

And then suddenly everything changed. Without warning, the Jaguaero plunged over a green world.

Trees rose up out of nowhere. Silvery creeks wound through cool shadows. Horses ran in a pasture, sheep grazed on rolling hummocks crowned by circular stands of cactus. At first he thought it a mirage, until he looked farther and saw sheer stone walls beyond which the desert went on as before. This narrow valley was a fertile oasis sheltered from the harsh Baja sun, spring-fed, secluded.

Within seconds, glimmering silver bodies appeared at either side of Cornelius's car: aircraft with a distinctly military look. The whole car shook as they seized it in mag-grips from either side.

"How do you do," Cornelius said, gritting his teeth against the vibration. He hoped they were decent pilots—a slight variance in their flights and they could tear the Jaguaero to pieces.

Their speed slowed considerably. The trees crawled below at a leisurely pace. He saw a brown stallion carrying a rider in a broad white hat, black boots, dressed all in blue with a touch of red at the throat. The rider looked up, startled by the aircraft. As she did, he felt an overwhelming relief.

It was Dyad.

More trees obscured her, then parted to reveal the pink tile roof of a large *hacienda* whose stucco walls shone as if freshly whitewashed. Ornate wrought iron gates were wide open on a fountain jetting blue water in a courtyard lined with tall-spiked century plants and agaves as big around as truck tires. The Jaguaero was placed almost tenderly on the earth outside the gates.

The jets were sleek, bullet-shaped things with swept wings and metal arms. With a buzz and a click, they released their grip on Cornelius's car. He punched open the door and leaped out, looking off through the trees to see if he could spot Dyad.

Someone ordered him to raise his hands. Cornelius turned slowly to find five guards surrounding him. The great wooden door of the *hacienda* swung open and a lean, thin-lipped young man stepped into the heat of the afternoon.

"Greetings, Raimundo!" Cornelius called.

Raimundo Navarro-Valdez stiffened, recognizing his visitor. He rushed forward.

"What are you doing here? You're that Figueroa!"

"Not quite, sir, but a close friend of the family. I come on behalf of Santiago Figueroa. At his request."

Raimundo looked unconvinced. "Is that him in the car? What's he doing? He looks drugged."

"I wish it were that simple. He needs the care of your best surgeon."

"My surgeon? What are you talking about?"

"Santiago desperately needs his wires removed, much as you did for your bride."

"His wires . . ." Raimundo looked incredulous. "It can't be. He's the worst of them, an incorrigible sender."

"So was Dyad once, I believe."

Raimundo hesitated, then apparently decided that all the advantages were his. He nodded the guards away.

"Who else knows you're here?" he asked.

"I brought Sandy in secrecy."

"Hello, Cornelius," said a calm voice. Cornelius turned as Dyad walked out from the shade of a nut tree. "What's going on?" She glanced into the car and saw Sandy. She slid into the compartment and put her hands on his cheeks. "Sandy, what happened?"

His eyes came open, but only slightly.

"Die, Hyperbolean dog!" he cried in a choked voice. Then: "Look out, Rooster Man! They're lice!"

She backed out of the car. "Is he out of his head?"

Cornelius began to explain. Once Dyad understood what was required, she snapped at Raimundo: "Well, don't just stand there! Call Dr. Vargas!"

As the sun set over the walls of the lush little valley, Cornelius sipped punch with his hosts on a flagstone patio. Raimundo meditatively plucked the strings of a twelve-string guitar, reflecting his mood in his choice of rhythms, which wandered from slow, stately classical tunes to a passionate flamenco. Dyad, in a white cotton dress, ladled sangria from a bowl afloat with ice, strawberries, and lemon slices. She sat down by Raimundo and watched his face and fingers. At first he did not seem to see her, but eventually he stopped playing and set the instrument aside.

"They should be finished soon," she said.

Almost as she spoke, Dr. Vargas appeared between the open french doors. Raimundo queried him in Spanish. The doctor nodded, spoke a few words, then bowed slightly and walked away.

"We can see him," Dyad said. "But he won't be awake for a while."

"That's it?" Cornelius said. "Did he pull out the wires so quickly?"

She shook her head. "He doesn't pull them out. He injects a chemical into the lymph nodes. It gradually works through the body, attacking the polynerve, breaking it down, letting the body absorb and then excrete it. Once it's injected, it stops the signals immediately. He's cut off from the network already, though it'll be a week or so before the wires have totally dissolved. Would you like to see him, Cornelius?"

Raimundo rose quickly. "Wait. I want to be there when he wakes. He'll answer a few of my questions."

"Of course, Raimundo, you can do what you wish with your *guest*. But he won't be awake before tomorrow. Remember how long it took me to recover? I just thought Cornelius might like to see that his friend is all right."

Raimundo sighed. "Very well," he said, retrieving his guitar. "But I'm calling my father tonight. He'll have many questions, if Santiago has seen all the sealman claims. If he came close to the child and received such damage, then there can be no doubt that she's the one we fear."

The nightmares and advertisements went away eventually. After them came peaceful sleep, dreams from which he could have wakened if he wished. But sleep was a balm that never lost its novelty, and he wasn't anxious to end it.

Finally, hearing whispers, he opened his eyes. A few people stood around him in a room bathed with sunlight. He lay in a huge soft bed, under fresh white sheets. It was so warm that he started to throw the sheets aside, then he realized that the people were strangers.

One was an old man, tall and dagger-nosed, dressed in a much-decorated military uniform. Sandy thought he knew him vaguely—had seen him years ago. Behind him stood Raimundo Navarro-Valdez. Ah, yes. The old man was his father. General Joaquim Navarro-Valdez.

"How do you feel?" the general asked, his voice surprisingly gentle.

Sandy listened to his body, searching for aches, finding none. Had he been sick?

And then he remembered.

Kali. The Holy City. The disconnection . . .

An unfamiliar silence permeated him; peace lay upon and within his nerves. Try as he might, he could find no commercials, no game shows, no programs of any kind, neither ludicrous nor educational. Nothing but his heartbeat, the twitch of his muscles, the soft background murmur of natural, original thought.

"You're in Baja," the general said.

"Cornelius brought you," said Raimundo. "You wanted your wires removed."

Sandy shuddered, gripping the sheets. "I don't think I'll ever wear them again, not while she's out there. Now that I know what can be done with them."

The general's eyes narrowed. "Then you felt it? The wires are puppet-strings, isn't that so?"

Sandy nodded. "They are now. She can use them that way."

The general looked at Raimundo, then at a dark-complected woman who stood at the far side of the bed. "I told you. It's exactly as we thought." His eyes returned to Sandy. "You were lucky to reach us. We got your wires out just in time."

"What's going to happen?"

And then he remembered. His mother, masquerading as High Priestess, hinting at things she couldn't tell him. The networks, conspiring to raise Kali as a goddess. He told them what Marjorie had said, as well as all he had seen.

"You think it's only the networks?" Joaquim Navarro-Valdez shook his head. "McBeth is behind it. The networks merely do his work. Who better to grab hold of so many people at once? Who better than Hollywood, with their vast propaganda machine? Only they can turn a weapon into a star, and tune everyone in for their own destruction."

"But why?" Sandy asked.

"To take control, why else? To have all the wired masses working together, with one mind."

"But it wouldn't be the president's mind—it would be Kali's."

"Easier for him to control one child than billions of adults. She's the natural focus for such power: a baby already believes itself to be the center of the universe."

The woman spoke: "Should we speak in front of him, Father?"

"He knows more than I do, Sebastiana," said the general. "I'm sure he will want to assist us in stopping this. Isn't that so, Santiago?"

"It was horrible," he said. "You can't imagine being so out of control."

The general nodded. "I've imagined many things. An entire nation, moving as one, could be turned against any enemy. They would be irresistible. Internal strife weakens and destroys armies and nations; but in such a group there would be no dissent, no resistance. A frightening challenge lies before us. You are free of the wires now, Santiago, but you are not yet free of what the other slaves may do."

The dark young woman, Sebastiana, leaned toward him.

"How did it feel when she took control of you? Did she inhabit your thoughts or merely your body?"

Sandy shook his head. "No, not my thoughts, though she could change my expression. I must have looked like I was thinking whatever she wanted me to think."

"Did she seem friendly? Did she frighten you? Or did she seem like a normal child?"

He stared at Sebastiana in something like awe, realizing that for the first time he was truly free of the self-consciousness that had come with the wires; for even when he hadn't been sending, those wires had reminded him of his invaded privacy. Even as an RO, he'd never known when his mood might cause the wires to kick in without warning. Many times his idle thoughts had triggered broadcasts, tuning him to channels that seemed to match his mood. During sex it was even worse.

Now he was free of that chatter, the constant interference.

He stared at Sebastiana as if she were the first woman he had ever seen. Dark hair, clear blue eyes, an olive complexion. There were no voices in his head, nothing but the sight of her. He thought he could learn to like it here in Mexico.

Leave California behind, forget about the wire slaves, live a quiet life . . .

She smiled and reached out to stroke his forehead. "I'm sorry, you must be tired. Forgive my questions."

"No, it's not that. I—well, maybe I am tired. But I feel better than ever. It's really incredible. There's a deep feeling of peace and quiet. I could lie here for hours, just soaking in it."

The general cleared his throat. "Get your rest, then. You will need your strength when you go back."

"Back?" Sandy said, his newfound peace suddenly threatened.

"To California. To find your sister. You know her better than anyone; and now she has no power over you."

"Find her?" he said. "And then what?"

"Then you'll do what must be done," the general said. "Whatever that may be."

11

Who Will Baby-sit the Baby-sitter?

Alfredo stood on the balcony, gazing down into the fissure of Beverly Canyon, hazy as the brown smoke that rose from his tofu cigarette. Filthy habit, but he couldn't help it. He had stopped worrying about his health, his image, everything; and still he felt constantly worried. Worried and numb.

Door chimes warbled and bleeped in the distance. He didn't move. Let the ilk answer it.

Hollywood again. Back into the 'Woods. How could he have been so stupid? The networks were closed off to him. He should have known! No one cared about a has-been, a refugee from a family show. The Figueroas were stale news, deep in the trough of that peculiar fifteen-year sine-wave between popularity and nostalgia. He might be dead by the time a full-fledged rerun cult began. Poppy lay in a coma. His wife was long dead, and his mistress freshly so. His oldest son had vanished without a word, as mysteriously as his granddaughter had. It was strange how numb he felt, as if pain and shock were gathering in a reservoir inside him, stored up for some future time when he was ready to drink of them. He'd suggested a series—"Orphan Dad." "Love the idea, Alf, it's just great, but without the whole family we don't have a chance of competing against the Magyks." Who were skyrocketing to unguessed-of heights even as he puffed and chewed the soya filter ragged. "Find yourself a new wife—get an interracial thing going, that would be best—adopt yourself some kids, then maybe we'll talk. But it'll have to be your money till then."

Meanwhile, out of pity, they offered him a pawnship on "Hollywood Chess."

Take that town by storm.

A far-off clatter on the ceramic tiles. Miranda started screaming.

He peered down the hall. His daughter backed into the living room followed by something like a robot, but baroque and crystal-gleaming rather than functional matte black. Miranda turned and ran, shrieking, her huge breasts heaving on her dinky frame, overcome by this terrific spectacle. Even Alfredo doubted his senses until he saw the small human head of the robot, and its orange eyes.

Miranda leaped over a sofa and crouched behind it. The robot filled the doorway, keeping eye contact.

"Grandpa?" it said.

His mouth moved uselessly. He knew who this was—had to be—wearing a robot like a pair of pajamas, talking like an adult. He didn't have the words to greet her.

"Cal—Calafia?"

"Kalifornia," she said, coming down hard on the name though she sounded relieved at the same time. A smile flashed over her little face, spontaneous, lighting up her features. "I left my escort outside, is that okay?"

"Escort?" asked Alfredo, still numb.

"They'll behave. At least while I'm holding them."

"Escort from where?"

"Originally? I didn't ask. But they knew *you*."

He started across the room, beckoning toward the sofa. "Say hello to your niece, Miranda."

"You scared the shit out of me," Miranda said, coming out of hiding. "Hey, where'd you get that outfit? It's tortious. Sort of an Iron Toddler look."

Alfredo put out his arms and embraced the hard carapace of his granddaughter, though he knew she couldn't feel him. Her cheek was soft, her eyes were alive. She returned the embrace gently, careful of her four powerful arms.

"Where's my mommy? Uncle said she was hurt."

"Your uncle? Do you mean Sandy? Where is he?"

"I don't know. He got left behind. I want to see my mommy."

"Yes, of course, right away. She's here; she's below. Come, come, Calafia."

"Kali*forn*ia," she repeated. "My name is Kalifornia. But since we're related, you can call me Kali."

Elevator doors parted, revealing a quiet room sealed behind glass. A man in a white uniform sat outside, watching a board of monitors. Kali walked past him, leaned her head against the glass, and looked in at the figure hanging in the harness.

Mommy, she thought.

She remembered what her uncle Sandy had said: Her mommy was a normal person, not a goddess. How could a goddess have a mortal mommy? A *wounded* mommy?

Her fingertips clicked on the heavy pane; it wasn't glass exactly, but some material similar to that from which her armor was made. Some part of her got busy analyzing it reflexively, for no reason. She shut off the babble. Not everything was important, she was learning. Information overwhelmed her from every direction, within and without. It wasn't all of equal value, but there was no algorithm for deciding what mattered.

She thought this did, though. Her mommy . . .

"You can go in," her grandfather said. "I'll be right here."

She went through the lock, into the clean-room, and stood over the woman in the wires.

She didn't even know her mommy's name. Seeing her mommy so quiet, still as a doll, made her very curious to know more. Mommy had wires inside her, that much Kali sensed. Everybody around here seemed to have wires—not like the Daughters. That was good; it meant that she could get into them. She could be in everyone all the time.

Back in the temple, Kali hadn't realized how much power was in her reach. Some sort of electrical barrier in the temple walls had cut her off from the cosmos of information that swarmed all over the rest of the globe. No wonder she had felt so tiny and helpless back there; they had deliberately held her down, convincing her she was no more than a baby. Now she knew she really *was* a goddess. If she reached out with her mind, every sort of knowledge was hers.

Now, for instance, when she wished to know more about her mommy, all she had to do was wonder—

And knowledge came rushing in.

Poppy Figueroa was her name.

Kali was inside her, in a dingy room, giving way to spasms of belly pain, watching a spill of wires and blood, the birth of a tiny girl with orange eyes.

Herself.

Strange. The reply triggered memories; they floated up from Kali's mind. She had seen all this once before. Yes, she had been there, in her mommy and in herself, watching herself being born as she felt herself coming out into air and light; looking up at Poppy as Poppy looked down at her, enduring a moment's pain of feedback before her mommy, protectively, looked away.

In that moment, they had been one entity. One mind. One life looking at itself through two sets of eyes. Her mommy's eyes were orange.

She decided to see if she could open them.

Orange eyes, under white lids.

She tried to put herself behind those lids. In a luminous silence. Floating, lost, going nowhere. No sensation. She had been there once before; she had been her mommy. No barriers existed now; no one could disconnect them. All she had to do was reach out and—

Lift, she told the lids.

The lids received mixed signals from Poppy's brain. They weren't sure what to do. Kali concentrated on making them pay attention to her alone.

Lift!

Her mommy's eyelids fluttered. Parted. Sprang wide open. Orange eyes.

She saw her mommy and herself. She was here in the clean-room but also cramp-legged on a dirty hotel bed; past and present merged in the network of polynerves.

Outside the room, Kali heard the monitor bleeping. The man in white was shouting. Alfredo rushed to the glass.

"What's happening?" he said. "Did you see that? Did you see?"

Kali took a step backward, maintaining the link. She worked her mommy's fingers, elbows, arms; flexed them in the cat's cradle. She turned the head from side to side and made the eyes blink normally.

Mommy's vision, from Kali's POV, was cloudy, the view eroded by ragged areas, spots of gray, signs of neurological damage.

"She's healing her," Alfredo said in awe.

Mommy, Kali thought. Sadness overcame her. She had come from this womb. What's wrong with you, mommy? Why won't you come to me?

Poppy's body thrashed in the cradle, gently at first but with increasing agitation. Poppy's arms went out longingly toward Kali. Animal noises spilled from her throat. She struggled to regain her feet, but the cradle and sheer muscle loss, after so much time in the harness, held her back.

Kali didn't want to be hugged by a puppet, but she

couldn't bear to be separated from Poppy's flesh now that she was inside it. Poppy fought free of the harness, tottering on the floor, reaching out for her armor-plated daughter. At last, an embrace. Kali lost track of whose head she was in. Part of her spilled out of control, buoyed by excitement and despair, and she found herself watching this scene through her grandfather Alfredo's eyes, touching briefly on the doctor's perceptions, too. She didn't want to be in them—it diffused her sense of reality—but she couldn't quite control it. Her mind felt cobbled together out of many different people. The sensation only added to her loneliness.

How could she, a goddess, feel like an orphaned child?

Suddenly the doctor pushed her aside, rushing to examine Poppy. Kali backed out of the chamber, but at the same time she stayed there, living through the doctor's hands, feeling them take hold of her mommy's arms.

Alfredo hugged Kali's crystal torso, kissed her cheeks of flesh.

"You healed her," he said, with joyous tears streaming down his cheeks. "You healed her! You are a marvel! This is the best day of my life. The day you came home to us. Oh, Calafia—*Kali,* I'm sorry. Of course you can change your name, if that's the one you like."

Poppy nodded as the doctor worked her back into the harness.

"She'll soon be her old self, won't she?" asked Alfredo, sounding sure of it. "We'll all be reunited. We'll all . . . what is it, Kali? Where are you going?"

"I don't feel well," she answered, heading toward the elevator. The doctor's flesh and her grandfather's hung heavy on her. Outside the house, the soldiers in her escort were beginning to fidget. She felt herself coming apart, into too many fragments. She needed to consolidate somehow. "Is there somewhere I can rest?"

"Oh, of course. You're still just a baby, aren't you? You need your rest. A nice nap. You can use a guest room while we fix up something special for you. I'm so glad you've come, Kali. Wait until I tell—oh, tell the world!"

The world, she thought.

It sounded so small.

While the "world" clamored to see her, Kali spent her first days at home in seclusion, reliving endless replays of "Poppy on the Run." She wanted to know her mommy as she'd been when she lived. If she got Poppy's body to reenact enough of its old behavior tropes, it might eventually reactivate the nascent will that hid there somewhere, sleeping in damaged tissue. Or so she hoped.

She played the kidnapping tape over and over again so often that giving birth to herself began to seem a commonplace occurrence. She gave birth to herself repeatedly. She leaned into the wires, inhabiting her mommy's body, feeling the corroded iron of the fire escape beneath her fingers, hearing the voices of the dogs, watching the little parcel of blanketed flesh as it fell into the station wagon stalled conveniently below. Back and forth, back and forth a hundred times she fell; a thousand; more.

Meanwhile, Poppy's body was in therapy. Kali couldn't bring herself to admit that she alone inhabited the form. Everyone believed it was Poppy herself, returning from the dead. Muscle rebuilt slowly. New joints slid smoothly beneath a webwork of fine scars. Poppy's face fell into accustomed expressions, though they were not always suited to the situation: Kali could use only what she had gleaned from the wire show.

"You'll never get me!" she would cry out of context. The therapists thought she was talking to them, but they smiled and continued to hurt her in various ways essential to her recovery.

Meanwhile, the crowd around the house grew steadily. Cars dipped through the canyon for a glimpse of Kali. Tourists crowded the balconies of restaurants on the opposite brink, overstressing the structures until, early one Sunday, a flock of gawking tourists—along with a handful of innocent brunchers—were precipitated into the abyss. Whereupon a mob of the deceased's relatives converged on the Figueroa manor, begging Kali to bring them back from the dead as she had done her mother. Kali's military escort were put to work holding back the agitated fans. The soldiers paraded the grounds of the house, patrolled the rooftops, even watched the doors and took up posts in the interior of the house. Kali watched through all of them; they served as her private closed-circuit remotes.

She was watching in this manner one afternoon when Alfredo approached the apparent captain of the guard with an unsettling question.

"Excuse me," said her grandfather. "How are you and your men holding out? Like troopers, eh? You're doing a fine job, I mean to say. But I have a question I wonder if you can answer."

Kali watched him through the soldier's eyes, playing peekaboo. She was half tempted to make the captain wink at him, or coyly whisper, "It's me, grandpa."

"How did you find Kali?" he asked. "Who hired you?"

It was a good question. Kali didn't know the answer herself. The soldiers, being so much in her power, never spoke of personal things—or anything at all. Any conversations they had were simply Kali talking quietly to herself, to create a semblance of normal behavior. This seemed important somehow, at least until she revealed the extent of her power.

Still, her grandfather needed an answer.

"Kali called us," she said the captain. "She signaled through our wires, showed us the way through the Holy City, and we rescued her."

Kali had told her grandpa a little about the temple, but not much. He nodded slowly, unsure if this made any sense, then strolled away.

The answer was good enough for him, but not for Kali.

Where *had* they come from? She supposed she could try relaxing her hold on a few of the soldiers and see if they started talking among themselves; but she was afraid they might do something unpredictable if she let go for even an instant.

One of the dog soldiers crossed the captain's line of sight. The fierce, loyal dogmen had followed the human soldiers faithfully from the Holy City, despite the fact that none of them was wired or controlled by Kali.

Her captain whistled to the dog. "Here, boy!"

The soldier quickstepped over. "Sir!"

"Is it true that you dogs have poor long-term memory?"

The dog looked mildly offended. "Sir?"

"I'm curious. Do you recall things only by their smell, or do you actually think about and remember things that aren't explicitly present?"

The dog was now plainly insulted. "I am more than eighty percent human, sir, and proud of my heritage. My exceptional sense of smell is enhanced by an exceptional memory. Nor is it true, as some humans seem to think, that I am color blind. I can appreciate a Motherwell or a Peter Max with the best of them."

"Hm. Then I suppose, just as a test, you'd have no trouble telling me who ordered us into the Holy City? Who sent us to find that young goddess?"

"I recall the circumstances clearly, sir, but I can hardly give you the name of the one who hired us. The orders were encoded through Snozay Central. Is this a trick question?"

"Snozay Central," Kali's captain murmured.

"May I go now, sir?"

"Yes. Good boy."

The dog walked off with a sneaking backward look.

Snozay Central was merely a dispatch office, sending trained soldiers to assist in private, small-scale disputes. Ideally the guards were on hand to prevent violence; but they were also licensed to use violence on behalf of their employers, provided they did not stray beyond certain broadly defined parameters.

Kali shunted her attention directly to the central dispatch office, of which the mercenaries and thousands of other soldiers were simple extensions, remote fighting-sensing units. Within a matter of moments, by ransacking records, she traced her escort's original orders to their apparent source. It was easy but tedious, methodical work. The order calling them to the Holy City had been placed by a command center at a higher level, of which the various mercenary centers were only branches.

She paused at this juncture, peering back through the wired flow of information as though examining a trail of crumbs. She could see, extending backward from her, a myriad of astral wires, each ending in a bulbous, human-shaped cul-de-sac: a human life—in this case a soldier. Mercenaries like these worked all over the nation, guarding banks and chemicals; some were at weapons practice, others eating lunch, while night watchmen slept away the day. She could enter any one of them right now, from where she hovered.

But looking forward, she saw that this main line was but a thin branch stemming out of a much thicker limb. She rushed ahead on the data boughs, climbing closer to the trunk of the tree, and as it advanced her consciousness darted lightning-like to fill wires that were becoming newly available. She found herself simultaneously in thousands of cities, listening to a babble of conversations, engaged in a million activities. Some tasks were overtly military, but others were bland desk jobs, people doing nothing. She could have entered them, made them move as she wished, but she sensed that it would take time to learn how to coordinate such complex actions; she might cause too much chaos.

Patience.

In the meantime, she had yet to find the source of that original order, which had trickled down to Snozay Central from somewhere very high in the information hierarchy. There were many more rungs on the ladder.

Up she went.

It was day and night at once now, winter and summer simultaneously. The planet's hemispheres were bridged. She was asleep and awake, speaking languages that at first she didn't understand, though she had access to so many speech interpreters that her comprehension grew instantaneously.

She was everywhere. Kali reached out and covered the world, waking up inside of everyone. She wondered if they could feel her coming to life inside them, peering out through their masks; she looked at herself and saw starts of recognition, though that couldn't last long before she had to look away. Feedback was a constant danger. Still, it was hard to control her excitement: earth was like a huge toy begging to be played with.

At the same time, she felt something odd going on inside herself.

It felt . . . it felt as if something were waking up and looking around inside of *her*.

As if somebody were looking out of her eyes just as she was looking out of everybody else's!

What was going on in her?

Was she being monitored from within? Was there some part of her disloyal to herself, some innate watcher planted before her birth? Whoever planted it, had they also sent the order to the mercenaries who rescued her from the Holy City? Only one thing was she sure of: if such a person existed, they weren't wired. She would have sensed them otherwise. They'd be her subject now. She'd have come across some trace of them.

Unless they knew the way to jam her signal. And were using it, expecting her.

With growing fear she realized that the mercenary dispatch had been sent in such a way that when she went to trace it, she would invariably work her way up through the branching paths to exactly this point. She had set off little alarms all along the way, no doubt. By her actions, she had inescapably woken the watcher.

She paused, frightened for the first time in her brief life, a coldness suddenly running through every polynerve on earth and the moon.

The moon . . .

She saw it in the night skies of earth. Setting, rising, and at the zenith.

The moon was underfoot as well. Some of her subjects stood in moondust, in the earth's reflected light.

"Who are you?" she whispered, talking to herself, to the thing in her.

All over the planet and in the malls of its satellite, these words were whispered. People touched their mouths, not realizing where the phrase had come from; none understood why they heard it everywhere at once. Something was happening . . . a quickening . . . something fearful. They said it in chorus, a timid universal whisper:

"*Who* . . . ?"

"Kali?" Her grandfather's voice. "There's someone here to see you."

She opened the eyes of her tiny source body, the one in the armored grown-up suit, the one sitting in a dark room in the Figueroa house. Her search for clues had yielded nothing; the sense of a watcher's presence within her continued to grow like an alien cancer.

"Kali?"

"Yes, grandfather. Come in."

The door opened a few inches; the light it admitted was broken by the entrance of two men. First came Alfredo, smiling, proud. The other was dressed in white and orange, covered with glinting bits of jewelry and crystal. She knew him instantly, although she had never met him.

"Kali, I'd like you to meet the Reverend Governor of California, Thaxter Halfjest."

Halfjest fell to his knees before her, seizing one of the robot's crystalline hands in his fingers and kissing it. She couldn't feel his lips.

"Kali, this is the greatest of honors. I've looked forward to this day since Alfredo and your grandmother Marjorie, bless her soul, first announced their plans. I'm so glad to see you're well. And the things you're doing—marvelous, just marvelous!"

Kali was at a loss for words. It took her longer than usual to rise from the depths of herself. She resented every instant not spent pursuing the watcher with every bit of her being. She wanted to root it out, to purge herself of the thing. She hated feeling it lurking inside her. She hated the thought that something else could use her.

Halfjest babbled on, gazing into her eyes, saying something about Hollywood now, how Kali would be its greatest star, a natural. . . .

"The networks approached me, Alfredo, and asked me, as a friend of the family, to talk you and Kali into doing a program. As her guardian—"

"A program? What are you talking about, Thax? Why couldn't they come to me directly?"

"Well, they said they'd be honored if I made the offer. Everyone is dying to meet Kali—to see her live, if you know what I mean. They've offered her a program of her very own. Since she's already wired, the connections are ready for her."

"A . . . a show? Her own show?"

"People want to get inside her; they want to feel what she feels. You know what they're saying about you, Kali, since you brought your mother back from the dead? They think you're divine. They want you inside them. A wire-show sacrament."

"Divine," Kali whispered.

The Daughters had said as much, and for a time she had believed it.

But a goddess, a true goddess, tolerated no parasites. No watchers inside. No . . . no baby-sitters! A goddess could not be manipulated.

She stared at Thaxter. Instinctively, because it was what she did best, she reached out to trace his wires, to slip inside them. His smile widened as if to make room for her; as if he felt her coming. The RevGov was live all the time, of course, constantly broadcasting to his fans. Which meant they were all there inside him, watching Kali.

Then why couldn't she find herself? Why no pain of imminent feedback when she looked at herself through his eyes?

Just to be safe, she tuned completely into Thaxter Halfjest's program.

How strange.

On his wire show, the RevGov was alone, walking in a park, looking at trees, smelling flowers.

His smile, out here in Figueroa manor, grew wider.

She didn't understand—

She was inside him now, but she didn't see what Thaxter really saw. She tried to play the wires of the Halfjest walking in the park, but nothing happened. It was an illusion, unreal, he wasn't in any park at all. He was here, right in front of her, but she couldn't touch him, couldn't get inside.

Then a voice from deep within her, the voice of the watcher, said, "Peekaboo, Kali. I see you. Can't you see me?"

Halfjest's voice.

She rose from the chair, needing all the power she could summon. Thaxter Halfjest was both here and not-here.

She raised her sheeny metal arms. "You!" she said.

"That's right, dear," said the Reverend Governor. "I am the fortunate bearer of these good tidings."

"It's *Kali's* show, then," Alfredo said, unaware of what Kali knew. "Not a family show? Only Kali's?"

She tried to speak but her mouth wouldn't work. Her wires

were being pulled for the first time, as she had pulled so many others. She lashed out at Halfjest, trying to injure his wires in self-defense—

And found herself in the illusory park. Sniffing illusory flowers.

She heard him chuckling. Here she was in Halfjest's body. It had a thin, unreal quality about it.

"Well, well," she heard him saying. "It's nice to finally meet you, Kali. I was afraid High Priestess Marjorie would find a way to keep you all to herself. But your talent—like mine—deserves to be shared with the world."

"What . . . what are you doing?" she asked. She could work this mouth, this body—but the ability was no more useful than the ability to control a dream.

"I'm taking your place, dear. You have far too much responsibility for a mere baby. I'm putting you in a lovely place much more suited to someone your age."

Ahead, through green trees, around the curve of a flagstone path, she spied a meadow. Swings, slides, a sandbox, and a wading pool. Thaxter walked her straight toward it; then his body, now her body, began to deflate. She sank toward the ground. The trees expanded, stretching out to the artificial sky. She glanced down and saw his hands shrinking, turning small and chubby; the hair receded from his arms, leaving them little pink columns. His steps covered a shorter distance with each successive stride; then they hardly carried her at all. She stumbled and landed on all fours.

Help, she thought.

She tried to reach back into her real body, groping for the protection of her grown-up suit, but she couldn't find them—or anything else familiar.

The RevGov said, "If it's any consolation, you're about to be a lot more popular than the Magyk 7."

She sat down on the path and wailed. "Why?"

Halfjest spoke out of her nerves, her blood, her nails: "California is the world leader in science, in technology, in fashion, art, and culture. It rules the world in so many things, I fail to see why it shouldn't simply *rule the world*!"

And then he was gone.

She was a baby again, or for the first time, really. Helpless, trapped in a snare that Halfjest had created to capture her. She howled and scraped the path till her soft fingertips bled. The pain was thin, but real enough.

No one came in answer to her cries. No one ever would. There was no one else here. From a world of billions—all company for her, all potential playmates—to this. . . .

After a while, when her eyes were finally dry, she started toward the playground in the meadow. It was a long way to go, for a baby.

12
Zing! Went the Strings

Poppy woke inside a dream.

She knew she was dreaming, but it was the closest she had been to consciousness for . . . for how long?

How long since she had run along a roadside that exploded into a river of stars and sounds which turned slowly to a Styx of stillness and silence?

How long?

In the dream she was looking for something, searching everywhere, feeling as empty as the hollow places that held her. And when she had found it, she almost woke—but not quite. The dream was too peaceful; she didn't want to leave it.

She was in a green place, singing quietly as though to a child. She sang to herself, really, because she was weak and needed healing. She cradled herself in her own arms, singing quietly, rocking and rocking herself. Holding her daughter, herself held, in a green place.

The child was very small, very frail, very frightened. Her mother's voice calmed her a little, though. She looked up at

Poppy with golden eyes, and Poppy could see herself through the child's eyes. As they had been at birth, but without pain: there was no feedback, only a current of warmth. This was her daughter, this little one.

In the dream, her daughter began to speak, voicing both of their fears.

"Help me," she said. "Help me, Mommy."

"I will, dear. I will."

"Mommy . . ."

"*Poppy.*"

That was another voice. An insistent voice, trying to take her away from her daughter. She had searched too long to lose the baby now, she thought. She could fight the voice—had to, in fact. But then the voice sent hands. Hands all over her, touching her, trying to be cautious but still ripping her out of the dream, tearing Poppy away from her child.

Not now. Not after all this. How could she lose her again?

Please, Mommy!

Not again!

"Poppy, it's me, Sandy. Come on, wake up. It's just a dream, you're having a dream."

Sandy?

She opened her eyes and saw him standing over her. She was—where? In a bed, of course. She'd been sleeping. Dreaming. Dreaming of a green place where someone sang and called for her. She felt a sense of great loss but couldn't place it. What had she lost? She was so confused.

"Sandy? Where am I?"

He looked relieved. "You remember me? They said you were amnesic. You're at home, doll. How are you feeling? Healing up, I see."

She tried to sit. Her muscles were sore; her whole body ached. Why was that?

"Sandy?" she said. "Was . . . was I in an accident?"

He stared at her as if wondering how to tell her. "You

can't remember? Oh, Poppy, I hadn't realized. I don't mean to push you too hard."

"My . . . my baby. I was dreaming about my baby, I think."

His face changed, darkened. "Kali?"

"Calafia," she said.

"Kali now. That's what she calls herself."

Poppy's heart leaped. She started to swing her legs out of bed. "She's here?"

"She's here, all right. They say she started you healing. I'm not sure how much to believe, but there's no doubt she's got amazing powers. She'd be here right now, except she's about to do a wire show."

Poppy felt a moment's desolation, wondering why they hadn't brought her daughter to her when she woke. Perhaps she did have amnesia. Maybe she woke like this every single day, forgetting all the days that had gone before, repeating this act each morning. Maybe they were tired of telling her the same things over and over again. To her, each day was a revelation; while to them, each awakening was an ever drearier chore.

"A wire show," she said. "Already? Sandy, how long has it been since the . . . accident?"

She hesitated when she named the event. Details were starting to return. She had fled; had been chased. Suddenly she remembered Clarry—

"It's been a few months, Poppy. What—what's wrong?"

"Clarry Starko," she said, looking quickly around the room as though he might be hiding somewhere.

"Dead," Sandy said. "He was murdered."

She lay back, asking nothing. It was enough to know he wouldn't be coming after her. No more midnight chases. Why ask questions? The answers would only confuse her. For now there was something more important to keep hold of, though she wasn't yet sure why it mattered.

A fleeting image. A glimpse of green, lingering from the dream.

Golden eyes.

Her baby!

She remembered holding the child. The memory of holding Calafia—Kali—in the dream was as real as any memory of sensation; it was as real as the memory of Sandy's hands on her arms when she woke. Perhaps *this* was the dream, and that green place was real. She wished she could be there again with her daughter.

"I want to see her, Sandy," she said.

"Well, you've got your wires. You can tune into her easily enough. This is a big event. She's a cult figure, a born star. The networks have her on virtually every channel. There's no way you can miss her. She's live. You'll be able to feel her completely."

Poppy closed her eyes and tried tuning in to her daughter's signal. She knew it intimately; she remembered the strong link coursing between them in the moment of delivery, like an intimate closed circuit. If only she could find that channel again. The memory alone should have been enough to tune her to the broadcast.

But something was wrong with her wires. Maybe the accident had fouled her reception.

She just kept remembering that dream. The green place was getting clearer, her focus sharpening.

The dream-memory kept changing, as though she were dreaming with her eyes open. The vision had moved on, so that she reentered at a later point.

She felt sand sifting through her fingers. Little fingers. She heard someone weeping. Lifting her eyes she saw treees against a blue sky. She seized another handful of sand and let it pour away. Then she sank down weeping.

"Mommy . . ." she said.

Poppy opened her eyes and looked at Sandy. "She misses me, Sandy."

He looked a little puzzled. "What's going on?"

"It's such a sad program. Why would they make her do something so sad? It seems too private, too subtle. Not a popular sort of thing."

"What're you seeing?"

"You can't feel her?" she asked.

"Sure," he said. "Sure I can. I just wondered how it seemed to you. Why sad?"

"Well . . . because she's in that park all by herself. She's playing in sand and crying and calling for . . . for me, I guess. All alone."

Now he looked very confused. "Are you sure? That doesn't sound like the program they—uh, I'm getting."

"What do *you* feel?"

He stood up suddenly. "Poppy, are you up for a walk? I mean, are you strong enough to come with me? Just to the car?"

"I think so," she said tentatively. Her legs felt strong; she wanted to stretch them. "Why? Can we go see her?"

"Yeah, I'd be really curious. She's in Studio City."

"A studio?" she said. "It looks so much like a park."

"Well, you know what they can do with special effects these days," he said. Even as he said it, his face changed. His eyes got wide; he looked frightened.

"What's wrong, Sandy?"

"I'm not sure. Come on, let's see if we can get you on your feet."

From the air, there seemed to be a riot going on down in Studio City. People were crawling over each other to get closer to the huge building where Kali was holding her live broadcast. Sandy carried VIP credentials so that the vehicle wouldn't be deflected as he dropped to a landing on the roof. He ushered Poppy toward the guest entrance. As they passed near the edge he looked down on the mob.

A tremor passed through the crowd. All at once the people

turned calm, peaceful. They began to form orderly lines, concentric rings surrounding the building and trailing off into the glittering streets. A hush fell over the city, the state, perhaps the world. Sandy didn't want to think about the extent of the broadcast.

The public had followed her story as if it were the Second Coming, though free of sectarian bias: no one with polynerves would willingly miss the broadcast. With unfortunate timing, Thaxter Halfjest had successfully passed Proposition 5,997, the measure prohibiting signal-scramblers in office buildings, so that even more people were being exposed throughout the state.

They had all tuned into Kali, their media goddess, and she held their wires. They were hers now. Like the thousands of neurons in a single brain, but linking up for the first time, switching on all at once, innumerable combinations creating a new personality, a thing different and greater than any of them. A new form of consciousness was coming into being right there below him in the streets of SanFrangeles, some kind of monster or god waking up. He feared it might see him and instantly know his deception.

He had dreaded this day, dreaded his return to California, putting it off until General Navarro-Valdez informed him that it could be postponed no longer. Arriving home this morning, he had found the house in an uproar, Kali already gone to the studio. Alfredo was amazed to see him but too busy to ask for explanations. Sandy, by delaying his arrival until the last moment, had been excluded from their plans. It was just as well; he had to act alone, knowing what only he truly knew.

Well, plenty of others knew it by now. They had surrendered to Kali. They arranged themselves in the streets with military precision and awaited her commands. They must have sensed, with some dim, inexperienced vestige of critical reasoning, that all this discipline and harmony did not come naturally. Surely somewhere inside the net of wires, some of them must be wondering what the hell was going on. When their rapture passed, they would find themselves trapped and helpless. Tremors of indecision might be passing through that vast, quickening brain, where pockets of synergistic psychosis waited to be discovered.

"She has already taken control of the world's wired militia," the general had told him. "But the citizens themselves remain largely untouched. With the upcoming broadcast, all that will change."

It was changing right now.

He felt it around him, all those people breathing, moving, acting in unison, with one mind. Controlled by a child. He wondered where a child could have learned such discipline. What use did she have for rank and file? Playful chaos, a creative frenzy, was more what he had imagined would follow when Kali took control, nothing like this. Nothing so grim. This foreshadowed a shift toward a horrible regime—something beyond tyranny or fascism—unimaginably worse than anything the world had seen before. This must be one of those kinks "Bob" had mentioned.

He was grateful to be watching rather than experiencing her control. She couldn't touch him, not from within, though there were any number of things she could do or have done to him from without.

After all, what scruples did a child have? Especially a child with such a keen grasp of military tactics?

Never mind my own scruples, he thought.

I'm only coming here to murder my niece, after all, and bringing her mother along to watch me do the job.

And look at that crowd! They'll tear me apart. There won't be a piece of me left intact—not a single mitochondrion. Unless Kali's death rips into them, stuns them all . . . the way I went into shock when she switched me off. Even then, they'll hardly look at me with pleasure or relief—they won't exactly *thank* me for killing their idol. Unless this sensation of being out of control really puts a fright into them. It sure scared the tan out of me. Bleached my bronze to fish-belly white.

It's all just so damn unpredictable.

He looked sidelong at Poppy, who seemed dazed and disoriented. He shouldn't have brought her along.

"How are you feeling?" he asked.

She shrugged. "She's so sad, Sandy. Alone in that park. Let's go in to her."

There was no putting it off. They walked past studio guard dogs and even more vicious teegees, entering the building. A hush rose up from below. Silence filled the place except for one small sound, a shrill voice speaking in stops and starts.

Kali's voice.

They descended through levels of catwalks and metal mesh that spanned the spaces above the theater. A motionless sea of bodies lay below, people crowded shoulder to shoulder, none protesting or fidgeting or squirming in the slightest. Thousands of faces were fixed on the center of the vast room, on a tall dais where Kali stood gleaming in her grown-up suit.

"Hold on a minute, Poppy," Sandy said.

He stepped off the stairs, onto a metal ramp, and tiptoed out over space. Glancing back, he saw his sister clinging to the stair rail, looking down at her daughter as if she didn't recognize her. Kali didn't look anything like the baby Poppy had seen for a few frenzied minutes on September 9, he reminded himself. There was little visibly human about her, apart from her tiny head, which was scarcely a speck at this distance. Even her speech seemed like something a robot would say.

Her voice was loud, though unamplified. There was no need for amplifiers when all the spectators listened, via wires, through Kali's own ears:

". . . humanity is one," she was saying. "It is our destiny to join together, to unite completely, to move with one mind, one heart, one body, one brain, one soul, one all-encompassing intent."

Sandy crouched down, watching her through the catwalk's metal mesh. He felt as if he were frozen in midair, forever falling. This was as close as he needed to get; he could fire from here and hit her. A cool blue line of fire would pierce that tiny unprotected skull. All he needed to do was sight the target and the gun would do the rest. The self-firing weapon required no marksman, but only someone to carry it. It could take care of the killing by itself.

He reached into his jacket, hands trembling.

Footsteps vibrated on the ramp behind him.

"Sandy," Poppy whispered. He let go of the gun. He would have to get her away from here somehow. If he found Alfredo, he could leave her with him. But he was afraid to delay what he had come here to do. He might lose his nerve—or his chance.

"Sandy," she said, "I don't know what's happening, but—"

"It's all right, Poppy," he said quietly, taking her by the shoulders. "Let's get you to a good safe place."

"That's not my daughter, Sandy. I can still feel her. She's in a park somewhere. That's not Calafia, it's someone else."

Sandy looked down at the babyish features, the rapt crowd.

It couldn't be anyone but Kali.

Poor Poppy. She really was confused.

"That's her all right," he said. "Maybe the grown-up suit makes her look different. I know you haven't seen her since she was born, but it *is* Kali."

Poppy began to weep. "You don't understand. She's here, she's inside me; I *know* where she is. I'm tuned to her right now. That thing out there has her flesh, but she's not in it!"

With growing exasperation, because she was starting to get too loud, he pushed her back toward the stairs.

"You don't believe me," she said.

"I think you're still disoriented."

"But that's not her! It's someone else using her body. She's been pushed out . . . she's lost. She needs me, Sandy. She—"

Poppy's frustration peaked. She let out a cry of rage and rushed away from him, down the stairs, into the crowd.

"Wait!" he cried. And then he was running after her.

It was odd, moving through the crowd. Despite all those faces fixed on the dais, no one actually looked at Kali. Their eyes were carefully and without exception averted. He recalled the tinge of feedback pain he'd experienced while in her control. If only there were some way to make them all look at her directly. The overload might shock them out of slavery—might even finish off Kali herself.

Sandy met no resistance. No one moved out of his way, but neither did they push back when he shoved them. Some tumbled, fell into each other, and lay there blinking.

Poppy, far ahead of him, clambered onto the dais. She grabbed Kali by her metallic shoulders and stared into her face, screaming, "Where is she? What did you do to her?"

Sandy reached the platform seconds later, but he was almost too late. The center of the dais was dropping, retracting into the floor of the studio while a huge protective lid slid into place above it. He hesitated, then threw himself over the edge before the lid closed.

The fall left him stunned. He heard Poppy shrieking, Kali's startled cries. People were rushing everywhere. Someone pushed him from the platform. They were underground, beneath the studio; technicians fought to separate Poppy from Kali, whose four arms whirred and clattered, beating at the woman. Poppy held on bravely but Kali's hammering crystalline fists brought blood and instant bruises, gashing her mother deep, reopening the wounds of her suicide attempt.

Alfredo Figueroa ran up to them.

"Stop it!" he cried. "Kali—stop! What are you doing, Poppy? Your own daughter—"

He hauled her away from the augmented baby.

"Where is she?" Poppy cried.

"Open your eyes, girl," said Alfredo. "Don't you recognize your own flesh and blood?"

"The body, yes, but not the soul. Where is she?"

Kali stared at her mother with a slight smirk, her arms whirring menacingly. There was blood on the shiny fingers. "Keep her away from me," she said.

"Now, Kali," said Alfredo mildly. "She's distraught, that's all, but she is your mother."

"I said keep her away from—"

Poppy tore free and threw herself again at Kali. Everyone in the room moved to stop her, but clumsily.

Perhaps they were numb from Kali's control; perhaps she hadn't yet learned to manipulate them all at once, except to keep them quiet and orderly. They moved jerkily and a bit unwillingly, even Alfredo, converging on Poppy and once more hauling her away kicking and screaming.

Sandy crouched back in the shadows, the only one to evade Kali's summons for aid. As he watched Poppy struggling, he thought of the weapon in his pocket. Could he get a clear shot at her now, while everyone was distracted?

He noticed a movement across the studio, a figure in the shadows like himself. At first he thought it was a teegee, an auggie-doggie or seal who lacked the wires and couldn't be controlled. You're the only ones who might evade her, he thought. For a while . . .

But it was no teegee. He saw a flash of tiny lights. Jewelry. Crystals.

Thaxter Halfjest.

Sandy watched the RevGov carefully, suspiciously, noting the way Thaxter studied Poppy as she was gradually—forcibly—quieted.

Why hadn't Kali seized and enslaved Halfjest? He was California's biggest sender, thoroughly wired, constantly live. He would have been useful to her.

Sandy wished he had wires, for just this moment. With wires, he could have tuned in to see what Thaxter saw.

He remembered his last conversation with the Reverend Governor. Thax had said something about a special-effects device he'd used to confound President McBeth. A synthesizer. Thax must have found a way to protect himself from Kali by using this device; a way of diverting her into some false scenario.

But what was he doing hiding back there? Why didn't he help Poppy, if it was in his power?

A synthesizer, Sandy thought. For special effects.

Effects like . . . a death on the moon?

An altered station wagon?

Sandy couldn't take his eyes off Halfjest. The RevGov stood quietly, not his usual flamboyant self at all. He stared off into space; and then his lips began to move, his hands to twitch.

Sandy saw him mouth a few silent syllables, like a lip-reader, and synchronously Kali spoke: "Take her away. I never want to see her again."

As Kali fell silent, Thaxter's mouth stilled. Sandy fought against disbelief, fought to trust his intuition that both had spoken the same words—but that Thaxter had spoken them a split instant earlier.

Poppy wept as they dragged her away.

A green place, he thought.

He could feel the change around him, the coming tidal shift in consciousness, and it prefigured nothing but evil. A vast conformist brain warming up to motivate the world . . . its ugly awareness rising like an immense, fearful wave.

A wave, yes. Thinking in such terms, he knew he could handle this. Remembering the surfboard under his feet, the water rising to carry him. Real as a wirecast, but of his own imagining. It was the thought he needed now to carry him through. Ride this wave, this moment, or miss it forever. . . .

And then he thought nothing at all. A perfect silence filled him.

The gun slipped into his hand; he kept it out of sight behind his back. He walked steadily from the shadows, counting on the effect of surprise.

It was his only advantage.

He walked straight toward Kali. She stood alone, her puppets all preoccupied with Poppy.

She heard him coming and turned suddenly in his direction. For a moment she looked fearful, but then, seeing him, a wide smile spread over her features.

"Hey, Thaxter," he said casually.

And Kali spread her four arms wide, in a gesture the Reverend Governor had used a million times, used so often it was more than habit. It was a trope, a reflex.

"Sandy, my boy!" Kali said. Not *Uncle* Sandy.

She faltered, furious, her voice choked off in her throat. She turned to the passageway, where her helpers were busy with Poppy.

"Help me!" she cried, her voice too deep. "Help!"

Thaxter moved in the shadows, starting forward. "Help!" he echoed in a cracking voice. His head swung toward Sandy; Kali mirrored the motion.

Gun out, aiming, firing. All in an instant.

The wave broke around him. He was still up, still riding through the roar of the surf that was really the voice of the crowd above. There was no arguing with the ocean, no coaxing a wave into breaking as you wished it. No chance to argue with Thaxter or toy with sparing his life. No place for situational consultants here. This was pure improvisation.

But he kept his balance.

With a crash of broken crystal, the Reverend Governor fell.

Halfjest twitched on the floor, the golden crown a molten dribble pooling in his eye sockets, hair sizzling, gemstones blackening and cracking from the blast of heat. Sandy had expected a clean hole in the middle of his brow, but Thaxter's head looked like a marshmallow barely rescued from a bonfire.

Another shape burst from cover, fleeing across the room

on thick legs, a red cape fluttering behind him. The Pope of Las Vegas. Sandy leaped on him from behind, knocking the pope to the floor, tangling him in his velvet trail.

The pope rolled over, gasping. Kali walked up beside Sandy and stared down at the fat man.

"What were you doing to me?" she said.

Sandy saw her eyes begin to burn. She leaned over the pope and glared into his face.

"Look at me," she said.

"Bad girl," the pope stammered. "You can't touch me."

"No?" She reached behind his ear and pulled out a small contoured device like the one Sandy had worn in the temple of Kali to jam the baby's signal.

"Now . . . look in my eyes!"

The pope tried to look away but she must have entered his wires to force the confrontation. His eyes fixed on hers. He began to scream, his florid face darkening, the vessels in his eyes beginning to blacken and burst.

"Kali," Sandy said, grabbing at her, finding the metal unyielding. "Stop it! Don't kill him—you'll only hurt yourself."

But her own face was white, locked in agony. She couldn't seem to let go. Sandy flung himself against her hard carapace, sending her clattering to the floor. The pope sobbed loudly, hands clapped over his eyes.

"It was all McBeth's plan," the pope whimpered, pleading for his life. "He and Thaxter . . . it was *their* plan. He's really fully wired!"

Sandy growled warningly: "Pope . . ."

"No—no, you're right, you've seen through me. It was Dr. McNguyen! He—"

"You're not blaming it on him."* Sandy tightened his fists

---

*At which the clairaudient, mind-hopping immortal alien intelligence, better known as Dr. McNguyen, breathed a sigh of relief and turned its full attention to a large stack of documents labeled PLAN B: TEEGEE REBELLION (WIRELESS).

in wads of red velvet, shaking the pope. "I know about Marjorie, and I'm the only one who'll ever know. If you say a thing to my father, if you hurt him, I'll finish what Kali started . . . or let her do it."

"I won't tell if you won't tell." The pope blinked demurely, his lashes matted with blood. "But please, I—I think I'm blind."

Sandy staggered to his feet.

From the passageway, after a stunned silence, Sandy heard footsteps. Poppy was at the head of the returning crowd. When she saw Kali, she let out a cry.

"You're here!" she said. "You're really here!"

Kali looked around at the cavernous basement, the technicians, her uncle, the dead governor, and the quivering pope.

She threw up all her arms and started to cry, letting out everything at once, hysterical with fear and relief. Poppy knelt and took her in her arms.

"Mommy," she said. "Mommy, I'm here, I'm here!"

"I know, baby. I know."

Poppy fumbled at Kali's hard casing, but her fingers were shaking so much she couldn't work the locks. Sandy dropped down next to them, remembering how it was done. "Sit," he told Kali. Then he undid the catches in the suit's chest, revealing a small child at the heart of the enormous cold contraption.

Poppy brought the baby to her breast, rocking and cradling her. Alfredo knelt beside them.

"Sh, shush, little one," Poppy said. "It's all right now."

Kali quieted, but kept weeping. The technicians, and all those who had tried to pull Poppy away, looked cowed and yet comforted, as if her words were for them as well. And indeed, Kali's signals still carried the words out through the studio, bounced them between satellites, blanketing the earth and rising to the moon. Each one of them, every last wired soul, received a mother's comfort, whether they lived in the dark or in the light, in summer or in winter, at the poles or the equator. And like Kali many of them wept when they heard that everything would be all right. It was over now, she promised.

The very short reign of Kalifornia.

13

Sequelitis

A TEEGEE TRAGEDY: HUMANIMALS IN HOLLYWOOD
Reviewed by Nigel Wadds-Wright

Last night's gala opening of McNguyen's Viet-Celtic Theater was distinguished by the premiere closed-circuit wirecast and screening of the first production ever by a humanimal, "A Teegee Tragedy: Humanimals in Hollywood." The semiseal Cornelius, better known as "Corny" from the lamented "Figueroa Show," follows in the footsteps of Ron Howard, Rob Reiner, and Maggie Simpson as the latest in a line of gifted young sitcom actors to step behind the wires and create their own programs.

Written, edited, and produced almost single-handedly by the sealman—who acknowledges an unabashed debt to the late Clarence Starko, controversial wirist of "Poppy on the Run"—this ninety-minute documentary contains more genuine insight, pathos, and emotion than a year's worth of Magyk-7 weddings, funerals, and bar mitzvahs all condensed into one "Best of" broadcast.

Boldly combining flatscreen and wire technology to great effect, the documentary focuses on the struggles of several prominent transgenics in the entertainment industry: particularly the hot new star Kai Corgi, the cryptic E. K. Shemhamphorasch, and the popular but (as we see here) clearly demented child-violence star, Wayne Clutterbuck, better known as "Rooster Man."

Kai Corgi, who rose to global stardom after successfully fighting an involuntary euthanasia order all the way to the Monday Night Court of Appeals, is unsparing with his savage analysis of how Hollywood (here, a microcosm for society in general) has led to global oppression of teegees through ignorant stereotypes. An active champion of animal—and not merely teegee—rights, Kai has lately withdrawn from wire-show performances, although he made an exception recently to portray his close friend Cornelius in an adaption of the Kalifornia story (airing tonight: see Schedule for times and channels).

We watch in sympathy as Shemhamphorasch, a trained Shakespearean actor whose highest aspiration is to "tread the boards" as Hamlet or Othello (but whose genetic sources remain a matter of open speculation) finds himself cast again and again in the role of menacing alien blobs with monosyllabic lines . . . if any. Let us hope that the industry's eyes are opened to the talents of this underrated actor, and that he gets the chance to play some of the roles he certainly deserves. I, for one, would tap deep credit for the opportunity to experience E.K.S. as Willy Loman.

The most depressing moments, however, come in the study of Wayne Clutterbuck. Here is a teegee at the peak of his career—and his salary is anything but "chicken feed"—trapped at the bottom of an abyss of personal torment. Cornelius ably targets the source of Rooster Man's anguish in his inability to come to terms with his transgenic roots. Straddling the vast moral gulf between man and rooster, unable to embrace or reject either identity, Clutterbuck is a truly tragic figure. The segments detailing his various drug addictions are shatteringly painful and sordid. This is a wirecast to experience with your children, and should open the eyes of any parent who expects the wires to play the part of unsupervised nanny and tutor.

In spite of Cornelius's proficiency with wires, it is the flat-screen segments that add the most dimension to the show, distancing us from the subjects and thus reminding us that we can never know another's mind completely, despite the misleading evidence of our polynerves. With the sharp eye of an insider, Cornelius takes us into a world he knows well—and a harrowing journey it is, rife with injustice and bigotry, yet ultimately full of great hopes for an expanded, enlightened view of . . . not of humanity, but of intelligence itself. For what is most noble in these creatures is not necessarily their human qualities: it is something I cannot easily name. We should be grateful to Cornelius for his daring and insight. I await with trembling anticipation his next foray on the wires, whether he follows his bent for serious social commentary or plunges straight on into nerve-tingling entertainment!

The Baja sun was hot in the afternoons, even in the green shade of the valley. Cornelius put down the review with which he had been shading his eyes as, sneakingly, he read it over again. Lying in a soft chaise lounge, he sipped a margarita and nibbled on some fresh chilled trout he'd hooked from the stream below the house just that morning. He thought of his relatives sunning themselves on craggy, barnacled rocks covered with sea-gull excrement, and had to pity them. They would never know the pleasures of a purely terrestrial existence. On the other hand, they didn't have to put up with so much nonsense. This afternoon was a distinct and rare departure from his recently hectic schedule. Real seals had no concept of—no need for—vacation.

Maybe there was something in all this for his next project. He was fishing for ideas with increasing desperation now that his first feature had been released. He must remain true to his roots, that much was certain. Despite the promised corporate sponsorship of McNguyen Industries for whatever his next effort might be, he had promised himself to liberate the suppressed humanimal energy he felt crackling around him every day, seeking avenues for release. So much injustice. If only he could focus all his ideas into one grand concept. An overarching plan eluded him, but he could feel it coming. . . .

He perked up as Dyad called him from the shaded depths

of the house. Going inside was like diving into cool water. She was waiting in the study. "It's time."

Among the shelves of antiquarian books was another antique, a twenty-seven-inch color television set. Because the three of them lacked polynerves, it was more than merely a curiosity. A leather loveseat and several padded chairs sat in front of it. Cornelius dropped down in one of the chairs, and Dyad took the loveseat. A few seconds later, Raimundo came in and sat beside her.

"I don't know why you force me to watch this garbage," he said with an aristocrat's pride.

"This is a big moment," she said. "Something to rank with a new episode of 'Gilligan's Island.'"

"I don't know how you can compare the two," Raimundo said scornfully.

"Oh, Raimundo, get a tan."

He appeared to be sulking, but that was his continual expression. Beneath his moody surface, Cornelius found him to be an agreeable fellow. He certainly couldn't blame him for disliking the wire shows. No one exactly trusted the wires right now. Television and holography were experiencing a renaissance—probably temporary—which pleased Raimundo beyond words, except when the programs themselves drove him to caustic criticism. He was a connoisseur of vintage sitcoms; the newer creations he considered pale, derivative crap.

The screen lit up with a blue glow. Baroque fanfare was followed by a somewhat embroidered version of a tune Cornelius had heard thousands of times before. It was music he heard in his dreams. The Figueroa theme.

"Tonight . . . finally it can be told . . . a stirring dramatization of the story behind the story everybody knows. 'The Rise and Fall of Kalifornia!'

"Starring . . ."

Cornelius watched bemusedly as the cast was unveiled: "Dane Magyk as Alfredo! Helouise Magyk as Marjorie!" So much for the pope's vow of silence to Sandy; he had sold his inside version of the story to the networks, risking prosecution for the chance to play himself. "Nona Magyk as Poppy! Danny B. Magyk as Sandy! Miggles and Pepé as Mir and Ferdi! Baby Wego as Kali! And Special Guest Star: Kai the Wonder Dog as Cornelius!"

The casting was bizarrely inappropriate, though Cornelius had given Kai his blessing. Alfredo was an eight-foot Zulu, Marjorie a tiny Filipino woman. They both, however, had beautiful singing voices and he had long enjoyed the Magyk 7's musical numbers. Sandy was the only remotely Caucasian member of the group, a short and somewhat pudgy redhead with a high-pitched nasal voice. And little Kali, plainly, was a dwarf.

As the story began, with a reenactment of Kali's birth in a luxurious suite of the Laguna Cliffs Marriott, Corny's attention began to recede. Fortunately, at that moment, the phone buzzed.

"Allow me," Cornelius said.

He moved to a corner of the room and switched on the screen. Sandy—the real Sandy—looked out at him. "Are you watching it?"

"It's on, but I can't say it has my full attention."

"I can't bring myself to . . . you know."

"I'm not sure I'll be able to give you an accurate report."

Behind Sandy was a cavernous region full of huge machines; sparks flew from blowtorches, illuminating the dark regions in bursts; the sounds of clanging and drilling and sawing nearly drowned him out. Sandy himself was smeared with oil and grime. He had discovered happiness in the Holy City, and had returned to finish his education—and perhaps live out his life—with the Celestial Mechanics.

"Who cares?" he said. "What's important is the kind of work you're doing. 'Grats on your show, man. I really thought it was tan, Corny."

"I'm glad you made it last night," Cornelius said. "It was good to see the family together again."

Their reunion had caused a small stir at the VC Theater. Miranda and Ferdinand were cresting on the popularity of "Child Bride" (Ferdi played the role of brother-in-law, a part somewhat smaller and far less controversial than the one he'd planned for himself), but Poppy and Kali had not been much in the public senses since the night of the Overload. Last night, they had looked much like any other mother and daughter. Kali, whose alarming growth rate had slowed quite a bit, was walking now—and on her own legs. Poppy had allowed Kali to keep her wires, but she remained tuned to her daughter constantly, supervising their usage. Alfredo, for once, seemed almost oblivious to the crowd's attention; he was more concerned with keeping an eye on Kali, playing little games as if she were in danger of being bored. Alfredo did not quite grasp the implications of her astonishing intelligence and her recent brush with world domination. To him, she was simply a grandchild, to be teased and adored and looked after.

Someone out of sight called Sandy. He held them off with a gesture, then nodded to Corny. "Well . . . let me know if it's any good. I can always catch a rerun. Later, Corny."

"Good-bye."

When Cornelius returned to the program, things had deteriorated further.

Raimundo made a noise, got up, and wandered away.

Dyad sighed. "Excuse me a minute, Cornelius. I think Raimundo's upset about something."

"I can certainly understand that."

The fat little Santiago character was waddling along breathlessly next to Kai-Cornelius at the oceanside. He tossed a stick far out into the waves, and the dogman plunged after it, barking joyfully in very poor imitation of a seal and apparently unaware of the fact that Cornelius had never learned to swim.

Cornelius licked margarita salt from his lips, thinking briefly of the sea. Genetic memories surfaced, tantalizingly, giving him a moment of fear before they subsided. He envied Kai the ability to splash about in the waves; in this respect, the program's portrayal was an improvement over the character himself. Cornelius was a seal who couldn't swim. What else had he lost when he gained his humanity? And what exactly had he gained?

Thumbs were the main thing humans had to be proud of. Even a teegee had to admit they were useful.

He used one of his to turn off the TV.

MARC LAIDLAW

A California native, Marc Laidlaw possesses a borderline-illegal Class-L(obster) epidermis wholly unsuited to the tanning requirements of the Golden State. Prior to the invention of SPF-500 sunscreen, Mr. Laidlaw was subject to exquisite burns and unsightly freckling which drove him into underground cartoons. As a lifelong alien in his own land, he has had plenty of time to compose the novels *Dad's Nuke* and *Neon Lotus*. Brief stints in Oregon and Long Island have done little to improve his complexion. He currently resides in fog-bound San Francisco, where his skin has taken on an unhealthy pallor which even his wife finds unsettling.